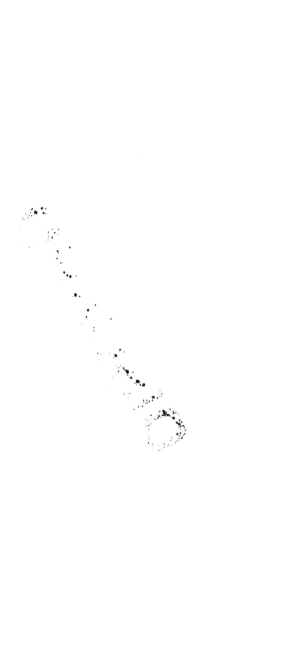

Davey's
Daughter

Center Point
Large Print

Also by Linda Byler and available from
Center Point Large Print:

Fire in the Night

**This Large Print Book carries the
Seal of Approval of N.A.V.H.**

Davey's Daughter

Lancaster Burning
—Book 2—

Linda Byler

CENTER POINT LARGE PRINT
THORNDIKE, MAINE

This Center Point Large Print edition is published
in the year 2015 by arrangement with Skyhorse Publishing.

The characters and events in this book are the
creation of the author, and any resemblance to
actual persons or events is coincidental.

The text of this Large Print edition is unabridged.
In other aspects, this book may vary
from the original edition.
Printed in the United States of America
on permanent paper.
Set in 16-point Times New Roman type.

ISBN: 978-1-62899-731-6

Library of Congress Cataloging-in-Publication Data
Byler, Linda.
Davey's daughter / Linda Byler. — Center Point Large Print edition.
pages cm. — (Lancaster burning ; book 2)
Summary: "Sarah Beiler's friend, Ashley, acts strange, even
nervous, when anyone talks about the rash of fires raising Sarah's
suspicions. But that is not Sarah's only trouble. She remains
distracted by Matthew Stoltzfus, who says that God is calling him
to leave the Amish community and begs her to join him"
   —Provided by publisher.
ISBN 978-1-62899-731-6 (library binding : alk. paper)
1. Amish—Fiction. 2. Lancaster County (Pa.)—Fiction.
   3. Large type books. I. Title.
PS3602.Y53D38 2015
813'.6—dc23
                                                      2015028957

Table of Contents

Chapter 1

Sarah Beiler, Davey's daughter, bent over, grabbed the back of the stubborn boot, and yanked as hard as she could. She groaned and threw the offensive footgear into a corner of the *kesslehaus* (wash house). Priscilla had worn them again and gotten them wet. Would she never learn?

Resigned now, Sarah found her old Nikes, undid the laces, shoved her feet into them, and tied them again—more roughly than necessary. She'd just have to tiptoe through the snow, unless Dat had shoveled a path to the barn, which was unlikely considering how precise he was with the milking time.

Grabbing a navy blue sweatshirt, she pulled it over her head, tied a men's handkerchief low on her forehead, and plunged through the door, bracing herself for the cold and snow of December.

Sarah quickly lowered her head to avoid the stinging flakes, then lifted her face to the sky, which was dark and gray but alive with the swirling whiteness of the first snowstorm of the year. Christmas was only a week away. They'd have a white Christmas!

Already, the snow was drifted against the corner

wall of the new cow stable, where the wind created eddies, same as a creek when it rounded a bend.

Excitement pulsed in her veins at the thought of an early snowstorm creating a wonderland for Christmas. It was just more festive with snow. Holly was greener, berries were redder, cookies more Christmasy, gifts wrapped in red and green glowed brighter when there was sparkling snow.

Sarah's early morning grumpiness had dissipated by the time she pulled on the door latch to the milk house, where the glass steamed from the hot water Dat had already used. She entered and set to work assembling the gleaming stainless steel milking machines.

The diesel in the shanty purred to life as Dat prepared to begin the milking.

When Sarah walked into the newly whitewashed cow stable, the two rows of clean black and white Holsteins were already being fed, jostling their chains, lifting and lowering their heads, impatient to taste the richness of their twice daily portion.

"Good morning, Sarah."

"Morning."

Dat went on with his feeding as Sarah prepared the first three cows for the milking machines and then turned to fetch them from the milk house.

She still appreciated the barn, the cow stable, and the milk house in a way she never had before their barn burned to the ground only eight months prior. It had happened one April night when the buds were bursting open on the maple trees in the front yard.

The whole family had suffered a night of terror, standing by helplessly as innocent animals, family pets, faithful workhorses, and driving horses had suffered horrible deaths. The battle against real fear occurred after the local police called it arson.

Davey, as a minister of the Old Order Amish who had lost his own barn, could freely sympathize with Ben Zook and Reuben Kauffman after each of their barns was also set on fire. He became a pillar of support for both of them.

His leadership in the community was thrown into question, however, when Priscilla, his daughter who had been deeply traumatized by the terrible, fiery death of her riding horse, Dutch, was questioned by a local reporter about the fires. She answered the reporter in a way that was considered inappropriate for the Amish, saying she hoped the arsonist would go to jail and die there.

Levi was the oldest of Davey's children and had Down syndrome. He was thirty-one years old, overweight, and clumsy, but he was the character of the family and was known and loved by everyone around him. He enjoyed a life of love and compassion, feeling pretty sure that he was an important part of Lancaster County, especially since the last meeting between prominent mem-bers of the church, when he was called upon to describe what he had seen the night of the Beiler barn fire as he had been up and about the house with a sore throat.

Levi had an exceptional memory and was astonishingly observant. He had informed the men at the meeting that a white car, maybe a Volkswagen, had driven by the house.

Sarah was now twenty years old, tall and lithe, with curly hair that never lay as sleekly as she wanted. Her seawater green eyes changed color with her emotions—gray and stormy like waves tossed by the wind when she was upset, dancing yellow lights like sunshine on rippling water when she was happy. She had grown up with a constant yearning for her neighbor, Matthew Stoltzfus, whose brown eyes never failed to melt her. He had always been the object of her affection, and she had never dreamed of marrying anyone but him. But when she turned sixteen years old, the time when she entered her years of *rumspringa* (running around), Matthew suddenly began dating her friend, Rose, a sweet and beautiful girl.

Their relationship had thrown Sarah completely off balance and stretched her faith to its limit. Now suddenly, a few years after they had begun dating, Rose called off the relationship with Matthew, which put him in an awkward situation as he strove to hide his emotions with pride and hurt battling for control. He had given Sarah enough reason to believe that he would now pursue her, and she now lived in constant suspense waiting to see what would really happen.

"Sarah!"

"What?"

Dat's call was urgent, so Sarah set down the milker she was carrying and hurried toward the sound of his voice.

"Is Priscilla up yet?"

"No."

She came upon an unforgettable sight. In the early morning dimness, the sputtering gas lantern swayed on its hook from the new, yellow post that had been erected by hundreds of men eager to show their charity by helping Davey back to his feet, lifting his spirits to new heights by erecting a new barn in only a few days. In the lantern's light, Dat's eyes were pools of shadow, the wide, black brim of his felt hat hiding the emotion on his face as he stood, helpless, in the face of the scene before him.

Sarah reached her father and grasped at the oak post, rough and splintered but a support as she beheld the horror. She let go of it then as both hands went to her mouth, and she uttered a long moan of denial.

In the light of the unforgiving lantern lay Priscilla's new riding horse, also named Dutch, a replacement for her first beloved horse. Dat had tied him in the stall with a neck rope—the soft, sturdy nylon rope often used for driving horses—when he was cleaning the box stall the day before.

Dat had intended to finish, but a distraught member of the church had come to seek advice, and Dat left the barn. He figured Dutch would be alright for a while. Then, with his mind filled with his church member's troubles, he had spent a distracted evening and hadn't been able fall into a restless sleep until after midnight.

Now Dutch's sides bulged, and his legs curled helplessly. But the real horror was his twisted, elongated neck, where the rope buried into his flowing mane, strangling the life from his veins as he had desperately struggled to free himself. It appeared as though his own panic had been the cause of his death.

"He's dead!" Sarah cried, her voice cracked with fear. Dat shook his head, his lips a grim line of resolve, but he did not utter a word. Slowly, he reached into his pocket, extracted his old Barlow knife, moved in beside the already cold form, and cut the nylon rope with a few precisely executed movements.

Dutch's head flopped to the floor with a "whumpf," and bits of shavings wafted upward, clung to the beautiful mane, and shuddered, as if attempting to give some sort of life back to the dead horse.

Dat did not look at Sarah, his voice like gravel pouring over stone when he said, "Go get her."

"I can't."

Dat was suddenly crushed by the emotional weight of too many barn fires, too many men bringing their petty disagreements, too many sleepless nights. He turned on Sarah, his large, work-roughened hands clenched, his eyes bulging, and he yelled in a voice Sarah had never heard before.

"*Harich mich* (Listen to me)!"

Her breath coming in harsh sobs, Sarah ran, slipping and falling to her knees, her bare skin exposed to the wet iciness of the snow. She got to her feet and kept going, blindly. She slipped again on the wet floorboards of the porch, righted herself, and fell through the door, her breath coming in ragged gasps.

Mam was sorting laundry on the floor of the *kesslehaus*. The safe, ordinary odor of moist, used towels, soiled socks and dresses and shirts and aprons brought Sarah back from the shock. Her mother straightened, looking at her in surprise.

"Sarah! *Voss iss lets* (What is wrong)?"

"Mam! Priscilla's horse! He . . . he hung himself."

"Oh my," Mam replied with complete hopelessness, a defeat so raw she could not utter another word, unable to draw the breath needed to say anything more.

Leaving her mother, Sarah moved heavily, numbly, up the stairs and found her way to her younger sister, Priscilla, who lay snugly under the warm comforters, sweet and innocent. Her hair was light brown with streaks of blonde running through it, and her green eyes were closed in trusting slumber.

Sarah reached out and shook her shoulder, then sat on the edge of the bed and whispered, "Priscilla. Cilla!"

Alarmed, Priscilla sat up quickly, her large eyes blinking.

"Sarah! It's your turn to milk."

"I am milking. Priscilla, listen, you have to be strong. Dutch . . . he . . . your horse is dead."

"What?"

It was plain she had not understood Sarah's words. She was sure she just hadn't heard right.

"He hung himself by his neck rope."

"No, he didn't. He couldn't have. He's not in a tie stall."

Priscilla was certain there was a mistake, so there was no reason for her to become upset. She remained calm and carefully explained it all away in her still somewhat groggy state.

Sarah persuaded her to get dressed and come to

the barn, where they found Dat, grimly lifting full, heavy milkers and dumping them into the stainless steel Sputnik vat on wheels. Wearily, as if he had suddenly aged far beyond his years, he told his daughter what had happened, flinching in the face of her inability to accept what had occurred.

"He'll be alright," she said and moved away toward the horse stables to find her beloved pet, still and cold and unmoving, her second precious horse now as dead as her first.

"He did," she whispered.

Broken, she fell on her knees beside him, her hands fluttering to his chest, reaching out to feel for just one steady heartbeat but defeated already.

"Why?"

She lifted her head, seeking an explanation.

Dat spoke reassuringly, taking all the blame, saying he should not have left him in a tie stall.

"But why?" Priscilla asked, struggling to understand how a horse as smart as Dutch could have panicked as the rope tightened.

"Well, it happens. Some horses just lose all common sense and keep jerking and pulling until their breath leaves them."

Priscilla remained quiet, her hands stroking the still, lifeless form of her horse. She was weeping but calmly, resignedly.

Sarah searched Dat's face, and he shrugged his shoulders.

"I'll finish milking," Sarah said.

Dat nodded, then looked past her as the figure of his wife came through the door. He was visibly lifted by the appearance of his unfailing supporter.

Mam did not go to Priscilla. She just put a hand on the side of the cow that was being milked and took over, instinctively handling the heavy milking machines and helping Sarah do what had to be done.

They left Dat with Priscilla and Dutch.

The cold and the snow whirled outside the rectangular blocks of yellow light at the windows. The purring of the diesel was muffled by the storm and the drifting snow as the milkers ka-chugged along, extracting the rich milk from the cows.

There was no singing, no humming, no whistling this morning. There were only two women who had once more been assailed by adversity and were now gathering the strength and resolve they would need yet again. They silently went about their duties, knowing that this, too, would pass, and the sun would shine again, for Priscilla, for them all.

In the horse barn, Dat stood, his head bent. Then he fell to his knees beside Priscilla, an arm going around her thin, heaving shoulders.

That was all.

But is there greater human support than that of a father's love? Feeling the undeniable strength of that strong arm across her back, a heart filled with compassion and caring propelling it, Priscilla turned her head and buried it in her father's coat as his other arm came around and held her close to his heart. He willed her to be strong, to be able to rise above this loss one more time.

"*Noch ay mol* (One more time), Priscilla," he murmured, his tone as cracked and broken as his heart.

Priscilla nodded and sniffed but remained in the circle of her father's comforting arms.

"God does chasten those He loves. Don't feel as if you did something bad to deserve this. You didn't. Perhaps He just allowed this to see what we make of it."

Sighing, he reached for his handkerchief, stood up, and handed it to her.

"We'll get another one, okay?"

She nodded.

"At least it's not one of us, Priscilla."

She nodded again. "Yes, Mervin was . . . so much worse."

The memory of his youngest son's drowning remained an ache in Dat's heart, one that would never leave him, and one he cherished, strangely. The memory of six-year-old Mervin served as an unfailing source of empathy and understanding when folks around him were hurting or grieving, grappling with their own losses.

"Yes, it was," Dat agreed.

"Well," Priscilla began. Her voice broke as she let out a long, unsteady sigh, and the soft weeping resumed as Dat stood by, his presence a support.

She rubbed the wrinkled, red handkerchief fiercely across her eyes and shuddered. Then she pinched her lips together in an attempt to show strength and steady her emotions.

"Well," she began again. "I should be glad maybe, Dat. You know he was going blind in one eye, don't you? The whole eye was clouding over, and when I went around barrels, he didn't always know what he was doing. So maybe . . . I don't know. I'll probably want another horse, eventually."

Dat nodded. "Yes, I'd noticed he had trouble in that one eye, but I figured it might not amount to much."

"It would have."

Dat knew Priscilla was probably right. She knew so much about horses, so he nodded.

She looked down at Dutch, lying so still and cold, and she squared her shoulders and said, "Will Benner have to take him?"

"Do you want him buried here on the farm?"

"Yes. I'd rather. I can't stand to think of him being used for dog food. Could we bury him beside the remains of the barn?"

"Of course."

When Dat and Priscilla reappeared, Sarah could tell by the set of her younger sister's shoulders that everything would be alright. Priscilla would rise above this. Hadn't she already weathered so much?

Mam headed back to the house with her arm around Priscilla's waist and sat her down at the kitchen table. She made a cup of strong mint tea with cream and sugar, brought her daughter warm slippers, and stoked the coal fire in the stove. Then she banged the big cast iron frying pan onto the gas stove and added a generous glug of canola oil. She turned to the refrigerator and removed the blue granite cake pan of cooked cornmeal mush. With an efficiency born of habit, she sliced it and placed the pieces in the sizzling oil, talking all the while, reliving disappointments of her own, and calling Suzie, all in one breath.

Suzie was the youngest daughter and was still in school. She was a miniature replica of Sarah, except for her straight, honey blonde hair and her love of dogs. The goal of her life was to own a Lassie dog, her name for collies.

Mam opened one of the oak cupboard drawers, pulled out an old beige, doubleknit tablecloth made with her own hands, and spread it quickly across the kitchen table. Then she thumped six Corelle plates and six clear plastic tumblers, her *vottags glessa* (everyday glasses), onto the table.

She set a jar of homemade ketchup, a dish of butter, one of homemade strawberry jelly, salt and pepper, the honey bear, and Levi's vitamins in the middle of the table.

She turned to slice bread for toast when Levi's voice cut through the comforting sounds of breakfast preparations.

"Malinda!"

So it was Malinda this morning, not Mam. She caught Priscilla's eye, and they lifted the corners of their mouths in unison.

"*Du mochst an hesslichy racket* (You make a big racket)!"

"Come on, Levi! Time to get up."

Levi's bedroom was on the main floor in the enclosed porch facing the driveway and barn. The many low windows were filled with tin cans containing colorful geraniums, Mam's pride and joy.

His hospital bed, a nightstand, dresser, recliner, and a few bright, woven rugs made up his pleasant bedroom. It was his area of comfort and belonging in the old stone house that had been remodeled over the years to accommodate a family of ten children.

Three married sons and two married daughters completed the David Beiler family. Anna Mae and Ruthie were each just a few years older than Sarah and already had babies and homes of their own that were filled with the aura of completion and contentment that seems to permeate young Amish homes.

They had a fit about Sarah and her senseless yearning. Although they usually kept their thoughts to themselves, occasionally a snippet of their indignant views would slip out, allowing Mam to glimpse the discordant note between her married and single daughters.

Well, Anna Mae and Ruthie had better watch out, she would think, setting her jaw firmly as she drove Fred home from sisters day. Those two had had pretty uncomplicated courtships.

"Malinda!"

"Levi, what is wrong now?"

"*Ich hopp ken hussa* (I have no trousers)!"

"*Yoh* (Yes)."

"*Nay* (No)."

Priscilla got up from her misery to help Levi find a pair of trousers, which were not in the usual drawer but folded neatly and stacked on top of his dresser, where she had put them the day before.

"You have to look, Levi."

"That is not where I look for my trousers, and you know it. You just didn't want to open the drawer and put them in. I know how you are. Always in a hurry."

Priscilla managed to laugh and tweaked his ear. He lifted a large hand to slap it away, but he was smiling, the crinkles beside his deep brown eyes spreading outward.

Breakfast was subdued but not without encouragement, as they heaped their plates with the crispy, golden slabs of cornmeal mush, fried eggs, stewed crackers, and chipped beef gravy. The plastic tumblers were filled with the orange juice made from frozen concentrate that Mam bought by the case from Aldi.

Levi's weight was a constant challenge. Some meals could turn into a battle of wills, but the first meal of the day was normally not restricted, so he was a cheerful person at breakfast, happily dabbing homemade ketchup over his stewed crackers and spreading great quantities of strawberry jelly on thick slices of toast.

Priscilla ate very little, and Sarah noted with concern the look of suffering in her eyes as she watched the snow swirling against the kitchen window.

Mam poured mugs of fragrant coffee and brought a fresh shoofly pie from its rack in the pantry. Sarah cut a fairly large wedge for herself and one for Levi, smiling at him as he thanked her over and over.

Dat said he'd have to ask Ben Zook to use his skid loader to bury Dutch. Then they had to explain to Levi what had occurred that morning, and he listened with great interest.

Wisely, he shook his great head. "Well, I didn't make it up then. A car drove in here. I was up during the night and walked to the bathroom. I saw it. I bet there was someone in the barn."

Dat slowly set down his mug of coffee, the color leaving his face. Mam turned, her mouth open in disbelief, her eyes wide, alarm clearly visible.

But it was Priscilla who began to shake uncontrollably.

Chapter 2

Dat questioned Levi extensively, and he answered with calculated precision.

No, it wasn't snowing then.

Yes, it was a white car.

White shines in the dark. It's a lot lighter than the darkness. The lights were round, down low, just like the time the barn burned.

Clearly, there was only one choice. The police had to be notified. The story made it into the *Intelligencer Journal* the next day. It was just a short strip with no picture, which was Dat's wish.

The police had urged the Amish people to invest in dogs. Big dogs trained to attack, but Dat was slow to be convinced, saying if they did get an attack dog, was it really worth the injury to another person? What if an intruder was accidentally killed?

As they discussed the article and the issue of the dogs, Sarah suggested allowing Suzie to get her Lassie dog, and Mam's face softened as she looked at her youngest daughter with so much affection that Sarah could hardly watch. Then Sarah caught Priscilla's eye and smiled, encouraging her to smile back.

Priscilla had been brave the day before, Sarah thought. Very brave. In fact, so courageous, it had broken her heart to watch her sister standing in the snow, a black figure, her head bent, her shoulders slumped, her eyes downcast.

Priscilla had been braver than she had been herself. For one thing, why did they have to send that Lee Glick with the skid loader? Dat could have driven Fred over to Ben Zook's and left him in the barn while he came home with the piece of equipment to bury Dutch himself.

Furthermore, wasn't it about time that Lee finished up his stay at Ben Zook's? Sarah thought he would have returned home months ago, but now he had a job and everything. Had he decided his home was now here in this community?

The thing was, Lee always unsettled Sarah— not really unsettled, but he left her feeling as if she wasn't quite getting it or didn't understand something he understood.

Or was she just remembering the night of Reuby Kauffman's barn fire, when she . . . Sarah lifted cold hands to cheeks that turned warm at the thought. Oh, he was just being kind, she told herself. He would help anyone. But would he help anyone in such a . . . thoughtful way?

At any rate, who showed up driving that skid loader but Lee Glick with his blond hair covered by a gray beanie? His gloved hands quickly dug a hole, drug out the sad black and white carcass with the skid loader, and rolled the great horse into the yawning, cavernous hole before covering it neatly and packing it down by running over it repeatedly.

Sarah could have stayed inside, she supposed, but Priscilla needed her support, so she stood beside her, watching the snow drift across the landscape creating a vast whiteness interrupted only by jutting buildings and trees and telephone poles, drooping wires hanging between them.

When the skid loader stopped and Lee hopped off, Dat reached into his pocket for his wallet, but Lee waved it away and stood talking to Dat for the longest time.

Lee was taller than Dat, something Sarah hadn't realized. As they turned, Priscilla waited, her eyes never leaving Lee's face. She was mesmerized, Sarah could tell, and was surprised to find her-self suddenly irritable, cold, her feet wet inside the soft lining of her snow boots.

When the men reached the girls, Lee looked only at Priscilla, and she lifted her eyes to thank him.

"Hey, no problem. Glad I could help. Must have been hard, losing another horse."

"It was."

"I feel really sorry for you. I sure hope the police can help."

"We talked to them this morning already."

"Really?"

Priscilla nodded.

Dat gave Lee more details, and he whistled low,

then shook his head. And he continued to ignore Sarah as if she had all the charms of one of the apple trees behind them as he asked Priscilla questions and listened closely to her replies.

Just when she was ready to walk away, Lee turned to Sarah and asked how she was. His eyes met hers with so much blue it was like a streak of lightning blinding her for a second before she could see clearly.

"I'm fine," she said curtly.

"You get home okay Saturday night?"

"Yeah."

Defiantly, she met his blue eyes, eyes that seemed to mock her now. She felt as if he knew everything that happened that night between her and Matthew Stoltzfus.

She felt the warmth rising uncomfortably in her face, and she lowered her eyes and kicked at the loose snow, her composure sliding away in a free fall along with the whirling snow.

Dat stood comfortably, his hands in his wide trouser pockets, his black coat bunched up above them, his wide black hat protecting his face and shading his eyes as he observed this exchange with seasoned perspective.

It wasn't Dat's way to say anything serious about matters of the heart. That was Mam's domain, but a small smile played around his lips as he noticed Sarah struggling to regain her air of aloofness.

So that was how it was with Sarah. Well.

The remainder of the day she thought of Matthew, his warm brown eyes, the way he had asked if she'd consider being his girl. She thought how it would feel to have finally attained the long awaited goal of being exactly that—Matthew's girl. Oh, the thought of buying and wrapping a gift for him! She'd dreamt about it for years but knew it couldn't happen this year, but the next one, likely.

As she mixed the butter and sugar for a batch of peanut butter cookies, she planned what she would buy. When she burned the first sheet of cookies, Mam was not happy, her cheeks a brilliant shade of red, her hair almost crackling with frustration, clucking and fussing, saying she'd never been so behind with her Christmas baking, and goodness knows she still had nothing for Anna Mae's baby.

"Sarah, stop being so dreamy. It upsets me."

Sarah watched her mother running around, accomplishing nothing. She told her to calm down—she was acting worse than Mommy Beiler ever had.

"Humpf."

It was a huge insult. Mam esteemed her work ethic far above that of her late mother-in-law's, but she was used to navigating the surprising waters of mother-daughter relationships, and so she drew her lips to an uncompromising line and remained silent.

After about a hundred Hershey's kisses had been pressed into as many peanut butter cookies, Sarah felt uncomfortably warm and nauseous, not to mention completely irritated by Mam's silence, so she said loudly, "I don't know what you're so mad about."

Mam burst out laughing, sat down, and slid low in her chair, her feet wearily stretched in front of her. She pushed up her white covering, extracted a steel hairpin from her bun, and scratched her head before replacing it.

"Huh," she sighed. "One of these years, believe me, I'm going to skip Christmas altogether. I'll just sit in a corner somewhere and read a Bible story about the Baby Jesus and let it go at that."

She stretched her arms over her head.

"Levi, get away from there!"

Mam sat up and leaned over, her eyebrows lowering as Levi tried to make off with yet another cookie.

This was when Sarah loved Mam best. When she was completely herself—just Malinda, humorous and comfortable and not taking things quite as seriously as usual.

"These peanut butter cookies make me sick after the chocolate on top gets cold," Levi said, as wily and slick as any thief trying to convince a judge of his innocence.

"They do not!" Priscilla retorted.

The door burst open, and Suzie exploded into

the house with her bonnet tied haphazardly over her head scarf, her boots covered with snow, and her coat buttoned crookedly.

"Hey! The English people's school bus is stuck on the hill past Elam's!"

"Oh my goodness. Is it still snowing? *Ach* (oh), it is. Well Suzie, I hope you were careful coming home. My goodness."

Suzie reached for a cookie. She watched Levi's hand snake out and grab one, too, before shuffling back to his card table and the display of cards spread out on it.

"Levi, put that cookie back," Mam said without turning around.

Levi stopped in his tracks, facing away from Mam, and said, "What cookie?"

"The one in your hand."

Quickly, Levi inserted the cookie in the gap between the buttons on his shirtfront and answered glibly, "I don't have one."

"You don't?"

"No."

"Okay then."

That was the most entertaining part of the entire day, aside from the hole being dug for Dutch, or rather, that chap driving the skid loader, Sarah decided.

Why did he do that to her? It seemed as if he kept planting his blond head into her thoughts when she did not want to think about him at all.

It was Matthew she loved, and it was Matthew she planned on marrying. It was just that . . .

She wished that she'd never gone to Reuby Kauffman's barn fire. All it had done was bring back the terror, the memory of the screaming animals, and all the helplessness their own fire had brought into her life.

And then Lee had held her securely in his arms as she struggled to recover from her fainting spell. Of course, he would have helped anyone. That was how Lee was.

He was the one who buried Dutch. And he was helping his brother-in-law, Ben Zook, finish the details in his barn, working every evening after work for months. He was always one of the first ones on the scene at barn raisings, one of the last to leave. It seemed as if that was all he did— work for other people and help them out.

Was that how someone was measured? Sarah didn't know. She just wished she'd never met him, the way he made his way into her thoughts like an uninvited intruder.

Sighing, she thought about making supper and doing chores. The usual routine suddenly felt like an insurmountable burden. All she wanted to do was roll into her bed and cover her head with the quilt to block out the snow and Christmas and Dutch and Priscilla and, yes, Lee.

That evening, Sarah walked to the barn and halfheartedly helped Dat with the milking. Her thoughts were a million miles beyond the cow stable, Lancaster County, or anyone around her. She missed Mervin and wished she could see him again, touch him, tousle his blond hair, just one more time.

When a cow lifted a heavy, soiled foot and kicked her shin hard, she yelped in surprise, then pain. She began howling in earnest, bringing Dat to her side as a dark bruise started forming beneath her woolen sock.

"Boy, she socked you one, didn't she?"

Grimacing, Sarah laughed ruefully, nodding her head. "She has a secret hatred for me."

Dat laughed heartily and agreed with Sarah that she was an ill-tempered cow. He had seriously considered turning her into steak and hamburger. Now he said he just might have to.

"Nothing broken, is there?"

"No, it was just enough to make me good and angry."

"You weren't too happy to begin with."

Sarah nodded. "Yeah, well. Sometimes you just aren't yourself," she said, making an enormous effort at cheeriness.

Dat watched Sarah and then took the golden opportunity to ask her if she had prayed for God's guidance in seeking a life companion.

He was shocked to hear the rebelliousness in his daughter's voice.

"You make it sound like one of those better-than-thou books. Of course I pray. The Lord showed me a long time ago that His will is for Matthew and me to be together."

The words were explosive, forceful.

Dat's eyebrows raised of their own accord.

"Alright, Sarah, alright. You know I'm not the one you talk to about matters of the heart. I get embarrassed talking to you about . . ."

"Say it," Sarah said harshly, unkindly.

"Sarah."

The tone in his voice stopped her downward spiral into a stream of hurtful and useless words.

"You don't want to be this way."

"How do I want to be?"

Dat didn't answer. He just turned to the cow being milked and bent to retrieve the milker. He poured out the warm, creamy milk and placed the machine on the next cow.

Straightening, he watched Sarah's face and said, "All I want is for you to be honest with yourself."

"I am."

"Alright. If you are, there is no need to defend yourself."

That sent Sarah into a miserable state of confusion. Dat had never mentioned Matthew's name, so what was all that supposed to mean? Now thoroughly confused, she walked out of the barn into the cold evening that was just headed toward dusk. The sun was spreading a pink and apricot glow beneath the remnants of the snow-storm, infusing the stone house with an other worldly brilliance as the snow piled in glistening heaps on the shrubs and bushes reflected the same beautiful radiance.

Well God, she breathed, her prayer a whispered need, a small cry of confusion from a bowed spirit. You're going to have to come through if . . .

She couldn't finish, somehow unable to lay her sacrifice on the altar, afraid to think or pray about what was hidden in the recesses of her heart, that delicate balance of her own will, God's will, and Matthew.

As if in immediate answer to her troubled spirit, a dark figure cut into the Beiler driveway, the black horse easily pulling a two-seater sleigh—a cutter—painted a glossy black. Her cousin, Melvin, waved wildly. He was wrapped in a ridiculous pile of outerwear, his prominent nose rising above his gaudy, plaid scarf.

"Sarah! Good! You're home! Come on. Let's go for a ride before every back road is cindered."

"Give me a minute!"

And that was all she needed. She washed her hands, donned clean socks, boots, a sweater, coat, head scarf, and warm gloves before limping and slipping out to the sleigh and the impatient horse.

"Here we go! It's unreal how quiet this is. There is not one sound except for the horse's hooves, and even they're muffled."

He talked as if he had invented the sleigh and the horse and created the snow, the sun, and the clouds himself, Sarah thought, knowing Melvin as well as she knew herself.

They sped through the waning light, the cold invigorating her, dashing all the confusing thoughts from her head. Like cobwebs, they were swept away with an unseen broom.

Melvin chattered away, and Sarah listened, nodding her head or saying, "Mm," or "Okay," or some other fitting word to assure him that she was listening.

When she did have the opportunity to tell him about Priscilla's horse, asking if he had seen the paper, Melvin's mouth opened, his eyes widened, and he shook his head in disbelief.

That was all it took to start another of his verbal explosions, his head nodding and hands gesturing as he spoke of the very real danger of someone losing yet another barn or more live-stock.

"It's just a matter of time. I bet you anything that horse reared back out of fright, seeing someone sneaking into the barn. But the nerve! Can you imagine someone doing this again? Still driving the same car? He can't be too smart, or he'd drive a different vehicle. For Pete's sake, Sarah. What a loser!"

Sarah reminded her agitated cousin that Levi may not have been completely awake or was imagining things, trying to create drama, enabling him to have the top spot at meetings.

Melvin disagreed vehemently, turning the sleigh at the end of Irishtown Road, skillfully handling the reins with one gloved hand as the other one waved in the air for emphasis.

That was the end of the conversation as the wind picked up and whirled their words away in its fury.

Sarah's shin throbbed painfully beneath the heavy blankets, and her face was numb with the piercing cold. She pulled the blanket higher, hiding her face behind it until they slowed to a stop back at the house, and Melvin jumped out.

"Come in for hot chocolate," Sarah said.

"You know I won't turn that down."

"Good."

Limping, her leg causing her serious discomfort, Sarah made her way into the house and hung her wet, snow-covered things by the coal stove to dry.

Levi was getting ready for bed, taking his blood pressure medication and his vitamins and minerals. He was dressed in flannel pajamas, navy blue ones with the white pin stripes. He had on brown slippers, and his hair was clean and wet from the shower.

"Melvin's here," Sarah told him.

Levi shook his head, slowly gathering the small pile of pills in his hand.

"I'm going to bed."

"But Melvin wants to talk to you."

"No, I don't feel good."

"But Levi, he's worried that our barn isn't safe, the way Dutch died."

"No, I'm sick to my stomach."

With the words spoken forcefully, Sarah knew his mind was made up, and he would refuse to cooperate at all.

Levi turned away and shuffled heavily to his room. He sat on the edge of his bed and muttered to himself before turning off the battery lamp and swinging up his legs, grunting with the effort of settling his large body comfortably.

Mam appeared out of nowhere, clucking, bringing an extra comforter to spread over Levi's great bulk. She tucked him in, worrying about the roaring wind outside as the snow blasted against the windows. She returned to her bedroom and opened the lid of the cedar-lined chest that had been her great-grandmother's and had the initials A.M.K. inscribed on the front.

She pulled out homemade comforters, pieced with blocks of fabric cut from remnants of fleece. They were knotted securely with brightly colored yarn from leftover skeins from afghans she had crocheted.

None of the colors matched, but that was not the purpose of the comforters to begin with. As long as the fleece patches were sewed firmly and the yarn was pulled through twice and securely knotted, they were well done and served their purpose.

Those comforters stayed in the cedar chest all year except for the coldest part of the winter, which had come early this year.

Mam bustled up the stairs, Suzie in tow, distributing the necessary comforters. She spread them over the beds, tucking them between mattresses and box springs, saying, "*Ach* my. *Siss kalt do huvva* (It's cold up here)."

She clattered back down the stairs, a cozy light shining from her kindly eyes, *fer-sarking* (taking care of) her children on a cold winter night, the way she had done ever since her firstborn lay in his crib in a corner of the bedroom in the old stone house.

She'd bustled then, and she bustled now and was fulfilled by her motherly duties.

"Just listen to that wind!" she exclaimed to her husband and her nephew, Melvin, who had followed Dat into the kitchen.

Dat shook his head, saying he'd watched those gray clouds just as the sun left that red slash in the sky. He figured a real wind would be kicking up.

Melvin looked around for Levi, clearly wanting to have him describe in detail what he had seen during the night.

"Where's Levi?"

The question was inevitable, and Sarah knew he'd be disappointed, knowing once Levi refused to talk, it was like trying to budge a two-ton rock. Impossible.

"He's in bed."

"Well, ask him to get up. I want to talk to him."

As always, Melvin's voice was clear and precise, and it carried well, producing a rumpus from the hospital bed.

"Melvin, just go on home. I'm not well."

"*Ach*, come on, Levi!"

"No."

"I'll give you some gum."

"No."

Melvin looked to Dat for assistance, then to Sarah, saw the futility of his attempts, and sank resignedly into a kitchen chair. Sarah served him hot chocolate and peanut butter cookies, and they talked far into the night.

The fear wrapped itself around Sarah, an unsettling cloak of mystery, the unknown a burden as Melvin's words rang in her ears.

"Mark my words, Davey. There's more trouble to come. If he thinks we Amish are all going to turn our backs and let him terrorize all of us, he has another guess coming."

Maybe we're the ones who have another guess coming, Sarah thought to herself.

Chapter 3

The wind wailed around the eaves, sending a section of loose spouting clattering down the side of the stone house with a metallic crash that woke the whole household. Levi cried out in alarm, and Suzie called from her bedroom in hoarse terror.

Sarah jumped out of bed, grabbed her woolen robe, and hobbled painfully down the stairs, meeting Mam already halfway through the kitchen, her small flashlight slicing a path across the darkened room.

No one went back to bed before Dat dressed warmly, lit a gas lantern, and searched the barn and the outbuildings, holding the lantern high, before finally coming upon the indentation in the snow left by the section of spouting. He carried it triumphantly to the porch, his great relief visible.

Mam sighed, the tension leaving her body, and told them they could now go back to bed. Sarah took two Tylenol tablets and swallowed them at the kitchen sink. She cowered at the window as a mighty gust bent the great, old maple trees in the front yard, erasing the vast bulk of the new, white barn for only a few seconds.

She shivered.

The cold lay around the baseboards along the walls and crept along the windowsills, where the coal stove's heat could not quite keep it at bay. Little swirls of chills shivered up Sarah's back as she turned to Mam, who was warming her hands by tentatively touching the tips of her fingers to the top of the coal stove. Mam pulled Suzie close against her when Sarah came to join them.

In the dark and cold, they huddled, the warmth a comfort, creating an aura of normalcy. Though they didn't say it, they all knew this whole scene contrasted sharply with the way they would have reacted previously to a noise in the night.

The truth hovered between them, driving them into isolation with their own thoughts. The shame of their fear, or the admission of it, would have to remain unspoken, a denial of the fact that it existed.

They were people of faith, weren't they? Christian folks of the Old Order who placed their trust in God. They were blessed by Him as seasons came and went, with the rain and the sun and the good, brown earth sprouting the seeds they planted and the barns bulging with the abundant harvests as the leaves turned colors, signaling winter's approach.

So what were they doing now, cowering around this stove and casting furtive glances over their shoulders, peering into the dark corners that had become hiding places for strange men, Bic lighters flicking as they terrified good, strong, sensible horses into a state of deathly panic?

Barns that stood tall and stately had crumpled and burned to useless black piles that no one could ever fully erase from their minds. The memories left apprehension lying thick and suffocating over Lancaster County.

"Go back to bed," Mam said curtly.

Everyone obeyed, silently padding their way up the staircase, knowing that in previous years, they would all have remained in their beds and later laughed about the great crash the spouting had made during the night. But that was before the ongoing mystery was wedged into their lives. Now, they would need to adjust, over and over, to overwhelming waves of fear.

In the morning, Leacock Township already had the great, rumbling snowplows shoving walls of snow to the sides of the roads. Heavy chains were secured around the big tires, and the machines clanged and banged as they scraped along, yellow revolving lights warning passing vehicles —if there were any—of their approach.

The wind remained stubbornly stiff and unrelenting, so Sarah helped Dat shovel paths to the barn and everywhere else anyone would need to go on the property. The wind had their walkways blown shut again in a few hours, so they kept at it. The sun was shining, however, and Sarah preferred the outdoors far above being cooped up inside with Levi.

His stomach pained him terribly as a result, of

course, of his over-consumption of peanut butter cookies.

Mam was on the phone half the morning. She was in quite a stew about Ruthie's two year old who had the croup. She worried he'd have to be taken to Lancaster General Hospital *ivver vile* (soon).

Suzie couldn't go to school, so she sang the same song over and over as she sharpened her colored pencils with a battery-powered sharpener that emitted a high whir as each pencil was poked into it.

"My Lord, my King, you're my—WHIRRR—everything—WHIRRR—Glory sing."

Sarah could only take about two minutes of that until the cold and the wind looked positively inviting. Back outside, she looked up to see her sister, Priscilla, wading through the snow on her way to find a sled, no doubt.

As Sarah turned in the opposite direction, she saw another familiar tall figure wading through the snow, coming over the small hill from Elam's.

Matthew!

As usual, her breath caught in her throat, and her heartbeat, though it was already elevated from shoveling snow, accelerated to an even faster rate. And, as usual, she felt her confidence slip away, afraid that this time she would need to accept that he was back together with Rose, the relationship resumed, and this time, they would remain together, inevitably being married the following year.

She was surprised to see he was waving, his arm swinging wide with enthusiasm as he caught sight of her. She stood still, awaiting his approach, a smile playing around her lips.

"Hey, whatcha' doin'?"

She lifted her shovel and turned her face to smile at him.

"Shoveling?"

She nodded. "What does it look like?"

"Shoveling snow?"

She reached out to hit his forearm playfully, and he smiled at her, his teeth dazzlingly white in his dark face, his black beanie pulled low on his forehead, his eyes warm and brown and inviting.

"Hey, Sarah. I walked the whole way up here through the cold and the wind and the deep snow to ask you to go to the Christmas singing with me. Want to?"

There was no shyness, no hesitation with Matthew, and she answered quickly and maybe a little too loudly with a resounding, "Oh yes!"

Her eyes were shining, her face glowed, the tendrils of her curly, brown hair swirled about her forehead, and she could not take her gaze away from him.

"Good. Good, then. I'll pick you up Sunday evening. Around six, six-thirty."

"I'll be ready."

"You have a Christmas dinner that day?"

"Yes, of course. Though it's a little strange with Christmas on a Sunday this year."

"Well, we have Monday off, too. Second Christmas."

"We have the Lapp Christmas dinner that day."

"Your mam's side?"

"Yes."

"That's cool."

Matthew stood, relaxed, unwilling to leave her, so she leaned on the shovel and watched his face, taking in the way his nose turned down just perfectly, the two black wings for eyebrows.

He said, "Your hair's a mess," as he reached up and lifted off his stocking cap. He set it firmly on Sarah's head, pulling it down well below her eyebrows, then stood back and laughed aloud.

"You look really cute like that."

Sarah pushed the beanie up, a warmth spreading over her face.

From the kitchen window, Mam's paring knife slipped, wobbled, then stopped completely, her jaw sagging in disbelief as Matthew put his cap on Sarah's head. Her mouth compressed, her eyes sparked, and her nostrils distended only a millimeter as she brought the paring knife through the potato with a new intensity.

Did that boy have no shame? In broad daylight,

traipsing right in their driveway to flirt openly with their daughter, who he knew was an easy target. In her day, in her *rumspringa* years, that was completely unthinkable, and here he was, larger than life, without a care in the world of what she or Davey thought.

A sharp pain shot through her thumb as the knife slipped again and cut a nasty slice into the skin. Quickly, she bent and opened the cupboard door, ripped a paper towel off the roll, and wrapped it around her thumb.

She wanted to cry. She wanted to bang her fists against the window and chase him away like an unwanted starling at the birdfeeder. Instead she walked calmly to the oak medicine cabinet, got out the box of Band-Aids, and applied one with all the concentration she could muster, avoiding looking out the windows as much as she could.

Taking a deep breath, she steadied herself and sat down heavily. She knew this was not right. So she bowed her head, the part in her hair perfectly centered, her hair sleekly falling away on each side. Her hair was graying but still retained most of its dark color under her large, snow-white covering with its wide strings falling down her back.

Her lips moved in prayer as tears hovered between her eyelashes and quivered there before dropping onto the gray fabric of her apron, creating dark splotches while her cheeks remained dry.

Mam had reached her Waterloo. It was such a maddeningly futile situation, and she knew she must let go, give up her own will, and replace it firmly with God's will.

How could her own precious, beloved daughter be so blind when the dashing Matthew was so obviously still in love with the beautiful Rose?

Or was she, herself, blind to God's will? She didn't know, so she gave herself up to God, following the advice handed down from generation to generation, the sound principle of the ages for every Amish wife and mother. You could never go wrong by giving yourself up.

Mam had just resumed her potato peeling when Sarah bounded into the *kesslehaus*, yanked open the door to the kitchen, and charged over to Priscilla at the sewing machine.

"Did you see Matthew?"

Priscilla looked up.

"Where was he?"

"Here. He came to ask me to go to the Christmas singing!"

"He did? What did you say?" Priscilla ducked her head and giggled as Sarah swatted her shoulder. "You said no, right?"

But Sarah was already on her way up the stairs, taking two steps at a time before bounding back down.

"Mam, may I go to Lizzie Zook's store?"

"Why?"

"I have to have a new Christmas dress. I have to."

Resigned, Mam turned, her face inscrutable. "Why?"

"Matthew was here. He asked me to go to the Christmas singing with him. I only have my burgundy dress from last year, or that homely looking dark green. I look sick in that one. Please, Mam?"

What Mam wanted to say and what she did say were two entirely different things.

"I suppose you can. How would you go? Surely not Fred and the buggy on a day like this?"

"Of course!"

Priscilla was elected to accompany her in spite of Suzie's protests. Levi came to the rescue and promised her a game of Memory, and Sarah promised her a new book.

The town of Intercourse was digging itself out of the snowstorm, but as it was only a few days before Christmas, plenty of cars crawled along Route 340. Horses and buggies clopped along the roadside. Pedestrians hurried along swept sidewalks and ducked into shops to frantically look for last-minute gifts. Trucks carrying fuel oil or tanks of milk geared down for the red light at Susquehanna Bank as the girls neared their destination—the fabric shop in the heart of the village.

Bolts of fabric stood upright along low shelves,

an endless display of colors and patterns making it difficult to choose. Sarah remained indecisive till Priscilla began tapping the toe of her boot and looking at the ceiling, accompanied by a hum that grated on Sarah's nerves. Her sister's impatience distracted Sarah and scattered her resolve to settle for the red that was not as pretty as a more brilliant shade—one that would be completely unacceptable to Mam.

Mam was so strict, Sarah thought. She never changed with the times. Well, not never. But not very often.

"Priscilla!" she hissed.

"Hmm?"

"Would you get this one?"

"You're crazy," Priscilla said flatly.

"Why?"

"You just are. You know Mam will never allow it. Don't even think of letting Dat see you in that orange red."

"They'll hardly see it."

"Not at the singing?"

"Oh, I forgot."

Her shoulders sagged with defeat. Well, it would have to be the dull red with the barely discernible stripe. That was all there was to it.

She took it to the counter to have it cut, paid for her purchase, and returned to the buggy, stowing the white plastic bag beneath the seat.

On the way home, they ate broken pieces of

Fifth Avenue candy bars from the plastic bag they had purchased at a reduced price from Nancy's Notions. They examined the Christmas wrap and bows Sarah had purchased for her gifts, and Sarah launched into a colorful account of the elaborate gifts she would buy for Matthew once they were dating. She shrugged off the look she was receiving from Priscilla.

"You don't like Matthew," she said out of the blue much later.

"I like him okay. I just don't want you to get hurt. I'm sure you know as well as I do, he likes every girl in a hundred mile radius."

"But he will like me best, once we're dating."

Priscilla pretended to read the new children's book that Sarah purchased for Suzie and shrugged her shoulders with an air of disinterest.

"Yeah. Could be."

The subject was over almost before it started, and nothing more was said.

On Christmas Day, the sky was a spectacular shade of blue, crowning the white snow, creating crevices of blue and gray where the shadows lay beneath the drifts.

Sarah was up early, helping her mother arrange all the wrapped presents in a large pile on the drop leaf table in the living room. It was over-flowing with gifts beneath and beside it as well, the way it always was.

The forest green of the roll-down blinds behind the sofa blocked the bright glare of sunshine on snow. The cushions on the couch had patterns of brown and red and, with the green blinds, created a scene of Christmas colors.

There were no other decorations for the holidays except for a few red and green candles scattered throughout the house. Since Dat was a minister, it was expected that their family would have a plain house, to lead by example, without worldly displays of expensive artwork or fancy curtains.

Not that Mam didn't think about it, she always said. But she had a nice, new house and nice furniture, so she was content and wanted to stay within the rules.

Anna Mae and Ruthie gave Mam nice things, saying what did it matter, but invariably the ceramic figurines and fancy candleholders and dried flowers ended up in the bedroom, out of sight.

The turkey was in the oven, the stuffing bursting out of its cavity, and by mid-morning the smell of celery and onion permeated the house. In the *kesslehaus*, the ham cooked in ginger ale and pineapple juice, moist and succulent, causing Dat to inhale mightily as he walked through the door.

Sarah was peeling potatoes at the kitchen sink when the first vanload of brothers and sisters-in-law arrived, followed by a team and buggy containing Ruthie and her husband. The chaos officially began.

Dat hurried into the bedroom in his stocking feet, tiptoeing, telling Mam to welcome them in. He hadn't changed clothes yet, and Mam's cheeks flamed red as she said, "*Ach* Davey, what were you doing till now?"

She opened the door, stood aside, and smiled as she waved her offspring inside and kept on smiling.

She cuddled babies, kissed toddlers, shook hands, and looked deep into her grown sons' eyes. She saw they were alright, life was good for them, and they were glad to be here.

"Where's Dat?"

"Oh, he's still changing clothes."

"What a loser!"

"Hey! Watch what you're saying!"

Dat emerged from the bedroom carrying his black Sunday shoes, his black socks in the opposite hand, and his hair uncombed. But a wide smile of genuine holiday welcome was shining from his face.

"Barefoot!"

"What's wrong with you? It's Christmas!"

Dat's eyes shone with a bit more than their ordinary moisture as he wrung his strapping sons' hands, telling them it was just wonderful to see them again. He shook hands with the daughters-in-law and gently held the grandchildren and marveled at their growth.

Mam's eyes sparkled, her color remaining high as she whirled between the stove and the long table, which was now extended with twelve leaves, allowing twenty-four people to be seated at once.

The tablecloths were green, the paper plates a patterned red, the plastic tumblers clear. These paper products were all Anna Mae and Ruthie's doing, Mam had lamented as she placed them on the table early that morning. She should be using her Sunday dishes, she said. Sarah told her times were changing, and she'd be thankful when it was time to do dishes.

Ruthie had made the Christmas salad in Tupperware molds, two of them, but told Mam she hadn't the slightest clue how to get them out of there. She knew they'd flop the minute the molds were inverted.

Mam's eyes sparkled as she filled the sink with hot water and lowered the molds into it for about a minute before turning them on a plate and slowly taking off the lids. She was rewarded by a sucking sound, and a perfect ring of red, green, and white Jell-O stood perfectly on the plate as Anna Mae's family and another vanload arrived.

The house was full, too warm, and extremely noisy. Levi held court by the drop leaf table, taking gifts as each new family presented them and thanking the givers repeatedly.

It was a wondrous Christmas dinner. Mashed potatoes heaped in Melmac serving dishes, puddles of browned butter pooled on top and running down the sides. Gravy—thick and salty—in Mam's best ceramic gravy boats. Wide homemade noodles swimming in chicken broth. Carrots and peas seasoned with a pinch of salt and plenty of butter. And coleslaw, deviled eggs, applesauce, and, because it was Christmas, cashews and the best olives in cut glass dishes with dividers down the center.

Dat had Abner believing he had cured his own ham and had a good laugh before he told him it was a John Martin ham. Allen said he probably raised the turkey, too.

No, Dat admitted, the meat was bought at the grocery store. Raising pigs and turkeys for meat was just not profitable, unless the farmer had a couple thousand of each and a good contract from the feed company.

"Sad, isn't it?" he said. "It used to be that my grandfather could make money keeping a few hens and pigs and milk five cows by hand, but no more, as the price of feed eclipsed the price per pound of beef."

This led to a discussion of times past, including the boys' antics growing up on the farm.

Sarah was careful, eating very little, knowing

Matthew would be picking her up at six. She'd have to look her best and being stuffed with holiday goodies was not an option.

Allen leaned across the table. "Don't you have a boyfriend yet?"

Sarah shook her head and busied herself feeding little Ruthanna.

"What are you waiting on?"

"Oh, till I'm thirty."

"You already are."

They all laughed uproariously at Sarah's expense. She laughed with them, so glad the secret in her heart was not visible, her joy a hidden treasure from prying eyes.

"Hey, you should come to Dauphin County to teach school. Next year three of our teachers are getting married. You haven't taught school yet, and that might fit you perfectly," said Rachel, Allen's wife, her voice carrying a seriousness that Sarah knew was not just banter, like her brothers.

"Maybe I should."

But, oh, I won't. I won't, she thought, exhilaration infusing her mind and heart. Next year, I might very possibly be married to Matthew.

Gifts were exchanged, the children wiggling in their seats, anticipation coloring their cheeks. They squealed with delight at the books and Legos, the dolls and coloring books.

Levi unwrapped his gifts with a great deal of

showmanship, folding the wrapping paper and telling Mam to keep it with a gruff commanding voice. He was simply speechless when he received a brand new air hockey game from his brothers.

That was what they played the remainder of the day, as they nibbled on the homemade candy and cookies, the leftover ham and turkey, the fruit and nuts and punch.

Dat watched from his seat on the brown recliner, a child on each knee, and whooped and laughed and forgot all his troubles for one blessed Christmas Day.

He remembered to thank God especially for Levi, who continued to bring them many moments of pure and unabashed humor. Lord knew, there were plenty of concerns to level it all out these days.

Chapter 4

True to his word, or almost, Matthew arrived at a few minutes before seven. Amid much loud teasing and banter, Sarah managed to get out of the house unruffled, a smile on her face.

Matthew greeted her warmly, kept a lively conversation going, seemed genuinely interested in her family's Christmas dinner, saying he couldn't imagine having a family that size.

Sarah laughed as she leaned back against the seat. Matthew asked if she was wearing a new coat.

"Yes."

"It's pretty cool."

"Thanks."

She became shy then, wondering if the new coat was trying too hard. Well, she'd needed one, so she guessed he'd just have to think what he wanted.

"You didn't buy the new coat on my account, did you?"

The question took her completely off guard, and she floundered, red-faced, caught in a hard place. If she said no, he'd think she didn't care, and if she said yes, it would appear a bit desperate. She just couldn't come up with a coherent answer.

Matthew seemed to enjoy her discomposure, a half smile playing around his features, his confidence allowing him to relax and remain at ease, even when Sarah was so obviously nervous. That was the only rough part of the whole evening.

He unhitched his horse, asking her to help and then wait until he could accompany her to the shop where the parents and youth were assembling.

The youth sat around a long table with the girls on one side and the young men on the other. The parents sat around the walls of the shop, and propane lamps hissed gently from their cabinets.

The singing had already started when they arrived, a sea of green and red and black dotted with white coverings, as everyone lifted their voices to sing the old German and the newer English Christmas carols.

Many faces turned to watch their arrival. Acquaintances' hands went to their mouths, and eyebrows lifted. Well, he hadn't waited long to move on, they thought.

Mam stared straight ahead, and Dat lowered his head. Matthew's mother, Hannah, watched them like an exultant hawk sure of its prey. Her husband, Elam, didn't care one way or another as he was sound asleep beside her.

"How'd you get here so fast?" Sarah whispered to Mam.

"The boys dropped us off."

"Oh."

"Rose!" Sarah turned to greet her friend, who was also dressed in red, but to Sarah's chagrin, the red she'd wanted so badly before deciding to take Priscilla's advice.

Oh, she looked like a Christmas flower, her blonde hair shining, her face glowing, catching the red of her dress. Her large eyes were luminous, her white teeth so perfect as she caught Sarah's arm.

"Come with me!"

Together, they made their way to the bathroom, giggling nervously, and then collapsed on the rug and talked as fast as they could, catching up on local news. They chatted about the farmer's market in New Jersey where they both worked and what a madhouse it always became over the holidays, when they were absolutely run off their feet.

Then, the inevitable.

"I didn't see you come in. How'd you get here?"

"Matthew."

"Is he taking you home?"

"Yes. I . . . I think so."

Rose said nothing after that, the silence thickening around them. Suddenly she blurted out, "Sarah, how does he . . . I mean, like, how does he seem to be? Happy? Sad?"

"He's . . . he's just Matthew. Sort of the way he

always was. Normal. The way I've always known him."

"Is he going to ask you?"

"No."

Her answer came too loudly and forcefully, and Rose knew it as well as Sarah.

Sarah's face felt burning hot, she reached both hands up to cool it, her icy fingers bringing their temperature back to normal.

"Rose, please don't be suspicious of me."

"Well, the thing is, I miss him, and I'm torn with horrible indecision. Are break ups ever okay? I mean, here I am, rid of what really bugged me about Matthew. His selfishness, his . . . I mean it, Sarah, don't you ever tell anyone this, but he's sort of lazy sometimes, and yet I find I miss him so much. His good qualities do far outweigh his bad ones. Love is so weird. Sometimes I wonder if I know what it is. Now that I don't have Matthew, part of me wants him back. It's so hard to know what is right. I'm afraid to go back, because what if I don't want him after all—after we're back together?"

She leaped to her feet, leaned across the narrow counter top, and checked her image very carefully in the mirror. Then she turned, taking a deep breath and clasping her hands in front of her small waist, the one-sided conversation obviously over.

"Well."

It was an ending, and Rose had pulled the lever of control on the conversation, her blue eyes infused with a sweetness that comes in a packet, Sarah thought, Sweet and Low and awfully artificial.

Obediently, Sarah stumbled clumsily to her feet, so ill at ease she could not meet her friend's eyes. She felt gawky, unkempt, only a shadow of Rose. Yes, she was a shadow. A darker version of the true Rose.

As they walked into the room, the singing was already going well, rising to the rafters of the shop where members of the Amish community had gathered for an evening of praise on Christmas.

Many of the songs were sung in the old German language, timeless old Christmas hymns that reached back to the homeland in the Emmenthal Valley of Switzerland. There the forefathers had come to a decision to move to the New World, and they had settled in Berks County but ultimately became cloistered around Lancaster, where the soil was dark, loamy, and very productive.

The German hymns were beautiful and easy to sing. The youth sang mindlessly as they waited for the more catchy English tunes that were allowed after the traditional ones had been sung.

Children were lined up in small groups on the benches along the walls, trying their best to behave. They were so stoked on sweets, they could barely hold still, so they swung their feet, wriggled, pinched each other, giggled, and laughed out loud. Then they clapped their hands over their mouths, their eyes rolling above them, before a stern father or harried mother came to straighten up their erring offspring, which also served as a reprimand to all the children for a while.

After all, it was Christmas. Tomorrow was another holiday and another Christmas dinner or get together or hymn singing, so the children remained in high spirits.

Sarah, however, remained subdued, singing without her heart or her mind in the music.

So, that was how Rose felt. She wanted Matthew if she couldn't have him, but if he was available, she was not so sure. What in the world was wrong with her?

For Sarah, there was no question, no doubt, no wondering. She would always be happy to be with Matthew, second best or however he wanted her. As long as she might have a chance to be his wife, to share the remainder of her life with him, she would be senselessly happy.

That was all she wanted from life. Wasn't that real love?

That dry-mouthed, heart-thumping sensation the moment she was fortunate enough to be in his company? Everything he did, everything he said seemed so right and fine and wonderful, and that was how it would remain after they were married.

Marriage problems were completely out of the question for her and Matthew, as they would be the perfect epitome of God's will.

And so Sarah's thoughts went swirling about here, rampantly wandering there, her will level with God's, she was sure. After all, wasn't He a loving benefactor who gave richly of all things to enjoy? Dat spoke of God's love every single time he stood up before his congregation.

In the Old Testament, if God was with the children of Israel, they were given the victory over opposing armies. Nervously, Sarah stole a sideways glance and figured if that wasn't a formidable foe, she sure didn't know what would be. She watched Rose singing prettily in her showy Christmas dress, knowing all eyes were upon her. She had to know.

A swift dart of anger found its mark in Sarah's heart, thrown skillfully by the one who deceives. Her countenance fell as she lowered her head, and the singing paused for a bit.

She'd approach Matthew. She'd ask him fair and square about Rose.

Immediately, she knew she couldn't. She would not be able to build up the nerve, the sense of self to ask. Nor would she have the strength to accept if his answer was a disappointment.

She'd just clothe herself with God's righteousness, as the men of old had done, and He would be on her side, so who could come between them?

These thoughts came to her rescue on the way home, when Matthew remained silent. The horse plodded through the drifts that kept blowing stubbornly across the road in spite of the frequent runs made by the snowplows.

It was when they were stopped by the barn that Matthew turned, looked at her in the light of the headlights, and asked, "What would you say if I asked you for a date?"

There were no words anywhere for Sarah, her mind scrambling to catch what Matthew had just said.

"Did you hear me?"

"Yes. You mean, what would I say?"

"Yeah."

"How do I know if you're serious?"

"Oh, I'm serious."

"Then, I guess it's a yes."

"Good."

Sarah sat, looking straight ahead, a statue of fright.

"Aren't you going to look at me?"

She did, slowly, always obedient to Matthew's voice no matter what he asked. It was Matthew, the love of her life, and she would do whatever he asked, if it meant being his.

So when he leaned towards her and found her

lips, there were none of Mam's urgent words of warning to keep her from joyously yielding to his passion.

It was much later when Sarah ran up to the porch, opened the door silently, and tiptoed across the kitchen and up the stairs with stars in her eyes.

Sleep completely eluded her now. With her eyes wide open and her thoughts so scattered she could only retrieve bits and pieces of them, she lay in bed and smiled into the darkness.

He loved her!

He hadn't said the words, but oh my!

Over and over, she relived the evening and the intimacy with Matthew. And knew she had conquered. Matthew loved her!

His mother would be so happy, the circle so complete now. Mam would be alright with time, wouldn't she?

She thought of telling Hannah and Elam, knowing her position in their family would be cemented from the start. Hannah had always wanted this.

She thanked God over and over, her heart singing an old song of love.

In the morning, she was allowed to sleep in, if half past six could be called that, rising from her bed after being awake most of the night.

Nothing, however, could now dampen her outlook on life. Her wide eyes and bright smile gave her away completely before the family even sat down around the cheery breakfast table.

"My, you're happy this morning!" Mam observed.

"Yes, Mam, I am. Matthew asked me last evening."

She couldn't stop the heat rising in her face nor could she meet her mother's direct gaze, creating a sense of caution between them.

There was a moment of silence as Mam struggled with her emotions, unknown to Sarah, of course, the way she busied herself with the pancake batter. Eventually Mam said brightly, "Good for you, Sarah. I'm happy for you, if this is what you want."

"It is."

At the breakfast table, the steaming dishes between them, their hunger slowly satisfied, they spoke of Matthew and Sarah. Dat succeeded at hiding his surprise, and Levi slid his gaze slyly to the side and announced that there would be a wedding soon. Sarah laughed happily and said yes, there might be, but not till next year.

Priscilla watched Sarah's face and kept her innermost thoughts to herself. She congratulated her with as much genuine honesty as she could muster, but all was lost on the jubilant Sarah.

Suzie was the only one to remain silent, keeping her eyes averted, pouring syrup on a buttered pancake with great concentration.

"Suzie!" Levi tapped her arm. "Aren't you going to say something to Sarah?"

"Yes, of course. I just guess my teacher will be disappointed. Matthew comes down to school almost every evening," she said.

Mam's eyes met Dat's, and both raised their eyebrows, their faces completely rearranged seconds later, although there was no need as Sarah was oblivious to their exchange.

"Who is your teacher?" Levi asked quickly.

"You know."

"No, I don't."

"Her name is Naomi Ann."

"Who?"

"Oh, you don't know her." Suzie waved a hand, eliminating the need for further questioning.

Soon the Monday that had begun so favorably was clouded when Sarah caught sight of her mother sitting alone in the middle of little Mervin's twin bed. Her shoulders sagged with the weight of her grief as she held a pair of his flannel pajamas to her face and inhaled their smell, her *zeit-lang* (longing) for her youngest child encompassing her spirit yet again. Sarah stopped as she passed the door of his room and then went in to sit silently beside her mother, her hands in her lap, her head bent.

Finally, when a broken sob rose to the surface, she slid a comforting arm around her mother's heaving shoulders and said, "Don't, Mam. Please don't."

There was no answer, only small pitiful sounds coming from the pajamas.

Sarah's own eyes filled with tears, but something—what was it?—kept her from feeling deeply sympathetic. Did Mam really have to be like this, now?

Choking, Mam dropped the pajamas in her lap, wiped her eyes with the always useful corner of her apron, and took a deep, shaking breath.

"Sometimes, on days like this, when I'm not really pushed to get a lot of work done, I come up here to Mervin's room, just to remember. It helps to hold his clothes, feel them, inhale the odor of him. Or I guess what's left of him."

Sarah nodded, unable to form the words expected of her.

Sniffing, her mother straightened and reached for the small cedar chest containing his treasures, her fingers lifting each one—a steel sinker, a pencil sharpener, a bit of paper, two quarters, a dime, a spool of white thread. Then she replaced them, closing the lid, a finality, once more grasping for strength to sustain her.

"Oh, he was just so small. The water so horrible and strong. It must have thrown him around like a rag doll. I always hope he bumped his head and passed out, that he didn't suffer, swallowing that awful water. He was so little, so alone, and I wasn't there to help him."

Lost in the throes of her agony, she stared, unseeing, at the opposite wall, unable to rise above the bitterness of her small son's drowning.

"Why do you still feel this way, Mam? It's almost eight months since he died."

"I know. Time passing by helps, but I still need my personal time to grieve every now and then. He was my baby."

Mam turned her head then, taking Sarah completely by surprise, and said, "Let's talk about you now."

"Why me?"

"Oh, I'd think you'd be so very excited about dating Matthew."

"I am, Mam. It's every bit as unreal as you imagine."

Mam nodded, flipped a covering sting behind her back. "So now we need to have the talk about dating, too."

"What do you mean?"

Mam watched Sarah's face, the color spreading across it, the averted eyes, and knew suddenly why she had felt this sense of sadness, the grieving for her lost son, which had to be faced as well as this talk with her daughter.

Her voice fell firmly on Sarah's ears.

"You know that I cannot be untrue to you, Sarah."

Groping for words, Sarah's mouth opened and closed again.

"I want you to be happy."

Mam watched Sarah's profile, the bowed head, the way the curls sprang from her forehead like they had done when she was a little girl. Mervin's age.

How precious these daughters had been arriving in succession after four boys! Little Sarah, her hair a riot always, the mothers clucking and exclaiming, saying that the paternal grandmother had given her that wavy hair—that's what.

Here she was, concerned about Sarah but grieving for Mervin when, after all, Mervin was *fer-sarked* now, wasn't he? But what about Sarah?

"You know I have my concerns about Matthew. He's always been a magnet for girls, and I'm just so afraid . . ."

"Stop it, Mam," Sarah's voice cut in, sharp, frightened. "You don't want me to be happy, or you wouldn't talk to me this way. Matthew really does love me, Mam. He . . . he kisses me. He . . . he likes me much more than other girls. I know I can keep him happy. I can be his girl, and he will not want anyone else."

Mam thought of backing down, of trying to believe her daughter. She thought of putting her up on the same pedestal where she'd perched

Allen, thinking he was so much more than he was. In her eyes, in those days, Allen had done no wrong. Whatever he thought, Mam thought. Whatever he did, Mam thought was just great as well.

That, she knew now, was the surest, fastest path to a very real tumble off the pedestal, hurting more than one person in a clumsy plunge seen by everyone who had predicted it.

Mam had learned her lesson when Allen had moped around the house, sighing and crying after his beloved Katie broke off the relationship. He lost his position as foreman of his uncle's framing crew soon after.

To exalt one's offspring, to esteem them with pride, was not the way of the fruits of the Spirit, the humility and love of Christ's way, she had learned and learned well.

"Sarah, you stop." Mam's voice was terrible, cutting through all the assurance Sarah had piled around her sleeping conscience.

"First of all, young lady, he kisses you? And how much do you think that has to do with real love? The kind that lasts."

"Everything!" Sarah burst out passionately now.

Mam shook her head in disbelief. "Have I not taught you anything?"

"Why would you have? I never dated. That should be reason enough, don't you think?"

"Sarah, you must listen to me. You said he asked you for a first date and yet he has already kissed you? More than once? I am having a fit, seriously."

"Well, you'll just have to have one then."

With that, Sarah propelled herself off the bed and strode purposefully into her room, closing the door with more force than necessary.

Up came Mam's head. She stretched both arms high, got off the bed, and followed her daughter's footsteps. She yanked open the door and stood there, her feet planted firmly, her eyebrows lowered, her fists on her hips.

"You will not slam a door in my face!"

"I didn't."

"Of course you did."

Then Mam talked, really talked. She warned Sarah of the dangers of confusing love with want or need. She said it was the confusion that follows the heels of living by your own will, tricking yourself into believing that God approves of your will.

Sarah calmed under Mam's words, spoken with authority, although not without kindness. Mam assured her she would stand by her choice, and only God knew what the end result would be.

"I think you are old enough to make sensible choices, Sarah, but this is not one of them, allowing yourself this intimacy with him before you are dating. It's just not good, and I'm afraid nothing good will come of it."

Sarah said nothing.

"I'll have to ask you to promise me you'll speak to Matthew about this."

"I can't, Mam!" Sarah wailed.

"Why not?"

"It's asking too much. It's . . . it's all I have."

Sinking down beside Sarah, Mam realized from this statement just how great the danger really was, and she quaked in her shoes.

Oh my dear, small Mervin! I grieve for you when you are so safe, in a much better place with the Heavenly Father and all the angels. Here on earth, we are faced by this real adversary. How should she go about this?

In her wise way, Mam decided to wait. She needed to talk to Davey. They had a Christmas dinner to attend, and Sarah must have a bit of time as well.

So she held her troubled daughter in her arms, rested her forehead on Sarah's cheek, and told her to be very careful and to pray. God always answers the prayers of the humble, and she had so much more to offer Matthew—a good personality, a sweetness of character, and, of course, she was pretty, if that meant something.

Sarah laughed softly. She shook her head, but she knew without a doubt that she could not do what Mam required of her. It was too much.

Chapter 5

By March, the customers at the farmer's market in New Jersey were always impatient for the arrival of new spring onions, red radishes, and asparagus from Lancaster County. Sarah worked at the bakery, which took up one part of the huge brick building where many vendors plied their wares.

Today, Sarah was in a sunny mood, laughing at a heavyset matron who asked her why anyone could ever be anxious when these warm cinnamon rolls were so delicious and available the whole year round.

She stood behind a Plexiglass wall, rolling a strip of soft dough for the cinnamon rolls, the wooden rolling pin making a clacking noise as she bore down on both handles, her arms rounded, muscular.

"Do you have a moment?"

Sarah looked up, surprised to find her friend, Ashley, from the leather goods stand. She was a thin, pale girl who seemed as if her world was filled with anxiety.

They had more than just a passing friendship now. Sarah felt sorry for Ashley and was often unable to put her large, frightened eyes out of her mind.

Sarah asked for permission to take a break, and the two girls walked together through the market. They slid into a booth close to the soft pretzel stand, where the warm, yeasty smells made their stomachs rumble.

"Did you eat?" Sarah asked.

"No."

"You want to?"

"It's okay. I don't have any money."

"I'll buy you a pretzel."

"No."

Ashley had never allowed Sarah to learn much about her, other than the fact that her father owned the leather goods shop. But she was a nice girl even if she was timid and shy. And she had shown an interest in the survivors of the latest barn fire, where the house had burned as well as the barn.

Ashley wore a dull, washed-out sweatshirt, not quite green and not gray, her hair hanging thinly on either side of her face, and a . . .

Sarah gasped.

"Ashley! What happened to your eye?"

"Oh, it's nothing. It . . . I . . . like . . . I hit the corner of a cupboard door. At night. It was dark. Dumb."

Ashley bent to retrieve her purse, winced, then let it go, placing both hands on the table before picking at her fingernail, examining her hands very closely.

"Ashley. Is something wrong?"

"No."

The word was emphatic, followed by a swift shaking of her head. Suddenly, she gripped the table's edge, her eyes opened wide, and she met Sarah's eyes with intensity.

"Well, not really. But . . ."

Sarah waited.

"Since you're dating, do you, like, know your boyfriend really well? Do you know where he goes and what he does?"

Catching the inside of her lip with her teeth, Ashley's eyes were pools of raw concern.

Sarah laughed softly.

"Well, Ashley. I can't always compare some things with you. Our people live very quiet lives, in a way. Usually Matthew goes to work, comes home, reads, helps his mother, or plays baseball or volleyball sometimes. Just ordinary, dull stuff. So I don't feel as if I need to know where he is or where he goes throughout the week."

"Oh," Ashley said softly. "So, if my, like, boy-friend, disappears sometimes, would you worry if you were me?"

"Disappears? You mean he leaves for weeks or months?"

"Weeks . . . sometimes just days."

"He doesn't tell you what he's doing?"

"If I ask, he says he's just working or going to school or visiting."

"Well, then I guess he is."

"Yeah."

Sarah smiled reassuringly at her friend, bringing a warmth to her eyes, which crinkled at the sides as a smile spread across her wan face.

"Well, yeah, whatever," she said, trying to reassure herself.

"I mean, if you love him, I think you should be able to trust him. It seems those two sort of go together."

"You're right."

Ashley looked off across the market at the lights, the signs, the milling customers, her eyes wide, unseeing.

"How's . . . those people?"

"You mean Reuben Kauffmans?"

"Yeah."

"Good. They really are strong people."

"That's awesome. I have to go."

Ashley slipped away, disappearing into the crowd, the way she often seemed to do, leaving Sarah to shrug her shoulders and move off in search of something to eat.

Sarah never tired of the market's wide array of foods. She tried something new almost every week, when she was working on Fridays and Saturdays.

She bought a bowl of creamy potato soup, ate it with a dish of applesauce, and started back to work. She was suddenly stopped by the sound of voices behind the crowded display of leather products.

"You can't go around asking questions!"

There was a murmured reply and a louder voice, threatening, angry.

Sarah shivered as she hurried on, looking back over her shoulder after she passed. Something just wasn't quite right.

The spring peepers kept Priscilla awake that evening, so she got up to close her bedroom window on the east side of the house, figuring the bit of fresh air could be sacrificed for some peace and quiet.

She was bone weary after helping Mam with the Friday cleaning, helping Dat with the milking, and washing the carriage for church on Sunday. She had begun to think she was about as handy as that Robinson Crusoe's man Friday, doing everything and anything no one else had time to do.

She could hardly wait until the year passed and she would turn sixteen years of age. Then she would be allowed to work at the farmer's market with Sarah. Life was just so boring at fifteen.

Priscilla pushed aside the curtain, and a flickering, orange light entered her line of vision only a second before she screamed and screamed, a long, drawn out, shrill cry of alarm that brought a yell of response from the bedroom below.

"Fire! Fire! Dat! Dat! It's a fire!"

She couldn't move. She stood rooted to the spot by the window, her hands grabbing the windowsill, her nails digging into the varnished wood. She could see the flames already, beginning to leap wickedly in the night sky, illuminating the billows of smoke.

Sarah rushed into Priscilla's room, confused, having just fallen asleep after her long day at market.

"Oh no!"

Her hands went to her mouth, as if to keep the words from escaping. They heard Dat. He was running, opening the kitchen door. Levi bellowed from his room, a cry of alarm asking for someone to tell him what was going on.

"It's . . . it's at Elam's!"

"No! It's up the road."

"Surely not at Lydia's!"

"Oh no!"

The girls dressed hurriedly, grabbed sweaters and headscarves, and followed Dat out the front door. They walked quickly, the sound of the fire sirens a comfort now, assuring them that help was on the way.

They hurried past Elam and Hannah's, whose house was dark, which seemed unbelievable, but Sarah didn't want to alarm them. Besides, she looked terrible and didn't want Matthew to see her like that.

"*Ach* my."

Dat said the only thing he could think to say, the pity so overwhelming.

Yes, it was the barn belonging to the struggling Widow Lydia Esh. It was a rather large, old one, the paint peeling like white fur down its sides, the roof in good repair even though the metal was mismatched.

She kept a respectable herd of cows, and her oldest son, Omar, a square-shouldered, responsible seventeen-year-old, managed the animals with surprising expertise.

"There's no one awake!" Priscilla gasped.

With no thought other than the poor widow asleep in her bed, the girls ran, their speed increasing as they rounded the bend, hurtled down an incline, and raced up to the porch, their breath coming in gasps as they pounded on the front door.

The night their own barn had burned was still fresh in their minds. They opened the screen door and banged harder, yelling with all their might, the cows bawling in the background.

"Get the cows!"

Leaving the porch, they evaluated the distance from the licking flames to the cow stable. They might be able to save some of them.

Priscilla was yelling, crying, spurred on by a sense of duty borne of her own heartbreaking experience. She had no thought for her own safety, only that of the very necessary cows, the widow's livelihood, her bread and butter.

They raced through the door and searched for chains, snaps, anything that would give them a clue as to how the cows were tied.

"Snaps!" Priscilla shouted.

Sarah fell and started to crawl along the floor but bumped into the large face of a cow that was clearly terrified. She groped along its neck, found the collar, then the chain and the metal clasp, and clicked it open.

Bawling, the cow backed out, followed by four or five more.

Silently, a dark form joined them, unsnapping the cow's restraints, his arms waving, shooing them out.

Omar!

"Do you have horses in here?"

"One!"

"It's getting hot!"

"I'll get him!"

The youth plunged into the far corner of the barn, only to be met by a determined Priscilla, hanging on to the halter of a magnificent Belgian.

"I got him. Get what you can from the milk house!"

Sarah had already headed that way and was met by a stream of firemen, their great pulsing beasts already parked, men swarming everywhere, shouting, organizing.

Lydia Esh was also in the milk house, blindly throwing out buckets, milking machines, water hoses, anything she could fling out the door, her mouth set grimly, determined to survive.

The night sky was no longer dark, lit by the roaring flames of yet another barn fire, and it wasn't quite April, the month of their own fire.

Sarah heard strangled crying and looked to the old farmhouse, where she saw a cluster of shivering, frightened children cowering against the wooden bench by the door.

Quickly, she wound her way between the fire trucks, saw Dat and a few neighbor men backing a wagon away from the barn, and went to the children, herding them inside, lighting the propane lamp, assuring them they would be safe there in the house.

Anna Mae was Priscilla's age, a dark-haired girl who was terrified senseless with the shock of the fire. She stood by the refrigerator crying, unable to help with the younger ones.

Sarah steered her to the couch, covered her shivering form with an afghan she found on the back of a chair, and then sat beside her, rubbing her back and speaking any word of comfort she could think of.

"Are we going to die?"

The quavering little voice came from a small boy. There was a hole in his pajama top, his hair was tousled, and he was hanging on to a raggedy teddy bear with one of its button eyes loose and dangling from a white thread.

Sarah scooped him up quickly, smoothed his hair, and assured him they would certainly not die. The firemen were there now, and they'd keep the house safe.

The neighbors poured in, standing in the yard, white-faced, disbelief stamped on their features. This time something would have to be done, their faces said.

To start a barn fire was one thing, but to take from a poor widow was quite another. It was a slap in the face to a community already downed by previous fires but a brutal blow for a woman who had already endured more than her share of grief and hardship.

The flames leaped into the night sky, but the steady streams of water sizzled and sputtered, battling the tongues of fire far into the night. The water from the great nozzles was not used sparingly. And the haymow contained less than a third of the year's hay, so that helped.

In the course of the night, they soon realized there was more saved and less damage done because of the fire company's timely arrival. Who had called?

Dat testified to hearing the sirens when they were barely out of their own driveway. And Elams hadn't even been awake yet. Someone English? Some Amish on the road late at night?

Lydia Esh stood by the old tool shed, her work coat pinned securely with a large safety pin, and watched with hard resolve as the firemen worked to save whatever they could.

In the light of the flames, the cows stood, backed up against the peeling board fence, and watched warily. A neighbor man had taken the Belgian stallion home to his barn, away from the terrifying blaze.

Elam and Hannah came walking together, their faces grim with fear and—was it only weariness?

Hannah came into the kitchen, clucked and fussed. She told Sarah that this time it was completely senseless. A widow.

She praised Sarah effusively, saying of course she'd be the one here. But didn't she have market tomorrow? Sarah nodded, but said she'd probably take off with an emergency like this in the neighborhood. She was willing to sacrifice a small portion of her wages if she could be of help to Lydia.

The widow seemed so alone, so gaunt, so determined. She had no husband to lean on, standing alone by the tool shed, and Sarah wondered what must be going through her mind.

Self-pity? Defeat? Prayer?

She moved to the kitchen window, still holding the small boy, in time to see Omar walk over to stand beside his mother. She turned her face to him, then slowly reached out and clasped his hand, before releasing it quickly as if that small gesture of love embarrassed her.

Then Priscilla also moved to her side, slid an arm beneath Lydia's, and laid her head on her shoulder. Obviously moved, Lydia laid her cheek on top of Priscilla's head, and they stood together, an example of shared experience, heartfelt *mitt leidas* (sympathy), a statue of neighborly love.

But what really moved Sarah was the figure of Omar, the oldest son, who stood with his wide shoulders held erect, mature beyond his years, holding heavy responsibility before his time.

As if Priscilla read Sarah's thoughts, she moved to his side shyly but touched his arm and spoke. He inclined his head and answered, and that was where Priscilla stayed as the fire burned steadily into the night—at Omar's side.

Sarah turned and opened a cupboard door to look for a kettle to heat water for coffee. She found one and filled it, then searched for coffee with Hannah's help. Quietly, trying to hide the truth from each other, they slowly closed door after door before settling back on the couch, their eyes speaking. There was no coffee. There was only a scant amount of flour and sugar, a bag of oatmeal, a box of generic Corn Flakes.

"*Siss net chide* (It's not right)," Hannah breathed finally.

Sarah shook her head dully.

Hannah got up, saying she'd go get coffee and wake Matthew. It was embarrassing, the way he slept.

Sarah had no idea Matthew was still in bed. My, he was quite a sound sleeper. Perhaps he was up, already starting the French toast he'd made on the morning of their own fire.

A smile of belonging played around her lips, and she cuddled the small Rebecca close. Always, Matthew's love sustained her, lifted her spirits, no matter what.

When Hannah returned, she was pulling an express wagon laden with groceries. Sarah helped carry them in, amazed at Hannah's "extras."

The children were falling asleep again, so Anna Mae carried a few of them to her mother's bed, emerging white-faced but helpful as reality sunk in.

They made coffee and then sliced bread for sandwiches. Lydia came into the house and said, oh no, they shouldn't go to all that trouble, but she said it softly, as though if she spoke too loudly, her voice might break into tears, and she could not display weakness now.

Sarah spread mayonnaise on one piece of bread, mustard on the other, then layered the sweet Lebanon bologna and Swiss cheese between the slices and cut them diagonally while Hannah finished the coffee.

They put bags of pretzels, cans of beans and

peaches and applesauce in the pantry. A large round container of oatmeal cookies and one of chocolate chip were stored away beside them.

Lydia watched and apologized. She said she was a bit short this month, but the milk check was due tomorrow.

Hannah was kind, telling her she'd get a lot more than that before this was all over, chuckling in a way that meant well for Lydia.

When the men slowly trooped in for refreshment, Sarah couldn't help watching for Matthew, who remained maddeningly absent.

Hannah sidled up to her.

"He wasn't feeling good last night. I think he took too much Tylenol for a headache."

So that was it. Good. Sarah was relieved now, and she stopped watching the line of men. Matthew would be here if he felt well, that was one thing sure. He was so good-hearted, so neighborly.

The last one to come in was Omar, his face streaked and black, his eyes weary. Lee Glick walked with him, his own face darkened, highlighting the electric blue of his eyes. They were talking seriously but stopped when they reached the light of the kitchen.

Lee thanked Sarah for the coffee, but she did not meet his eyes, finding a certain safety in avoiding them.

Lee stepped to the side of the kitchen with

Omar following him the way a stray dog follows his benefactor, a look of adoration on his young, traumatized face.

Priscilla tried to be discreet, but her ears were tuned to everything Lee was saying, her eyes opening wide, snapping, alert. Finally, she just gave up and joined in the conversation. Whatever it was they were discussing, it was apparently an interesting subject for her as well.

Weariness overtook Sarah soon after the refreshments were served, and she looked around for Dat, caught his eye, and gestured to the clock.

He nodded. Relieved, Sarah moved to his side.

"Ready?"

"I'm falling asleep."

She told Lydia they'd be back in the morning after a few hours of sleep. She told Priscilla to come, they were going home now.

"Hey, thanks. You . . . you saved the cows," Omar said, talking mostly to Priscilla.

"You're welcome."

"Thank you, Sarah."

"You're welcome. You know we experienced the same thing, so we know exactly how you feel."

He nodded shyly.

"Good night, Sarah."

She looked up and met Lee's blue eyes and immediately wished she hadn't. The light in them questioned her, mocked her, put her on guard, as if she needed to explain her position in life, for being here, for dating Matthew, for . . . so many things.

She decided then that he was *gros-feelich* (proud) and she had chosen well, being with Matthew.

"You could at least have said goodnight to him," Priscilla grumbled as they wound their way between the throbbing fire trucks.

Sarah said nothing.

"Did you hear what he was telling Omar?"

"What?"

"He's interested in raising Belgians for profit. Lee is. He doesn't think Omar knows the value of that big stallion. Oh my goodness, Sarah! That horse could walk right over you and not even know it."

Sarah plodded along beside her sister as Priscilla babbled on about Omar and his Belgian and how kind that Lee was. Sarah's head spun, and she wished Priscilla would just be quiet.

"Where was Matthew?"

"He didn't feel good."

"Poor baby."

Sarah didn't feel the remark deserved an answer, so she walked on under the early spring sky, the night air still sharp with cold. But she could hear the sweet sounds of the earth waiting to burst into new life. The peepers were still persistent, their shrill mating calls stirring some old, bittersweet memory for Sarah. She became nostalgic, thinking back to when life was less complicated, soft and innocent, the way the years of her youth had been for so long.

The stars twinkled down from the black velvet sky as if to remind Sarah of their steadfastness. They were a guiding light, a trusting age-old light that God had planned the same way he had planned the spring peepers, the changing seasons, and, above all, the design He had for her.

Unbidden and mysterious, two tears emerged, quivered, and slid slowly down her soft cheeks, lit only by the light of a waning moon and about two million stars.

Chapter 6

Dat said if Lancaster County had responded well to disaster in the past, the caring was doubled, tripled, quadrupled for the poor widow after Hannah spread the word effusively and colorfully about the under-stocked pantry.

Even conservative members of the Old Order Amish voiced their outrage now. Something had to be done about all the fires. Old Dannie Fisher talked to the media, a vein of anger threaded through his dialogue, and no one blamed him. His old, bent straw hat was the focal point of the photograph on the front page of the Lancaster paper.

Ya, vell (Yes, well), they said. Enough is enough.

That poor Lydia Esh.

She's so *geduldich* (patient).

Aaron had passed away after a long and painful battle with lung cancer. The medical expenses had climbed to phenomenal heights. Always she'd accept the alms and the deacon's visits with a bent head and a strong face, any sorrow or self-pity veiled and hidden from view. She expressed gratitude quietly, showing no emotion, and no one could remember seeing her shed a tear at her husband's funeral.

And now, with hundreds of men swarming about her property, vanloads of people arriving daily from neighboring counties and states, her situation spoken to the world through the eager media, she showed no emotion—only a certain clouding of her eyes.

Sarah was in the small wash house, sorting through boxes of groceries—tin cans of fruit in one box, beans, tomato sauce, and other vegetables in another, and cereal, flour, sugar, and all the other dry staples in another. Many friendly faces she did not know assisted with the pleasant work.

The day was sunny, as if God knew they needed good weather to begin building the widow's barn. The mud was the biggest hurdle. Great deep pools of water had turned the already soaked fields into a quagmire. Load after load of stone was poured around the barn foundation, and still vehicles became hopelessly embedded in the wet ground.

Men called out, hammers rang, trucks groaned through the dirt and the mud and the gravel, and the sun shone as folks from all over came to the aid of Lydia and her children.

Someone had the idea to paint the interior of the house after noticing the stained, peeling walls and the lack of fresh, clean color. They'd buy paint after the barn was finished. They'd organize work days for different districts, have frolics to paint and clean, freshen the entire house. They'd plant the garden, mow the grass, plant some shrubbery, and build a fence.

Sarah approached Lydia that Monday, her eyes bright with the plans the women had devised. Lydia sat at the kitchen table, her angular frame so thin, her black apron hanging from her waist. Her hair was combed neatly, dark and sleek, her eyeglasses were sparkling clean, her covering clean but limp with frequent washings.

It was her eyes that concerned Sarah. They were veiled with a cloudiness, yes, but the inner light that everyone's eyes contained simply was not there.

Sarah hesitated to let the word enter her mind, but Lydia's eyes looked dead, lifeless, as if the spirit in them had left.

"Lydia."

"Yes?"

She turned her head obediently, and Sarah shivered inwardly at the darkness—that was it—the darkness in her gray eyes.

"What would you say if we painted your house?"

"Oh, I guess that would be alright."

"Are you sure?"

"Yes."

"We'll wait till the barn is finished. Wouldn't it be nice to have a fresh, clean house?"

"Yes."

Lydia was speaking in monosyllables, dully.

"Lydia, are you alright?"

Sarah leaned forward, put a hand on Lydia's as a gesture of comfort, and was appalled when Lydia pulled her hand away from Sarah's touch. Her lips drew back in a snarl, the darkness in her eyes became blacker, and she hissed, "Don't touch me."

Sarah gasped and turned her head as tears sprang to her eyes.

"I'm sorry."

Immediately Lydia rose to her feet and left the room.

The remainder of the day was ruined for Sarah. She felt as if she had inadvertently overstepped a boundary, been too brash, too . . . she didn't know what. She had only wanted to help.

She assisted the other women by mashing the huge vats of potatoes. She poured water into endless Styrofoam cups and washed dishes, but her heart was no longer in the duty she had previously performed so cheerfully.

Lydia moved among the clusters of people and did her tasks swiftly and efficiently, but alone.

When Sarah noticed Omar watching his mother, she decided to speak to him. She moved to a position where he could easily see her motioning to him with a crook of her finger to come outside with her.

"Omar, do you think your mother is alright?"

Omar was frightened by Sarah's question. She could tell by the swift movement of his head, the wide opening of his eyes—so much like his mother's but with a shock of dark hair falling over his forehead above them.

"Why do you ask?"

"She just seems to be half aware of . . . of everything."

Omar said nothing. He just turned his head, his eyes searching the crowd, before speaking.

"She's strong. She'll be okay. It's not like she hasn't weathered a lot more than this."

"Yes, of course. Your father's illness. I realize that. As you say, she'll be alright."

Priscilla came out of the house to stand beside Sarah, and Omar's eyes brightened immediately, the gray dancing with flecks of blue.

"Hey Priscilla."

"How's it going, Omar?"

"Alright, I guess. I just can't keep up with everything. Or everybody. Sometimes I get the feeling this barn is taking on a life of its own, building itself."

He grinned, his wide mouth revealing his perfect teeth, his face alight with a new energy.

"Oh, it's wonderful, Omar!"

Priscilla spoke eloquently, and he looked away from the undiluted eagerness in her eyes. Lowering his head, he kicked at an emerging tuft of grass, then looked up, revealing the veil that had moved across his own eyes, darkening them—just like his mother's.

"Yeah, well, we don't deserve any of this."

The words were harsh and imbedded with irony, self-mockery.

"Don't say that, Omar."

"I know what I'm saying. We're not worthy."

He turned on his heel and disappeared into the crowd, melting into it as if to find safety in the numbers. Sarah and Priscilla stood numbly, watching, keeping their thoughts to themselves.

The long lines of men snaked toward the house. The men filled Styrofoam trays with the good, hot food that had been donated and cooked by people from many different denominations or no denomination at all. All kinds of human hearts had been touched by the need of a poor young widow, and her situation had served to remove any fences of superiority or self-righteousness.

A need was being met, quite simply. More than one minister stood in his pulpit, or just stood without one, as was the Amish way, and spoke of the goodness of the human spirit in a world where pessimism is often the norm. Hadn't the loaves and fishes been distributed and twelve baskets left over?

Stories circulated about groceries being stored in the cellar and every available cupboard, even the attic, at Lydia's home. A brand new EZ Freeze propane gas refrigerator from Indiana also arrived out of nowhere.

Lydia hadn't had a refrigerator all winter, but she said she was thankful for the ice chests on the front porch. Sarah knew she probably didn't have much to put in them anyway.

Lengths of fabric, buttons, spools of thread. Coats and shawls and bonnets. The donations were endless. It was enough to make a person cry, Mam said.

The Beiler family hummed with a new purpose —that of making a different and a better life for the Widow Lydia. Dat had dark circles of weariness under his eyes from lack of sleep, and Mam was way behind with her housecleaning. March was coming in like a gentle lamb, just right for opening windows, airing stuffy rooms, turning mattresses, and sweeping cobwebs.

Sarah missed another week at market, and Priscilla traipsed over to the Esh family farm with any weak excuse. Sarah had a feeling her visits were more about Omar, Lee Glick, and the Belgians than anything else.

Then another bolt shook the community. Lydia Esh simply disappeared.

A frenzied knocking on the front door of the Beiler home was the beginning. Dat stumbled to the door in the dark, his heart racing, his mind anticipating the sight of the familiar orange flickering of someone else's barn burning yet again.

Instead, he found a sobbing Omar, completely undone, his mother's disappearance stripping away all the steely resolve that had upheld him after their barn burned.

Davey steered him into the dark kitchen with one hand and buttoned his trousers with the other before going to the propane lamp cabinet and flicking the lighter that hung from a string below the mantles.

As a yellow light flared across the room, Omar sank into the nearest chair. He covered his face with his torn, blue handkerchief, shaking his head from side to side, the only way he could think to show Davey Beiler, the preacher, how bad it was.

"I'm not surprised. I'm not surprised," he repeated over and over.

Dat remained calm and said nothing. Then he looked up to find his loving wife and steady helpmeet—dressed with her apron pinned on and her white covering in place—padding quietly across the kitchen in her house slippers.

When Levi called out loudly, insisting that someone tell him what was going on, Mam spoke to him quietly and said he must stay in bed, which seemed to comfort him. He obeyed, grunting as he turned on his side and muttering about "*da Davey Beila und all sie secrets* (that

Davey Beiler and all his secrets)" before falling asleep.

Omar spoke quickly. He couldn't seem to stop, his seventeen-year-old voice rising, cracking, falling, telling a journey of pain that had been repressed far too long.

"It wasn't the way you think it was in our family," he began.

A story of such magnitude had never before assailed Dat's heart. How could the children have appeared so normal? Omar was saying his mother had always been abused.

"Abused?" Dat asked.

"Whatever you call it. He called her horrible names. He hit her across the face, across the back. He pushed her into the gutters when they milked and laughed when the manure surged around her legs. He seemed to hate her and wanted to make her cry. But he couldn't stand her crying either. If she didn't cry, he quit easier than if she did."

"What about you children?" Dat asked grimly.

"It wasn't us. He was good enough to us. Not always nice, but he never laid a hand on any of us—just her."

"Why?"

Omar shrugged, wiped his nose, and then fell into a silence steeped in abject misery.

"I don't know what to do."

"Was your mother . . . How shall I word this?

Did she do anything to deserve your father's behavior? Did she fight back? Treat him miserably so that he retaliated? Was it just a bad marriage?"

"Mam always did the best she could. She finally got to blaming herself, assured us she just hadn't tried hard enough, spent too much money, overcooked his eggs, threw away some food. Whatever trivial thing he accused her of, she believed him and took the blame."

He began crying uncontrollably then, unable to form coherent words.

Mam came to stand beside Dat. She placed a warm hand on the worn, white T-shirt covering his shoulder and massaged it, a gesture born of habit, telling her burdened husband she was there for him and supported him always.

"I'm so afraid. I'm afraid to look for her. I'm . . ."

Omar looked up, the terror in his eyes a palpable thing.

"She . . . What are we going to do if she . . . killed herself?"

Dat spoke. "Omar, she wouldn't do that. She was not mentally ill. Your mother is a strong, good woman. She may have gone to her parents for advice or to a minister."

Vehemently, Omar shook his head.

"No, she didn't."

"Why do you say that?"

"Her parents blame her for the abuse. She told me."

A shadow moved across Dat's face, and he swiftly rose to his feet.

"Call Sarah, Malinda."

His voice was terrible in its purpose.

"Come, Omar. We must find her."

"Why . . . why are you in a hurry now?"

"She may be like a trapped animal. We need to search."

Together they moved out the door, Dat shrugging into his old, black work coat and setting his straw hat firmly on his head.

Sarah was awakened by the urgency in Mam's voice. She dressed quickly and ran down the stairs, followed by Priscilla.

Mam's face was pale, grim.

"Go help look for Lydia. She just disappeared, late this evening. Omar talked. It's frightening."

Sarah shivered, thinking of Lydia's aversion to being touched.

"God, please go with us now."

The prayer was simple but sincere as she grabbed her sweater and ran down the porch steps and out to the road, her long legs propelling her easily, her breath coming fast but comfortably. She was fit and young, strong with the physical labor to which she was accustomed.

Dat had a lantern, Omar a powerful flashlight.

They gave the girls a battery lamp and instructions, their faces tense with the reality of this night.

"We'll stay within the farm's boundaries. If we don't find her, we'll have to call 911. You girls search the house first."

Priscilla whimpered, an almost inaudible sound, but Sarah heard it and reached out to take her hand.

"Do you . . . Would you rather go back home?"

"No. I want to stay with you."

Quietly, not wanting to wake the children, they tiptoed down to the basement, holding their breaths. They held the lantern high, the white light casting weird shadows on the aged walls. The paint was peeling, and greenish mold grew along the bottom of the stone walls.

A pile of empty potato bags almost stopped their heartbeats. Sarah kicked them aside, relieved.

The basement produced nothing. There was no sign of anyone having disturbed anything at all, so they tiptoed back up the dusty staircase. They searched the kitchen, living room, the main bed-room, even beneath the unmade bed. Then they inched their way upstairs.

"We can't wake the children."

"I know."

"The attic?"

Would they be strong enough to face something as horrifying as . . . ? Sarah refused to think the word. She wouldn't.

Turning the old, porcelain knob on the attic door, Sarah grimaced as it squeaked loudly. Then she stepped cautiously on the first old stair tread, which groaned forcefully. Hoping for the best, they made their way steadily up the stairs, every step sending out a new and strange squeak or groan, until they reached the top where they stood together, their breathing inaudible.

Sarah held the battery lantern up and sighed. Boxes, bags, old furniture, torn window blinds. There was nothing of value, but the huge jumble of things could hide a person well. The rafters were low and dark with age. Nails had been pounded into them, no doubt having held hams and onions and strings of dried peppers in times past.

"You hold the lantern," Sarah whispered.

Priscilla obeyed and held it high as Sarah moved boxes and bags and got down on her knees to search beneath the eaves. Priscilla's large, frightened eyes searched the rafters, thinking the unthinkable.

Suicide.

God, we've come this far. Please stay with us.

When Sarah yelped in alarm, Priscilla clapped a hand over her mouth to stifle the shriek behind it, but it escaped around her fingers. She couldn't hold back the high-pitched scream.

No matter now, Sarah thought resolutely. They'd have to know. Her hand had made contact with a thin form lying behind an old quilt frame. She was on her back, her face turned to the side, her skin translucent, her eyes closed.

Sarah crawled closer and put an ear to Lydia's chest. She raised exultant eyes to Priscilla, who was now trembling.

Muffled bumps and cries from below told them of the children's rude awakening by the awful sound in the night.

"She's warm! She's breathing. Lydia!"

Sarah shook the limp shoulders gently.

"Beside her," Priscilla said.

Sarah's eyes took in the bottle of ibuprofen. The cheap brand from Walmart. Equate. Suddenly it angered her, and her mind refused to accept this bottle of pills lying empty, the cap carefully replaced.

"Get Dat! Tell the children to be quiet."

She guessed anger was a good replacement for fear. It could get her through the worst of times if it had to. Sarah was braced up by it, strong because of it, as Dat and Omar pounded up the stairs, their eyes wide, the fear mixed with relief, and, yes, anger.

"Let's get her down," Dat barked.

"Omar, call 911. Now."

"On my cell phone?"

"However."

In his moment of terror, he wasn't thinking straight, Sarah knew. It was only later that she allowed herself a small smile, thinking of Omar asking her dat, the minister, if he should use his cell phone. Cell phones were forbidden instruments of encroaching technology, but they were used by many of the youth and some older people as well.

Grunting, Dat reached for Lydia's still form, pulling her away from the eaves and instructing Sarah to hold her below her knees. He'd take the shoulders.

Sarah was not sure she could carry this poor creature down the attic stairs. Even a thin woman was dead weight in that state.

She hesitated.

"I . . . I don't know."

"You can do it, Sarah."

Together, they inched their way down the creaking attic stairs. Lydia's head rolled to the side awkwardly, her legs flopping on either side of Sarah's hands and her feet slapping randomly against the steps.

"*Kinna. Bleivat drinn*! (Children. Stay there!)" Dat called, his voice loud with authority. They were crying, asking questions, and Anna Mae refused to obey, charging through the doorway of her bedroom, crying uncontrollably.

"She's sick," was all Dat said.

"Come, Anna Mae. Come with me. The ambulance is coming."

Priscilla slid an arm about Anna Mae's shoulder, explaining, consoling. Her sobs turned to sad, hiccupping whimpers.

By the time they'd finally reached the living room on the main floor, the high, wailing sirens were already audible.

Sarah met Dat's eyes, visibly relieved. They both looked at Lydia, her frame swallowed by the old green sofa, the holes torn in the upholstery covered by a crocheted afghan, discolored from frequent washings in the old washing machine.

A sadness spread through Sarah's heart as the knowledge of this pitiful situation spoke to her. Lydia looked so young, her skin pearl white, her wide eyes closed, her mouth still determined, strong.

How old was she?

Omar was seventeen years old.

Please let her live, dear God. Just let her live. Sarah wasn't aware that she was praying until she saw Melvin come charging through the front door, and she burst into tears of shock and relief all at once.

Sarah had forgotten that Melvin belonged to the fire company now. Since the barn fires had started, he was determined to be of value to the community. But nothing had ever prepared him for this sight, and he had to step aside, grappling with the overwhelming emotion, and let the trained personnel take over.

Lydia was hospitalized, and the deadly quantity of ibuprofen removed from her stomach by the greatest invention, the stomach pump. Her parents were at her side, the beginning of a deep remorse entering their hearts.

Sarah and Priscilla stayed with the children, and they talked with Melvin and Omar for hours. Anna Mae hovered around the conversation, her face white with fear and disbelief.

Melvin listened, dumbstruck for once in his life. It was an uneasy situation for him, being cornered by an unbelievable situation and rendered helpless without knowing what to say. He had never in his life felt the kind of pity that swelled up inside him and took away every other emotion. Even his bravado was gone and his skill of planning, of moving and shaking. He simply did not know what should be done, except maybe get down on his knees and admit to God that he didn't understand how he felt, and He'd have to make it plain.

Chapter 7

In the morning, when Sarah was frying cornmeal mush for the children and Priscilla was helping Omar do chores, there was a soft knock on the door, and Matthew entered.

Sarah was giddy with happiness to see him. She lay down the spatula she was holding, her eyes weary with the events of the night, and said, "Good morning!"

"Sarah!" Matthew greeted her as joyfully. Without a thought of the children, she flew into his arms and was held, secure in a haven of comfort.

Her Matthew. Still unbelievable, after these months of dating.

"Tell me what happened," he said, his face alight with interest, his eyes soft and kind, such a rich brown and filled with caring.

Sarah obeyed. She spoke quietly to protect the children from more fear, then turned to the stove to finish breakfast.

Matthew listened and then responded kindly but with a sort of petulance, inquiring about her having to be there.

"Oh, we're neighbors, Matthew. Omar came to our door."

"Every time there's a scene, and that seems to

be happening with a certain regularity, there you are in the middle of it. Why?"

His tone was high, anxious, mocking.

Sarah remained at the stove, her back turned, and she stood very still, breathing slowly, gathering control.

Turning, she said levelly, "It's my duty. My parents always stress that."

"Well, mine don't."

There was nothing to say in response.

As if he had suddenly been given a new license, he began to barrage Sarah with his ideas about the barn fires.

Quite clearly, these fires brought out what was in the Amish, which wasn't very much, he said. He rambled on about this woman who was so worldly she'd attempt suicide and how Mervin was drowned by the devil's hand.

"I mean, Sarah, look around you. God is trying to say something here. All this isn't happening to the Mennonites or the other churches around us that are much more spiritual."

A dagger of fear shot through Sarah, but she quickly gathered her composure and calmly broke eggs into a pan. She bent gracefully to lay slices of bread in the broiler of the old gas stove.

"I think the Amish church is way out of line. All we think about is *ordnung* (rules). There's a reason for these barn fires."

Sarah slid the door of the broiler shut with her

foot and gave it a small kick to make sure it closed all the way. Then she slid a spatula beneath a sizzling egg, still remaining quiet.

"Well, aren't you going to answer?"

"Yes, Matthew. You have a point. Of course."

He came over and stood a little too close to her. He whispered in her ear about how he wanted to kiss her, but there were too many eyes around. Then let himself out the door with a silly wave, leaving Sarah smiling foolishly at the eggs. She kept on smiling as the children sat around the table and ate their breakfast.

Oh, that Matthew was something. She sure hoped he wasn't going to get some idea about leaving the church into his head, just because of the fires.

She watched as the teams began to arrive, the kindly women entering the kitchen, asking questions, clucking, caring. The police and private investigators came, asking questions, interrogating Omar, Priscilla, and Dat as well as herself.

They tried to remain as truthful as possible but knew, ultimately, that the real reason for the attempted suicide would have to come from Lydia herself.

The news reporters and journalists went wild with the nature of this story, the barn fires projected on TV screens across the nation, sensational half-truths filling the members of the Amish community with dread.

Where would it end? How much was simply too much?

At home again together, gathered around the kitchen table, Dat spoke at length, sparing his family nothing. He said these were hard times, spiritually as well as emotionally, and they would all need to remain steadfast in prayer and supplication and draw close to God to ask his guidance.

Levi said God was angry at Lancaster County, and everybody better sit up and take notice. Dat reprimanded Levi sharply, something so unusual even Mam looked surprised.

"God is allowing this to draw us together. Look at poor Lydia. A family in dire straits, robbed of a chance to have . . ." He stopped and broke down, his eyes filled with so much tender pity, Sarah imagined his eyes looked like God's somehow.

Sarah, however, kept the small tidbit of Matthew's attitude hidden. He was likely just going through a bad time, unable to do anything about these fires continuing and feeling helpless because of it. Bless his heart.

Despite the somber topic, Priscilla was beaming and smiling, unable to contain her excitement about the new barn Abner Fisher had just designed for the horses, those Belgians. She said if Omar didn't mind, she'd like to work with them, and if she was allowed, she wouldn't need another horse to replace Dutch.

"Priscilla," Levi said forcefully.

"What?"

"You can't go over there and work with Omar. He's a boy."

"I know. But his sister, Anna Mae, is there."

"You're not going," Levi said.

Dat smiled widely and winked at Mam.

"We'll see," was all he said.

The Widow Lydia came home from the hospital. Sarah and Mam walked through the tender spring sunshine, carrying a freshly baked carrot cake made with pineapple, nuts, and raisins and covered with cream cheese frosting.

Lydia was propped up on pillows, the fresh, white pillowcases framing her thin, tired face. Without her glasses, she appeared so young. The light in her eyes was genuine now, a small flame of hope burned there, the deadness gone.

Her mother and father were both present, hovering about, finding her glasses, arranging her pillows, asking if she was cold, bringing a blanket, quietly wiping their own tears.

The outdoors hummed with activity, as usual, the projects still going on but with a difference since word had circulated of Lydia's illness.

Tight-lipped wives packed their husbands substantial lunches, saying enough *ga-mach* (to do) was enough. They'd cook a good hot supper in the evening, but a packed lunch was enough for today.

At the end of the day, many of the wives raised their hands in dismay after finding all the food still in the Ziploc bags. The men sheepishly admitted that the dinner had been catered again by the folks at Kentucky Fried Chicken.

There was no contest between a cold lunch or that chicken. All this, however, was spared the Widow Lydia. She remained in bed and talked, shared, and cried with her parents asking her forgiveness over and over. They had no idea it had been so bad, they really didn't, and Lydia believed them. They made an appointment to go for extensive counseling at Green Pastures in Lebanon County, at David Beiler's request.

Mam and Sarah left the cake, their hearts immeasurably relieved to see the healing in Lydia's eyes. Again, the Amish folks as well as many of their English neighbors had rallied around the poor, the needy, the hurting, and the wounded in spirit, and life resumed its normal pace.

The trust fund at Susquehanna Bank grew to mammoth proportions, but Lydia did not know. She went back to her duties slowly, but she sat and cuddled little Rebecca and her thin, small Aaron most of the time. She thanked God for David Beiler, though he did not know that he had done anything at all.

The wind was a bit chilly when Mam asked Dat to hitch up Fred. She wanted to pick up her sister and go to Ez *sei* Mamie's (Ez's wife Mamie's) quilting, over along Route 897.

Dat did his duty, and Mam sat happily on the driver's side of the preacher's *doch veggley* (carriage), took up the reins, and thanked her husband.

"Be careful," Dat said. It was the same thing he always said, and Mam smiled.

The preacher's carriage had no front, just a heavy, black canvas duster that those in the front seat pulled up over their laps. There were doors on either side to slide closed when the weather was inclement, but today Mam kept them open and enjoyed the brisk little winds that flapped the gum blanket and swirled about her face.

She wondered if all Amish carriages had been preachers' *doch vegglin* in times past. Probably, the way most things changed over time, the storm fronts (windows with a sturdy dash) were a new and modern addition at one time. That had probably followed on the heels of the market wagon, the heavy, versatile carriage used to haul produce or baked goods—wares of all kinds—to open air markets in Lancaster City.

Mam adjusted her black bonnet and was grateful for her shawl. The black, woolen square of fabric pinned securely around her shoulders guarded against the chill in the wind.

Turning into her sister's driveway, she noticed the new growth of her hostas. The wide green leaves pushed the mulch away, new life springing from the earth everywhere, although Davey had told her it was still plenty wet to plant peas. She had the cold frame filled with early lettuce, onions, and radishes. She had checked them herself this morning and was surprised at the growth.

"Whoa."

Fred stopped obediently and then pulled on the reins to loosen them. Mam watched the side door, eager to see her sister, Miriam. She emerged, pulling the door shut behind her, one hand going to her covering. As usual, she wore a black sweater, but no shawl or bonnet.

Lifting the gum blanket, Mam exclaimed, "Where's your bonnet?"

Miriam plopped down on the seat, wiggled her shoulders, and said, "Boy, we fill up this front seat pretty snugly."

Mam smiled and thought, you mean you do.

Miriam weighted a bit over two hundred pounds and frankly stated that fact to any who inquired. She'd been heavy all her life. She was who she was, she carried it well, and tough if someone thought she was fat.

"Where's your bonnet?" Mam repeated.

"You know I hate bonnets."

"Now, Miriam."

"Sorry, Malinda. But I'm not a preacher's wife."

No, you're not, Mam thought wryly, knowing her sister was undoubtedly not cut out to be one.

"Well, alright. I like my shawl and bonnet on a chilly day."

They had gone a few hundred yards when Miriam said, "Poo!" and reached for the gum blanket, pulling it up well above her waistline.

"Should have worn your shawl and bonnet."

Miriam shrugged and said the good, thick buggy blankets would keep her warm.

Fred trotted briskly. The two sisters talked non-stop, catching up on community news, family gossip, the highs and lows of raising large families, clucking, lending listening ears, always sympathetic, understanding. It was the way of sisters everywhere, confiding in each other, the trust so complete, so cushioned with unconditional love, that conversation flowed freely, unrestrainedly.

"How's Sarah doing with her Matthew?" Miriam asked.

"Fine, I guess."

"You don't sound too enthused."

"I'm not."

"*Ach* Malinda. Come on. He's quite a catch, and you know it. You're just trying to be humble. Duh!"

"Miriam, I think looks is about as far it goes with that one."

She held up one hand to hush Miriam.

116

"Let me have my say. I can't talk like this to anyone else, not even my husband, who is always a pushover where Sarah is concerned."

Mam stopped, looked at Miriam.

"Isn't a pushover a baked item?"

"You mean a popover?"

They laughed heartily, rich chuckles of shared humor. Then Miriam told Mam if she didn't watch her horse they were going to have a wreck, and she meant it. Mam said no they weren't, she was a good driver, but Miriam didn't really think she was. She just didn't say it.

"Anyway, you were saying?"

"Oh, Matthew Stoltzfus."

"Yes."

"You know I think the world of Hannah. She's my best friend. But she had those two boys long after her girls, and . . ." Mam's voice became strong, forceful. "They're both spoiled rotten!"

Miriam gasped. "Malinda! I can't believe you said that!"

Mam sat up straight.

"Yes, I said that, and it feels good to be completely honest. She caters to those boys. She thinks they can do nothing wrong. And Matthew is less than ambitious. He flirts with any girl who will look at him, and there are plenty of them. I'm not convinced he loves Sarah at all. She's just second best because Rose doesn't want him."

"Wow!" Miriam mouthed.

"Yes. It's that bad."

"Are you sure you're not being too hard on Sarah?"

"No."

"Boy, Malinda. You sound like someone I don't know."

"Well, don't know me then. I'm just so sick of tiptoeing around Sarah and turning a false face decorated with an artificial smile. I know it's not going to make a lick of difference what I say. She fancies herself in love with him."

"Malinda! She is! That poor girl has always wanted Matthew."

"Wanted and loved are two very different things."

Miriam nodded.

"You are absolutely right."

"I know I am."

"Let's not talk about this anymore. It makes me sick to the stomach. Your Sarah is such a nice girl. I know she deserves genuine happiness with an extra nice guy."

Mam flicked the reins across Fred's back, urging him on. They'd be late for the quilting, and Mamie made the best filled doughnuts in Lancaster County.

Ez *sei* Mamie had pieced the plum-colored quilt by herself, a new design, she thought, until the contrary Emma Blank informed her that the

Courthouse Steps pattern was as old as her grandmother's grandmother.

"Well, it's new to me."

So began the day at an Amish quilting. The colors of the quilt in question were called plum and sage, whereas years ago, they would have been called green and purple. They still were by the older generation.

The fact that Mamie made the best filled doughnuts was widely discussed and finally accepted, after weighing the pros and cons of using doughnut mix or stirring up batter from scratch.

"You can't beat the ones made from fresh ingredients. And you have to have real mashed potatoes in the dough, not potato flakes," Mamie said, her cheeks like ripe apples, her eyes popping. The overwhelming pressure of having all those talented women in her house automatically cranked up the volume that was loud to begin with.

"I don't believe it," countered Emma Blank.

"Me either! We make thousands and thousands of them for bake sales and auctions. Every single one of our doughnuts comes from a mix. We buy it in fifty-pound bags," another voice chimed in, "And they are amazing."

Mamie's eyes snapped, but she smiled and, with a grand gesture, set a beautiful glass tray of perfect filled doughnuts in the middle of the table, surrounded by carafes of coffee and *vissa tae* (meadow tea).

Much oohing and aahing followed. Eyes rolled, and exclamations of "*Siss net chide* (it isn't right)" and other approving statements mingled with giggles and outright laughs of appreciation. Hands repeatedly reached for more doughnuts, everyone knowing full well that they were unbeatable.

Miriam whispered to Malinda that she guessed she'd have to stick a bag of pretzels in her pocket to keep that cloying sweetness from staying on her tongue till lunchtime. Then she admitted she'd eaten three doughnuts.

"Not three!"

"Three."

The women set to work. Their needles were plied expertly, up and down, in and out, the sturdy off-white thread pulled between the layers of fabric and batting.

Thimbles flashed, silver or gold. Occasionally *naits* (thread) was called for across the frame as the spools lay in the middle of the large quilt out of everyone's reach.

Someone would quickly press down on the quilt, allowing a spool to roll toward a hand where it was snatched up and thrown to the person asking for it.

Inevitably, the conversation turned to the barn fires and the latest victim who had been unable to face her life anymore. It was spoken of quietly, reverently, and without malice. Mam knew the most. She knew the truth as the well-informed minister's wife. Yet she spoke only what was necessary and then passed out Post-it notes with Lydia's address written on them.

Women blinked back tears of sympathy, blew their noses surreptitiously, and avoided eye contact, each one bearing the news stoically. The poor, poor woman. Oh, it hurts to hear it, they said.

Mam assured them all that healing was well underway, and her counselors were well pleased with her progress.

"You know she always was quiet. I suppose we just accepted her as that. She hid so much."

"What do you think became of Aaron?" Emma Blank asked, her words falling like rocks on macadam.

No one answered.

Mam finally spoke in a quiet voice, reminding Emma of his long and painful battle with lung cancer, the suffering that provided opportunity for him to repent.

Miriam said nothing but thought her sister had such a nice way about her, always soothing ruffled feathers, looking for the good in people, no matter what the circumstances.

That's why she was more than a bit surprised by her dislike of Matthew. Well, time would tell.

The men of Leacock Township held another meeting about the fires, this time speaking at length about the need to either get large dogs or sleep in their barns. It had to be one or the other. Mastiff. German Shepherd. Doberman. Whatever it would take.

Some farmers installed alarms with wires encased in durable rubber stretched across their driveways, but they needed electricity, so only a few actually used them.

Dogs were acquired, or sleeping bags and air mattresses. But sleeping in the barn lasted for only a few weeks for many as the meticulous housewives turned up their noses every time the well-meaning boys of the household came in the house after spending a night in the barn.

Men tilled the fields as the sun shone and birds wheeled their ecstatic patterns in the sky. Tulips pushed the soil aside and grew tall and stately, tossed about like hula dancers in the spring breezes.

Women bent their backs in their gardens, purple, blue, green, and red skirts tossing about them as they planted fresh, new onion bulbs and wrinkled, grayish peas, tiny radish seeds, and lettuce seeds so fine they threw them in slight indentations in the soil and figured at least half of them would grow.

Children skipped through the fields, holes in their school sneakers, longing to go barefoot, but their mothers remained adamant. The earth was too cold. They must wait for the first bumblebee.

The children searched the fence rows for new dandelion growth and picked the greens joyfully. They carried them to their mothers, who washed and steamed them. Then they fried a good bit of fat bacon, stirred flour into the cooked and crumpled bacon, added chopped hard-boiled eggs and the steamed greens, and had a fine supper.

The Widow Lydia walked carefully among her new shrubbery, unable to take it all in. She marveled at the bulbs that had produced wonderful red tulips, a gift from Royer's Greenhouses.

And then because they were so red, and the leaves so green, and the fresh mushroom soil around them so brown—everything a rainbow of vibrant color—she folded her arms on the new PVC fence surrounding her house and cried.

She cried because she was grateful that she could. She could let great, wet tears flow down her thin, pale cheeks and never once feel any guilt. It was alright to cry. In fact, she was supposed to cry. They said it was healing.

The barn stood at the bottom of the small incline below the house, new and shining, as if it grew from the earth itself, sprouting from a bulb like the red tulips. In a sense, it had. A bulb was a small thing, but with God's power, it grew to a much larger thing of indescribable beauty. The men had been tools in His hands, bearing the ability to wield a hammer, operate a saw, read blueprints, all the while their hearts holding goodwill toward their neighbor.

So the earth bore its new life, and the barn stood solid and charming, one complimenting the other to form a picture of beauty, as hearts that are hidden from sight grow by the Master's Hand, in love, in forbearance, and tender pity.

Chapter 8

Sarah kicked her bare foot against the moist, new grass below the swing by the grape arbor and thought about the words Matthew was saying. She rolled them over in her mind, trying to decipher their meaning, but none of it made any sense at all. He wanted to go away. He wanted to travel, see the world. He needed to get away on a spiritual quest.

Sarah felt herself becoming hysterical, imagining his perfect profile with the dark hair and brown eyes climbing a tall mountain with no trees, just grass and a small, wizened little man sitting on top.

A spiritual quest? He hadn't committed himself to the Amish church yet, as she had done the previous year. But how could he want to seek anything other than the faith of his fathers? She simply could not grasp what he was saying.

He'd be gone for a few months. Months? Not weeks. Or days. Months. The time was too long, the distance too great.

Feebly, she tried to explain that she couldn't allow this. They'd never make it apart, but she floundered, wallowing in the misery of her useless explanations and refusing to accept his words, hoping her refusal would keep him from leaving her.

He took her willing body into his arms. He kissed her with the usual enthusiasm and promised her he'd be back if she'd be patient with him. She traced his face with her fingertips and tried to memorize the exact dimensions. Her heart was already aching with the pain of missing him.

He was going with a single man from the Charity group, one of the other Amish youth groups, he said just before he left. Lester Amstutz. She nodded dumbly and stood up woodenly. She was surprised her limbs didn't creak and clank, as if made from tin, when she turned to go inside.

She stood with her hand on the doorknob for a long time, unable to face the suffocation her bedroom would subject her to. Turning, she reached out a hand and whispered, "Matthew?" It was a question, as if she was unsure about what he had told her. She wanted to run after him, hold him, keep him from going anywhere without her, but she could only stand on the front porch and whisper his name again.

What was that about loving something and setting it free? If you loved something and set it free, it would return? Or "he" would return. Not "it."

Reality finally reached her senses, and Sarah

turned the knob, made her way up the stairs, and lay on her bed, fully clothed. Sleep eluded her and the night stretched out long and black and filled with sorrow.

Somewhere inside, she knew Matthew was trying to be gentle. He did not want to be Amish. He didn't appreciate the heritage of his family, the old linage of conservatism, the traditions, the way of life.

Well, when he returned and had made a decision to leave his family and join a worldly church—was there such a thing?—she'd go with him.

Dat and Mam would get over it, eventually.

Wasn't that the most beautiful verse in the Bible? That part about Ruth going with her mother-in-law? "Thy God shall be my God." But she already had a God.

The old rooster in the henhouse crowed, and through the heavy blackness, Sarah squinted at the alarm clock and rolled out of bed. She surprised Dat by being the first one in the barn at four thirty. She wasn't tired, she said.

That spring, Sarah's world became tumultuous, her mind and spirit tossed about, surging forward, drawing back. The only description fitting of her inner turmoil was the stormy waves of the sea.

It was funny, the way doubt changed her perspective. The kindly people in church, sitting on their hard benches with their attention levels varying to some degree, all made her wonder if it really was the way Matthew had said—unspiritual.

There was Henry Zook, sound asleep, his head rolling to one side, his mouth sagging open slightly. If that wasn't unspiritual, she didn't know what was.

In the kitchen, a group of young women were gossiping, covering their mouths as they glanced around, their eyes stealthy like cats. Catty, that's exactly what they were. Well, perhaps Matthew was right.

She saw the yellowed covering set haphazardly on the head of the aged deacon's wife, a fine dusting of dandruff across her black cape. She thought of the snowy line veils the women in the Charity group wore instead with their hair combed up over their heads in a loose, attractive fashion. They wore pure pinks and yellows and blues. And Sarah suddenly didn't like the sloppy old Amish *ordnung*.

Then she became thoroughly miserable, remembering the day of Matthew's departure, the eagerness in his eyes, the new light of expectation. She would have done anything to keep him.

Lester Amstutz had waited in his sports car, keeping an eye on every move they made when Matthew stopped to say his final good-bye. Lester's head remained turned in their direction, watching shrewdly like a lion inspecting its prey, unsure what the outcome of its stealth would be.

Matthew had not held her hand that day. He only held her eyes with his own, his voice quiet, smooth, like water gliding quietly over oiled rocks, without turbulence. His voice was even, flat, whispery in its reverence. Had he already made a decision?

Fear had clawed at her heart, raking its fiery talons through her, producing a pain so great she had reached out with both hands, her palms upturned, and stepped toward him, a great sob catching in her throat as the words poured from her pain.

"Matthew, you can't! You can't do this to me. Does my love mean nothing to you? Does our God, our way of life, our heritage mean nothing? Don't go. Please, don't go. You'll be enticed into a new belief, to a place I cannot follow."

Matthew drew himself up, his voice quiet, reserved, as smooth as silk.

"I must go, Sarah. I have prayed. I want to become born again. Whosoever cannot leave his father or mother or sister or brother is not worthy."

"Don't, Matthew." Anger consumed her now. "You know better than to spout that verse at me. If you do that, you are clearly calling me an unbeliever. I am not. Neither is your father, or your mother, or . . . or Chris!" she spat out.

"By your anger, I know you are not born again."

She wanted to draw her arm back and smack him across his face, beat his chest with her fists, rail and cry and break down this new barrier between them. What she did do was draw a deep and steady breath and say, "It certainly has not taken you long to descend into self-righteousness."

A small, sad, smile played around Matthew's lips. His eyes became heavy-lidded, almost sensual. "I found Jesus last night at the revival meeting. I have not, as you say, descended into self-righteousness, but I've been clothed by the righteousness of Jesus."

"So you're not coming back?"

"Oh, I wouldn't go so far as to say that. I'm on a search for the true call of Jesus Christ."

There was nothing to say to such piety.

"I am a new creature, alive in Jesus."

That was the sentence that threw her off balance, hurling her into a vortex of uncertainty, wavering unsteadily on the brink of a precipice as he turned, still wearing the small, sad, conquering smile, and walked placidly away from her.

Would she always have every single angle of his body imbedded in her mind? His dark hair, cut just right, his wide shoulders, the way he swung his arms, his loose gait, even the way he placed his feet, so athletic, so Matthew. Her Matthew. No one else's. Not the world's, not a church's, not a new belief's.

Oh, come back to me, Matthew. Just come back.

And so her spring had turned gray. She no longer enjoyed the beauty of the azure sky, the birds' songs, the smell of fresh soil and newly mown hay, the wonder of a newborn calf. Her life was too full of indecision, longing, fear, and, above all, the strange new way she now viewed the Amish through lenses of doubt.

Was Matthew right? Was not one member of the Amish church born again? Did they all live in ignorance and suppression? She thought she might eventually go mad as the darts of confusion slowly entered her heart, draining the life from her.

Desperately, she hid her turmoil from her parents. They knew Matthew had gone on a trip to see the western part of the United States. That was all. That was all Hannah knew, or Elam. They went about their busy lives, working from sunup to sundown, happy and talkative, their ignorance about their son's travels a blessing, Sarah supposed.

Was it pride that kept her secret intact? Sarah didn't know. All she wanted was for Matthew— the old, happy, genuine Matthew—to walk back up on the porch, take her in his strong arms, say

131

there was nothing out there for him, that he was staying Amish.

She prayed frequently and fervently, with tears squeezing between her stinging eyelids, which were red and swollen from lack of sleep.

Mam watched her daughter, bought allergy medication at her request, and said nothing.

One fine spring evening, when the air was mellow with summer's warmth, Sarah could no longer hide the fact that her life had turned completely upside down. Mam sat on an old lawn chair on the porch, sewing buttons on a new pair of denims. The thimble on her third finger flashed in the pink glow from the setting sun. Her face was serene, the dark wings of her sleek hair now showing an extraordinary amount of gray, her homemade covering large and snowy white, the wide strings pinned behind her back with a small safety pin.

Mam's hands were calloused and work roughened but somewhat softened each day by the same lotion, the large yellow bottle of Vaseline Intensive Care, which she applied liberally at bedtime. She was humming softly, contentedly. Then she stopped, laughed, and said she didn't even know that song. It just stuck in her head, the way Priscilla kept singing it around the house.

Sarah smiled. Knowing she would burst into tears and thereby lay bare her secret, she got up and said she was walking down to Lydia's to see how she was doing.

Mam nodded assent and then shook her head at Priscilla, when she rose to accompany her sister.

"Better not, Priscilla."

"Why?"

"I'm afraid you're spending too much time with Omar. You're only fifteen."

Priscilla blushed furiously. The color in her face did not escape Levi, who watched her with a calculating expression, pursed his lips, and asked Priscilla if she hadn't heard that the younger daughter should not marry before the elder.

"Oh hush, Levi!"

"No. You shouldn't be going to the widow's house."

Mam smiled but said nothing.

"The barn fires made a mess of many people's lives," he said, shaking his great head sorrowfully.

"What makes you say that?" Mam asked.

"That poor widow. My, oh."

Mam said, yes, he was right, but there was also much good that had come of it. Every trial, every adversity in life serves the purpose of making people better, whether they are aware of it or not.

She clipped the strong black thread with her small quilting scissors and looked at Sarah, whose eyes became liquid with her own hidden feelings, guarded for so long. She propelled herself off the porch and away from the love in her mother's eyes, the one thing that would bring down the wall of reserve around her.

Sarah found Lydia relaxing on her own porch, the children around her. Omar was in the new horse barn building stalls for the large draft animals.

She waved, and he answered with a hand thrown high over his head.

Sarah grinned and greeted Lydia gladly.

"Such a pretty evening!" she responded.

"Sure is. Hi, Anna Mae. How is everyone?"

"We're doing well, Sarah," Lydia said. "Too good, I'm afraid. It doesn't seem right that we just take and take. It's overwhelming."

"Don't you worry, please, Lydia. I'm sure many families have been blessed by their charity."

"But it isn't really right, is it? I mean, I could take the cost of this."

She spread her arms to indicate the yard including the new white fence and the shrubs bordering it. She could live on the price of that fence for quite some time.

"*Ach* now, Lydia. You must stop that."

Lydia asked the children to see if Omar needed help, and Anna Mae left with them obediently.

Lydia turned her head and looked squarely at

her newfound friend. She began to talk, hesitantly at first, then with more conviction.

"It's hard for me, Sarah. Too hard. I talk to my counselors but . . ."

Lydia stopped and looked away, unseeing, across the yard. Her gaze went down to the hollow where the new red barn stood resplendent in the evening's glow.

Sarah remained quiet, biding her time, allowing the widow the space she needed to gather her courage.

A small vehicle drove by slowly. The occupants turned their heads to peer at the new barns. From the wide door of the smaller building, Omar straightened his back, throwing a friendly wave at the car's occupants.

For a second, Sarah thought it was Ashley, from market, in the passenger seat. Her eyes were wide, her face thin and white.

Must be her imagination.

But when the car returned and slowly made its way past in the opposite direction, she had a full view of Ashley through the front window. Hastily Sarah stood up, waving a hand eagerly, wanting to catch the girl's attention, but her gaze was focused on the barns.

It was clearly Ashley, Sarah realized. Why hadn't she returned her wave?

Like a bolt, the memory of Levi describing the car he had seen the night of their fire came back to her. He had described the taillights as being low, like a Volkswagen's, and this car was certainly a Volkswagen, and light-colored as well.

Was there a connection? Was Ashley involved in these fires somehow? Sarah thought of the girl's fright, her frequent questions. She didn't even hear Lydia ask her a question.

"Hello, Sarah?" Lydia laughed.

"Oh, sorry, Lydia. I just thought I knew the girl in that car, but she obviously didn't see me."

"Well, you probably don't want to hear about my boring, messed up life, anyway."

"Stop it. Please do continue."

"Well, I was just saying that it's hard for me to accept all this. Soon after I married Aaron, I learned life is easier if you kept blaming yourself when things . . . stuff, you know, goes wrong. That way, you don't see all the bad in the other person. Do you understand?"

"Well, not really. How can you place the blame on yourself for something you didn't do?"

"Well, I could. I wasn't a good wife."

"You weren't?"

"No."

"Why?"

"Oh, there were lots of things. I don't think Aaron would have lost his temper so easily if I would have tried harder to keep things going smoothly. Sometimes I just gave up and didn't try, figuring it would make no difference, and that was wrong."

Sarah shrugged. "I don't understand."

"Maybe I'm not saying this right. When the barn burned, I blamed myself. I figured I must have done something wrong, and God was chastening me for my wrongdoing. You know we can bring a curse on our own heads for not having enough fear of God in our hearts, don't you? Sometimes I feel cursed, Sarah. The night I no longer wanted to live—that was only the easy way out. Not easy, but the only way. A life of wrongdoing, then Aaron's suffering and death, the bills, the children crying, my baby so thin and sickly, never enough money, then the barn, and always, I felt cursed. It's as if God placed a special accountability on my head, and I literally had to pay here on earth for every one of my missteps, known or unknown."

Sarah sat on the wooden rocking chair, her thoughts slowly clicking into place, a typewritten message, easily deciphered. Here were the two opposite sides of Christianity.

The message was drummed into Sarah's mind, and she grasped it eagerly, greedily. The truth was a thing she could hold and cradle and care for with a genuine and sound mind.

There was Matthew on one side, aloof, with great quantities of redemption given to him, but so sadly unaware of the great gift he could not obtain because of his exalted, prideful state.

Lydia, on the other hand, was cowering in fear of her own wrongs, feeling cursed, unable to lift her head and accept as much as one ounce of forgiveness. She was not even able to believe. And both of them were missing Jesus's greatest gift.

Love. The love of their parents, their neighbors and friends, their church. They were missing it all as they grasped for the truth of Jesus. Hadn't He dwelt among sinners and shown His love to all?

With sadness in her heart, Sarah told Lydia the details about Matthew's leaving, revealing that it wasn't what Elam and Hannah thought it was.

Lydia listened, her eyes soft and luminous with sympathy, as Sarah poured out all the misery of the time since Matthew had left.

"He's not coming back?" she questioned softly.

"I am still hoping."

"Why are these revival meeting so *fa-fearish* (misleading)?" Lydia asked.

"I think they are misleading only to the Amish. I don't think the basic content is wrong. It just leads us away from what we have been taught."

"We can't judge others, I know."

"Absolutely not."

"But Matthew is not honoring his parents."

"No."

"Surely that must bother him."

"I doubt if it does. He feels free. He has Jesus now."

Lydia nodded, understanding.

"I would say he'd have more of Jesus by loving and obeying his parents and remaining humble, esteeming others above himself."

Sarah nodded, then asked bluntly, "Are you born again?"

"Oh, I wouldn't talk about that. The fruit of the Spirit is the only way we know. Isn't that what we believe? And I couldn't say I have any fruits at all, or . . . or all this bad stuff wouldn't have happened."

Sarah laughed softly.

"Well, Lydia, I'd say Matthew is floating somewhere close to the moon, but you're tunneling below the surface of the earth."

"*Ach*, I know. My counselors say I'm getting somewhere, though."

At that moment, Omar appeared, his face lined with fatigue, his shoulders rounded with the weight of responsibility far above his years, a tired smile lighting up his face.

"Hi, Sarah!"

"Hello, yourself. Hard day?"

"Sort of. Trying to do too much during the daylight hours, I guess. I don't know what I'd do without Lee Glick. He's over here every chance he gets. Did you know he's helping me get started raising these Belgians? He claims that with the cows' income and the farming, we can turn a profit. Sometimes though, when I'm tired, like now, I just want to go work for him. By the hour. Less worry. Less responsibility."

He looked around.

"Where's Priscilla?"

"Levi wanted her to stay home."

"Oh."

Omar was clearly disappointed, but he said nothing further. He just smiled and let himself through the door to the kitchen. Anna Mae followed him, clearly idolizing her older brother.

The soft, velvety darkness gently folded its curtains across Lancaster County. The two women sat side by side on the front porch of the old farmhouse, united by the shared calamities they had experienced, coupled with troubles of entirely different kinds. Their personal heartaches brought them together in ways they could never before have imagined.

Lydia was a member of the same church district as Sarah, but she had only been a slight acquaintance, someone Sarah had spoken to only occasionally. Now, however, she had shared her deep and personal secret about Matthew and had lent a sympathetic ear when Lydia shared hers. What a rare and appreciated treasure!

Only time would disclose the real nature of

Matthew's spiritual adventure, which is exactly what it was, Sarah decided as she walked home through the mild, dew-laden evening. She walked with her head bowed, her thoughts wandering as she sifted through new information. Was it okay for Matthew to do what he was doing, in God's eyes? Did his parents' pleas and broken hearts mean nothing at all? Who was right and who was wrong? Were they both wrong?

And there was the poor Widow Lydia, unable to lift her head, so burdened by her own shortcomings.

Well, Sarah wasn't going to figure it out in one night, and, very likely, she didn't have to. All she needed to do was allow Jesus to carry her yoke, and she'd be just fine.

That was why she was humming when she walked past Elam's house. For once, the pain wasn't quite as blinding even though she knew Matthew was not upstairs in his room. He was somewhere on God's earth, and where there was life, there was hope.

But there was still one other thing. What was that frightened Ashley doing in a cream-colored Volkswagen driving past Lydia's farm? As Melvin would say, "The plot thickens," she thought and chuckled.

Chapter 9

Sarah shifted her weight, pulled up her knees, and braced them against the seat ahead of her. She was searching for a measure of comfort to grab a few minutes of sleep before arriving at the market in New Jersey.

"Hey!" Ruthann reached behind her head to tap Sarah's knees.

"Relax. I'm not disturbing you."

With a snuffling sound, Ruthann slouched down and went back to sleep.

Sarah was cold, but she didn't have the nerve to ask the driver to turn the air conditioning off. He was overweight and was drinking his coffee in great, hot slurps, so he probably needed the cool air to stay comfortable. Meanwhile, the group of young passengers was freezing, many of them huddled under the small, fuzzy blankets they'd brought from home.

Sarah couldn't find her blanket that morning. She had scrambled wildly about her room looking for it as the van's headlights sliced through the darkness of the early summer morning. Priscilla had probably borrowed it again. She was always too lazy to go to the cedar chest to get a blanket of her own.

Sarah managed to doze fitfully, but she was

glad when the vanload of workers reached their destination. She was happy to jump down out of the van, stretch, and start her day after a quick trip to the restroom to fix her hair and pin on her freshly ironed covering.

She had dark circles lurking beneath her green eyes, and the pasty beige color she was wearing did nothing for her complexion. There was a coffee stain on the front of her white apron, but dabbing at it with a towel only made it worse, so she gave up and went to work, greeting her employers and fellow workers with half-hearted attempts at imitating her usual cheerfulness. Everyone knew Matthew was still away, so they shrugged their shoulders and left her alone.

Sarah measured ingredients and turned on mixers but kept her eyes averted, sending a clear signal for everyone to leave her to her thoughts. As the morning wore on, however, she became steadily caught up in the grinding work of the bakery. Her thoughts were occupied completely by her ability to turn out enough fresh cinnamon rolls, bread, dinner rolls, and sandwich rolls. She also helped out with any other pastries as needed.

An hour after her usual break time, she was exhausted, hungry, and completely fed up with her job. She felt as if no one cared whether she had a break at all. She figured that all the other girls probably had had theirs by this time, but because she was stuck back with the dough

143

mixers, who would even care if she got one or not?

Fighting the waves of self-pity that threatened her, she looked up to find her boss, Emma Glick, handing her a ten-dollar bill and saying Sarah was always the last to go for her break. She said to take an extra long one, and here, use this.

"You're doing an excellent job," she said, patting Sarah's shoulder.

Lifted from her pit of despair, Sarah gratefully accepted the money and thanked Emma. She went and bought the largest sandwich she could find and settled herself into a booth, not caring whether she saw Rose or not.

It was pure bliss—the homemade hoagie roll, browned and crisp from the oven, layers of ham and cheese toasted and melted with mayonnaise. The sandwich was then filled generously with shredded lettuce and onion with fresh red tomatoes peeking out from underneath.

She munched happily, wiped the mayonnaise from her lips, then smiled at Rose when she approached her table.

"Hey, stranger!"

"You hungry?"

"Not anymore."

Their small talk was just that—very small. In fact, it was ridiculous the way they circled around the subject of Matthew.

Sarah finally realized it was only her pride that

was coming between them. Swallowing that pride, she slowly revealed to Rose the agony of her heart, knowing she just couldn't hold it in much longer. Rose completely caught Sarah off guard with her gentle sympathy as she lowered her face into a used napkin, smearing mayonnaise across her nose and leaving a thin shred of lettuce dangling from one eyelash. Rose laughed hysterically when Sarah told her and reached to remove the lettuce.

Rose then filled Sarah in about Lee Glick, how much fun they had hanging out together, and how her heart skipped about seventy beats last Sunday evening at the singing, when he loitered around their buggy. She thought sure he was going to ask her.

Rummaging in her purse, she found a small mirror, checked her appearance, batted her perfect eyelashes, and smiled at Sarah.

"I wouldn't get too miserable about Matthew. Lee is much better for me."

"What does that mean?" Sarah asked sourly.

"Well, you'll get over him. Find someone better."

"It's not that easy, Rose. I have always loved Matthew."

"You never told me."

"You knew."

"Not really."

Sarah had no answer for Rose's denial, so she

sighed and changed the subject. She told Rose about the vehicle going past Lydia's house.

"You go hang out with that Lydia? She's mentally off, isn't she? She gives me the shivers. I don't know how you do it, helping her."

Sarah was surprised at her friend's lack of empathy.

"She's so pitiful, Rose. You have no idea."

"Whatever. I think it's creepy to spend time with her."

There was nothing to say in response. Wanting to show her disapproval, Sarah left the booth hurriedly, leaving Rose staring after her.

Sarah was seething now. Her day had started poorly to begin with, and now Rose had suddenly made her feel small and inadequate, the way she looked down her nose at Lydia. Sarah stormed past the meat stand, disregarding the friendly smiles of the proprietors and leaving them with raised eyebrows and questions in their eyes.

Her head down, her step quickening, she rounded a corner and hit something solid and immovable. She lurched to the right but was caught by a strong arm. She heard a "Whoa!" as she steadied herself. Then she saw a navy blue shirt, open at the neck, a pair of broadfall denims with a pair of gray suspenders attached.

"Watch where you're going!"

Sarah caught hold of the corner as she stepped back and looked up into the face of Lee

Glick. His blue eyes mocked her, but not unkindly.

She rose to the challenge.

"Watch where I'm going? What about you?"

Only for a few seconds, he allowed himself to watch the restless colors dancing in her eyes, completely losing any measure of time. It was a nanosecond, and it was an eternity. It was the most mesmerizing moment of his life, acknowledging the depth of this girl's spirit, her goodness, her sincerity.

"I didn't know you worked here," he said. What he wanted to say was something so much more profound, so filled with longing, questioning, wondering.

"At the bakery."

"You on break?"

"Just finished."

"Let me buy you dessert."

Ill at ease, shy, Sarah turned her head to look behind her, thinking of Rose.

"You don't have time?"

Sarah nodded, incapable of speech now, his blue eyes captivating her.

He bought two raspberry twist ice cream cones and led her outside where picnic tables dotted the narrow strip of grass by the parking lot. Young pear trees were planted at measured distances, their small leaves rustling in the summer breeze and creating a bit of shade across the graying, splintered top of the wooden table.

Sarah sat opposite him, swung her legs beneath the table, ate her ice cream, and was suddenly aware of an all-encompassing shyness gripping her throat. She could not speak.

Lee watched her face intently, following the shadows of the pear leaves as they played across her golden face, her startling eyes, the honey-colored waves in her chestnut hair.

He wanted to paint her portrait, silly as it seemed. He felt he could sit there for the rest of the day and say nothing at all. He could just watch her expressions, the eyes that gave so much away.

Finally she said, soft and low, "Why are you here?"

"We're roofing a house about a block from here."

"You came to see Rose?"

"Rose? You mean Rose Zook?"

Sarah nodded, bit down on the cone, afraid he had, afraid he had not.

"I didn't know she worked here."

"Oh."

Then, without thinking, having already thought far too much about this subject, he said, "How's Matthew? Heard from him?"

He wiped his mouth with his napkin and averted his eyes, too chicken now to meet hers as he was consumed with fear in anticipation of her answer. For a long moment, she didn't answer. When she did speak, her voice was barely above a whisper.

"I don't know how he is. I haven't heard from him."

Lee raised his eyebrows, ashamed of the joy that flooded his very soul.

"He doesn't write? Call?"

Lee drew his breath in sharply when she leaned her elbows on the table and hunched her shoulders. Her eyes became almost brown with shifting forces, waves whipped to foam by the strength of her emotion. She paused, breathing hard.

"He's on a spiritual journey, he says. He thinks Amish people are not born again, that these barns are burning because we aren't who we should be, we aren't really spiritual. Too much *ordnung*, he says. The thing is he doesn't even want to be Amish. He's threatened to leave the church ever since he broke up with Rose."

She stopped, biting her lower lip.

"Lee, what do these barns have to do with it? What?"

She'd said his name!

"I don't think someone lighting fires has too much to do with the spiritual health of the Amish church. If anything, the Amish spirituality has only increased . . . I don't know. It seems just about everything good there is to practice is being done even more."

"That's what Dat says."

"Maybe I shouldn't give my opinion. I'm not worth a whole lot when it comes to Bible stuff. I don't know a lot about anything. But you only know what you feel, and if a barn raising isn't the fruit of the right spirit, then I don't know what is. It's a coming together, everyone, and the whole reason is to help the poor guy who lost his barn. I always think the whole thing in a nut-shell —as far as religion goes—is giving a hoot about what happens to your neighbor, helping out whenever someone needs you, simply because you care."

Sarah breathed in slowly, blinking her eyes as if to truly grasp the meaning of the words he was saying. She realized that Lee spoke, and thought, along the same lines as her own revered father.

Lee's eyes found hers. There was not a word spoken between them, and yet Sarah felt as if they had talked at length.

Cars came and went, passersby strolled along, carrying purchases, or eager to make them. Despite the bustle of the market, Lee was oblivious to any motion around him, consumed by his strong feelings for this troubled girl.

Suddenly she spoke. "Are you born again?"

"You shouldn't be asking me that question."

"Why?"

"It's not our way."

"It's Matthew's."

His hope was dashed in an instant, leaving scalding burns like a kettle of boiling water dropped to the ground. Sarah's words splashed a dangerous wetness against his heart and left angry blisters of pain. Unable to stop himself, he leapt to his feet, his blue eyes blazing with a new and terrible light.

"If you want to follow Matthew, then go. Just go. Get out of my life, out of my mind, out of my knowing you even exist. Okay?"

He placed both palms on the rough, weathered surface of the picnic table. The muscles of his shoulders strained against the navy blue fabric of his shirt, the heavy veins in his tanned neck bulging as he fought the overpowering emotions that threatened to consume him.

"You seem happily oblivious to the fact that you are already misled, going around asking people if they're born again. Do me a favor, and stay away from me, okay?"

With that, he abruptly straightened, turned on his heel, and stalked away. As he threaded his way between the parked vehicles, his closely shorn blond hair shone like a beacon of sun-shine.

Sarah lowered her head into her hands, but her eyes remained dry. She felt cold and barren, windswept like an arid land without rain, without sustenance of any kind. Flat and unemotional. That obviously had not been the correct thing to say.

Well, he couldn't blame her for wondering if Matthew was right. He was, after all, her boyfriend, her fiancé, her intended. Obviously, her intended.

A great weariness enveloped her now. It folded her in seductive arms and whispered words of defeat into her tired ears. Perhaps it wouldn't be a bad idea to leave the Amish. If she was with Matthew, she'd be sure. She would have made a decision, and she would stick to her choice. No more doubting and wondering.

She would know she was born again, have a sure pass into heaven, and she could join the people who thought the same way she did.

Matthew would marry her. She would be forever secure and loved, and she would be knowledgeable, growing in wisdom from the Bible.

Back at the bakery, Sarah burned a tray of sweet rolls and was sharply reprimanded by her boss. She wept furtive tears into a paper towel and wondered if her life would ever right itself. If only Matthew would come home.

Sarah rushed to compensate for her mistake with the sweet rolls and cut her index finger with the dough cutter. She slashed it horribly, and blood spurted from the long gash. Her day's work was now finished except for standing at the cash register, her finger throbbing painfully inside its heavy bandage.

When Sarah stumbled in the door at home, Mam looked up with her usual warm smile of welcome. The smile quickly slid away and was replaced by a lifting of the eyebrows, a clouding of concern.

"How was your day?"

"Fine."

Sarah's tone was short, clipped. The word was hard, like a pellet.

"You don't look fine."

"I cut my finger."

"Did you take care of it?"

"Yeah."

Mam sighed and decided to take action. Enough was enough.

Resolutely she poured cold mint tea over ice cubes in tall glasses. She placed the glasses on a tray along with slices of sharp cheddar cheese, some Ritz crackers, hot pepper jelly, and the soft, raisin-filled cookies she had just baked before supper.

"Let's have a glass of tea," was all she said. She was soon joined by the rest of the family. Levi heaped crackers and cheese with large spoon-fuls of the quivering hot pepper jelly.

Sarah joined them reluctantly, her tears on the verge of spilling over. Dat plopped on the wooden porch swing and slapped Levi's knee with a resounding whack.

"Davey Beila!" Levi said, greeting his father and calling him by his given name as he occasionally did.

"How much of that pepper jelly are you going to eat?" Dat chortled, slapping Levi's knee again with affection.

"All of it, Davey. Then you can't have any."

Smiling, Mam handed Dat a glass of mint tea. The humidity produced beads of moisture on the outside of the glass, and a ring of water remained on the tray after she lifted it.

The night was coming on, but it did nothing to lift the blanket of oppressive humidity. The heavy green maple leaves hung thickly, completely still, not a whisper of a breeze stirring them.

"A storm will come up later tonight," Dat observed.

For now, the routine of the evening, the homey atmosphere, the completely relaxed setting surrounded the family. It provided the foundation of their home, a place where each was accepted and loved without having to be told. And it finally broke Sarah's resolve to hide away her doubts and fears about the future.

Hesitantly at first, then with stronger conviction, she told them of Matthew's quest and the real reason he was traveling.

In the fading summer light, Dat's face appeared

shadowed, patriarchal. His graying beard flowed across his chest, and his hair lay close to his skull where his straw hat had pressed against it all day as he worked the fields. He looked away across the porch and the neatly cut lawn, past the new barn and the fields beyond. He said nothing to interrupt the flow of words that now rained from Sarah.

Mam clucked, put a hand to her mouth, and shook her head, but she remained as quiet as she could.

"So, I'm no longer sure what is right and what is wrong. Everything is blurred. And my *zeit-lang* (longing) for Matthew to return is almost more than I can bear.

"And what if he's right? What if we Amish are blind, misguided individuals who have grown up in the shadow of the *ordnung* and all the Old Testament stuff that doesn't amount to anything at all?"

The questions vibrated above them, static with a sense of the unknown. Levi smacked his lips appreciatively after a long drink of the icy mint tea. Then he slid forward clumsily, balancing himself by grasping the chain attaching the swing to the hooks above it, and reached for two raisin-filled cookies.

"Levi," Mam said.

"We didn't have much supper, Mam. *Kalte sup* (Cold soup)!"

"Just one, Levi."

Resignedly, Levi returned one cookie, asking Dat if he was full on *kalte sup.*

"We had fish, too."

"I don't like fish too good."

Dat smiled at Mam, knowing Levi would eat another cookie eventually.

"Well, Sarah, you likely asked the most often asked question among the Amish people nowadays. It really surprises me how long you've kept this to yourself."

She hung her head. "I'm sorry," she whispered.

"Don't be. I just hope you aren't planning on following Matthew."

"I want to."

"I believe that."

Then Dat told her that he believed any individual could search the Bible and could pick out verses to justify their own beliefs. But too often, a belief was an attitude, a way of thinking, a way of looking at the world with either an air of superiority or an inflated ego. Call it born again, if you want, he said.

"When Adam and Eve were in the Garden of Eden, the serpent misled Eve by saying if she would eat the forbidden fruit, she would know what was right and what was wrong, like God. To this day, we completely mislead ourselves—and others—by thinking we know who is born of the Spirit and who is not."

Sarah interrupted her father. "But we have to! Matthew said!"

"Let me continue. When a breeze stirs the leaves on the maple tree, as the Spirit stirs the hearts of people, we know the leaves are moving because of the wind, but we don't know where the breeze is coming from or where it's going, in Jesus's words. We really don't. Tell me, Sarah, where does the wind come from and where does it go?"

She shrugged her shoulders.

"That's right. The power of the Spirit is God's, and only His to know. We are mortals. That is our way, Sarah. Yes, I know exactly what you're going to say, Sarah.

"Many *ausre gmayna* (other churches) accept powerful testimonies. They accept the faith of each individual by their moving reports of visitations by the Spirit. They highlight the condemnation, the repentance, the saving of their souls by the blood of Christ. That is all good and right. That is our way as well but with less fanfare, of course. You know that we cannot exalt ourselves by that alone.

"It is only by the fruits that we can know someone. And the fruits of the Spirit are a gift of God. They are nothing we do ourselves. So we choose to remain humble, exalting only the Father above and no mere mortal."

"What about Matthew? He's a new person, in Jesus."

"For awhile. He'll be back down."

"Dat!"

Sarah was shocked, angry.

"I'm serious. An English man told me once that a person who has come to the knowledge of the truth should be incarcerated for a while. They're on fire for the Lord, handing out tracts, just sure they are sent to save mankind.

"Likely they still disagree with their wives, spend money unwisely, and lose their tempers. They are human. Just like us. So our set of man-made rules—the law, if you will, the *ordnung*—serves its purpose, keeping our exalted selves restrained."

"So then, who will go to heaven, the Amish or the . . . the . . . others?"

Dat stroked his beard thoughtfully in the light that was visibly fading into the night.

"I think we all have the same chance. It's God's job to separate the weeds from the healthy plants, and not ours."

"What about Matthew?"

"I think he's on a dangerous road, but it's not in my hands at all. It's up to God to judge, to know what he will need in later years to mold him and purify him."

"What would happen if I chose to leave the church and to follow him?"

Darkness erased most of Dat's features, but the silver trickle, the trail of Dat's tears, sliced through her heart, leaving a physical pain somewhere in the region of her stomach.

He breathed in, a long, shaking inhalation of love.

"Eventually, you'd be excommunicated for your disobedience."

"I thought so."

"Are you seriously thinking it over?"

"I'm waiting to see what Matthew will do."

"Then, we'll leave it at that."

"What do you mean?"

"Just that. I can't tell you what to do."

Chapter 10

When Matthew's letter arrived, Sarah could not hide the shaking in her hands, so she escaped to the privacy of her room in spite of the sweltering afternoon sun burning through the glass panes of her windows. The screens below allowed only short puffs of hot air, sullenly ruffling the silky panels and barely stirring the air in the room.

A fine line of perspiration beaded her upper lip, and stray curls clung to her damp forehead as she sat on the edge of her bed. She pressed her knees together, her bare heels inches off the floor, the tension distributing her weight over her bent toes.

The envelope was plain white, and the folded paper inside plainly visible. The letter was thin—surely only one sheet.

With shaking hands, she lifted the flap and ripped open the top of the envelope, hurriedly extracting the one folded sheet of lined paper. He had always had good handwriting.

Dear Sarah,
You must come to me. I am leaving for Haiti in two weeks, on the 15th of August. I want you to be with me, flying above the earth.
I think I can make you understand my

way. Please come to me. This freedom is unbelievable. The chains that have kept me bound to the Amish are gone.

I'm free!

My cell phone number is 717-555-0139.

Call me!

Matthew

She could not contain the conflicting emotions that surged through her body. She held the paper to her heart, a sob catching in her throat. Her breath came out ragged, edged in pain and suffering.

She would call him. She knew she would.

Rocking forward, then backward, she opened her mouth as if to cry, but only a raw moan of misery emerged. The inner conflict was an unbearable thing. She could never leave Dat. She knew he was a barge of truth, plowing steadily through all kinds of weather, waves crashing around him, and he never faltered. The closest he had ever come to being undone was in the aftermath of their fire and then losing little Mervin in the flood.

But she could not live without Matthew. She loved him. Unconditionally. English or Amish, Mennonite or Catholic, Lutheran or Baptist. What really was the difference?

If the leaves on the trees were like human beings the way Dat said, did they all look alike to

God from way up there, and did he love them all the same?

Immediately, she flew down the stairs, burst through the door, and sprinted across the lawn, the grass crinkly and dry in the late afternoon sun. Her feet only skimmed the ground before she yanked open the door of the phone shanty, bent over the dusty white telephone, and punched in the numbers. The desperate need to hear his voice surpassed every other emotion.

On the fifth ring, his voicemail greeting washed over her aching heart, the sound of his voice a drop of water to a dying soul. Instantly, she dialed again and listened to his message a second time before replacing the receiver and slumping down into the old, cracked vinyl seat of the phone shanty chair.

Should she leave a message for him? No, she'd try later.

With a song in her heart, she went to the wash line and took down the black socks, denim trousers, and red men's handkerchiefs. She tugged on the line to bring in the multi-colored dresses, the black aprons, and pale shirts.

Whistling softly under her breath, she carried the large basket of clothes to a kitchen chair, took up a pair of trousers, and began folding them. Her thoughts raced, hysterical with the joy of Matthew's invitation.

Suzie came into the house, letting the screen

door bang behind her, which provoked a snuffling sigh from the recliner, where Levi lay stretched out for his afternoon nap.

"Shh! Levi's asleep!"

"Time for him to come help in the garden. We have about a mountain of green beans waiting to snap, and now Mam says we have to hoe the rows yet today. It's at least a hundred degrees, and I am not kidding you."

Sarah smiled at Suzie.

"Well, see if you can get him awake."

In the evening, the air turned uncomfortably humid, the lowering sky threatening, ominous. Sarah perspired freely, sitting in the phone shanty, unsuccessfully making another attempt at reaching Matthew. She held the receiver to her ear and was amazed to hear the beep indicating a message had been left on their voicemail. Quickly she checked the caller ID panel and found Matthew's number.

With bated breath, she listened to his voice. "Hello, Sarah. This is Matthew." His voice! But it wasn't really Matthew. It was low and smooth and polished, with a hint of a western accent.

"I hope you are well. I'm sorry I didn't answer my cell phone, but where I am, the service is sketchy at best. Call me, leave me a message. I need your answer by the second of August." No goodbye.

Well, the second of the month was today. She

couldn't make a choice of such magnitude in a few hours. It would break her parents' hearts. The church would eventually cast her away, shun her. She needed to understand excommunication better.

Sarah looked anxiously around the property. The wind was strangely stilled, the black clouds churning above the barn roof, jagged knives of lightning breaking out of the restless thunderheads. A fear of times past enveloped her. Surely not another flood!

There was another thin, high crackle above her, followed by a distant rumble. Immediately the heavy foliage on the maple trees danced to life as the wind kicked up with the approaching storm.

She couldn't leave a message now, so she turned away from the phone shanty, shutting the door firmly behind her and running swiftly across the lawn.

Mam was on the porch, grabbing the Ziploc bags she'd washed and hung on the small clothesline with wooden clothespins.

"Close the upstairs windows!" she called out as Sarah bounded onto the porch.

When she was in Suzie's room, she was surprised to see a team come in the driveway at breakneck speed. She peered anxiously through the window that was already splattered with fat raindrops. She recognized her cousin, Melvin, leaning forward, his eyes searching the sky as he surveyed the oncoming storm. Sarah greeted him in the forebay, just as the hailstones came crashing down on the new metal roof and the wind reached a high crescendo as it whined around the corner of the barn, bringing the hail and rain along with it.

"Melvin! What are you doing out on an evening like this?"

"Oh, nothing much. I was on my way to meet Lee at Lydia's, but I saw that I better find cover immediately."

At the mention of Lee's name, Sarah averted her eyes, her bare toe pushing bits of loose straw across the packed cement.

Dat suddenly burst through the milk house door. He greeted Melvin effusively, wiping the rain from his face with a soiled, wrinkled handkerchief.

"Whew!"

"Some storm. I'd let you know how bad it's going to be, but I can't check my cell phone with you around, Davey."

Dat grimaced and said he shouldn't be so worldly or so outspoken. Melvin grinned cheekily and clapped Dat's shoulder and told him not to worry, that he was raised to be respectful of the ministry.

Dat's eyes twinkled, and he shook his head.

"*Ach* Melvin, you're as full of hot air as you always were. If you were as respectful as you want me to believe, you wouldn't have mentioned the cell phone at all."

Melvin floundered about as his face turned red. He could not come up with a decent reply. Sarah burst out laughing, understanding Melvin and his need to look good wherever he went. Dat laughed, too.

"Probably the weather forecast would say it's stormy with a chance of hail in Lancaster County."

"Southeastern Lancaster County," Melvin corrected him wryly.

They all grimaced as the storm worsened. The sound of hailstones hitting the roof was deafening, like the din of thousands of projected golf balls. Speaking was impossible, so they stood in companionable silence. Each of them winced as the square barn windows turned an electrifying shade of blue for an instant, followed by dull rumbles of thunder. The peals reverberated among the storm clouds as if God had ordained a heavenly roll call in an attempt to catch his mortals' attention.

Finally Dat raised his voice.

"Good way to start a barn fire!" he shouted.

"You betcha!" Melvin agreed, vehemently nodding his head.

As the brunt of the storm abated, grumbling its way reluctantly to the south, they splashed into the house, dodging puddles and low hanging branches dripping with water.

Mam met them at the door, a worried expression erasing the serenity that was so commonplace.

"Thank goodness!" she said. "Sarah, I wasn't sure where you were, and I guess as long as the world goes round, storms will bring back memories of our little Mervin."

Her mouth wobbled visibly, and she blinked back the tears that so easily rose to the surface.

Melvin settled himself comfortably in a kitchen chair, his expressive eyes watching Mam's face, mirroring his own emotion. Mam shook her head, composed herself, and disappeared into the pantry as Levi stumbled from the living room, pure delight written across his face.

"Levi!" Melvin shouted.

"What's up, chap?" Levi said, loudly imitating the English man who drove the large rig that hauled their milk.

Melvin laughed.

"Not too much, Levi. How about you?"

"Oh, I think we got the barn fires stopped. Nothing going on since the Widow Lydia's."

"It hasn't been that long. Don't hold your breath."

"I don't look for another fire. The Amish are more aware of what that guy did. They're sleeping in barns, got big dogs that bite hard, alarms. Everyone has something," Levi said, his voice rising with excitement, aware of Melvin's attention.

"Levi's right," Dat said.

"Yeah, maybe the fires themselves aren't the real danger now. What about that Elam's Matthew taking off like that? Sarah, did you know he's texting the youth all the time? Surely you've broken up with him by now."

With Melvin, there was no tiptoeing around feelings. Everything was blunt, spoken in plain words, his recipients allowed to accept his words or disagree.

Sarah's face colored with misery, and she blushed self-consciously.

"No," she said in a cracked, hushed tone.

"What? Why not?" Melvin asked, his eyes popping in disbelief.

"Well."

"Well, what?"

"I thought perhaps he'd change his mind yet."

"Ha! Ever hear of that happening? Once they get ahold of their Jesus, they're GONE!" Melvin brought his arm up and swished it through the air, a vivid symbol of the disgust he felt.

Dat's eyes watched Melvin. They were sharp in their disapproval, but his voice was gentle.

"Melvin, it's a good thing for someone to be concerned about his soul, finding Jesus, accepting redemption, any way you want to word it."

"Yeah, but those holy rollers that take their vows and then break them—they'll be surprised on judgment day, let me tell you."

"Be careful, Melvin. It's a narrow and slippery path when we condemn, and when we refuse to try and understand, we do not have the right kind of love in our hearts."

"Well, they're wrong—people like Matthew."

"There's a huge possibility we're all wrong if we fight about Scripture."

"What do you mean? You're a minister, and you're uncertain?"

"Let me explain, Melvin. I don't agree with Matthew doing this to his parents, to the ones who love him, especially Sarah. But we have to be careful. We need to carry our own cross, let Matthew carry his, and leave him to God's hands."

"So, Sarah, knowing you, you'll probably go puddling off after him."

"I doubt if I'll puddle."

Melvin didn't acknowledge the humor. An angry blush crept across his cheeks, and he became almost belligerent.

"You'll be put in the *bann* (excommunicated). Then you'll slide straight to hell." He addressed Sarah angrily, his face working with suppressed feeling.

"I wanted to ask Dat about the true meaning of excommunication, as I have to make a decision today," Sarah said. "Matthew left a message for me. He invited me to go to Haiti with him on the fifteenth."

Dat's face was a mirror of Mam's with the color receding, leaving only fear and pain. They tried to grasp the fact that Sarah may actually want to leave, thereby breaking parental and godly rules. They knew they would be unable to restrain her if she wanted to go.

Pushing back the urge to cry out or hold back his darling daughter bodily, Dat calmed himself as a thick veil of confusion drew over Sarah's features. Her misery was so apparent, the reason for it so obvious. It drew its strength from the deep root that was her overwhelming infatuation with Matthew Stoltzfus, the single object of her desire.

No one spoke.

The rain still streamed down the kitchen windows, but the wind had died down and no longer whistled around the corners of the house.

Melvin was pouting, his mouth drawn firmly into a line of disagreement. He refused to accept the fact that his favorite cousin just could go skipping off scot-free, leaving his uncle's family with broken hearts. He'd love to have ahold of that arrogant Matthew about now.

The dripping from the faucet turned into a steady trickle, so Mam got up to adjust the handle. She checked the coffee in the stainless steel drip coffee maker, settling the top back with a bang to hasten the hot water dripping through the grounds.

She stood at the sink, her back turned, watching the rain creating a pattern of tears on the window pane. Her mind just could not grasp what Sarah was actually contemplating.

Dat drew a deep breath.

"And you want to go?" he asked, his voice gravelly with pain.

"Oh, of course. I'm just afraid of the *bann*."

"You should be!" Melvin exclaimed, leaning forward with intensity.

"Sarah, it is not fear of excommunication that keeps us together. If the pattern of life is as it should be, your love toward us is what should secure you to your heritage. The whole thing in a nutshell is love. Even the *bann* is a form of love. So many don't understand that, even our own people. But when we place someone outside of our church, we are acknowledging that they need chastening—trials and adversity—to become a better person, so their soul may be saved.

"Sarah it would be wrong for you to go with Matthew, because it would be blatant disobedience. It would be completely without love. In this day and age, we Amish believe in the saving grace of our *Herren Jesu* (Lord Jesus), and you would be turning your back on that.

"In the end, the choice is yours. Of course,

you would be welcome to return, to visit. But our spiritual unification would be gone. The freedom from guilt would be lost as well. Matthew promises you freedom, but you would not be free."

Mam watched Sarah's face, the struggle darkening her once carefree face. She missed that face from the years prior to Matthew.

"So, you're saying I have to choose between you and him."

"Yes."

"Why? Why do the Amish have to be so thickheaded? Why can't I go off and do what I want with your blessing?"

Dat never faltered.

"It is not the way of Jesus's cross."

"Why? How?"

"We are taught from childhood to deny the flesh, our own will."

"But I love him!" she burst out.

"I believe you. But he obviously does not love you."

Dat's voice was firm, cemented in true conviction, and Sarah's eyes opened wide in astonishment at his statement.

"You know how it is, Sarah. Sometimes a disobedient youth joins the wild *rumspringa* crowd. But then if he truly loves a girl, he gives up the ways of the world for her. Matthew obviously isn't doing that. He doesn't love you."

"But he wants me to come and accompany him to Haiti!" Sarah burst out.

Far into the night they reasoned. Dat and Mam listened with great patience and forbearance, allowing Sarah to express her point of view. They were considerate, temperate, while Melvin bubbled and hissed with attempted restraint, his eyes bulging with the force of his own emotions.

In the end, Dat conceded wearily with drooping shoulders. He got up, put a hand on Mam's shoulder, and they said good night, leaving Melvin and Sarah alone in the kitchen.

They lay in bed, side by side, the way they had for almost forty years, and they never fell asleep. All night, their lips moved in prayer, two steadfast warriors, their pillows soaked with the many tears that slid down their cheeks. All through the night, their hands remained clasped, symbolic of the strength of their partnership in the face of this spiritual hurricane that blasted their very souls.

Sarah told Matthew she would go.

His voice was still as flat and smooth as before. Without raising or lowering it, he said he was glad.

"Just glad?" Sarah said.

"There is only one source of true joy," he told her in a much quieter tone than before. "That is our Lord and Savior, Jesus Christ."

"Oh," was all she could think to say.

She replaced the receiver with shaking hands and sat alone in the darkened phone shanty, senselessly pleating the skirt of her nightgown.

Had Matthew gone a bit overboard or something?

Priscilla had a fit—what Grandmother King called a conniption. Anna Mae and Ruthie were horrified and demanded an explanation. How in the world could Mam let Sarah get away with this secrecy, this rebellion? Why was she allowing Sarah to run after that spoiled Matthew? He always got his own way with everything, and when he couldn't have his gorgeous Rose— the one time he had ever hit a brick wall—he acted like the spoiled brat he'd always been and just left, taking it out on everyone. It was his battered ego, his pride that was driving him.

They were reprimanded sharply by Mam. "Such talk! Such *unlieve* (hatred)!"

Ruthie bit into a raspberry and cream filled doughnut, leaning over her coffee cup. The cup only caught about half the powdered sugar, leaving the rest to sift onto the black bib apron covering her ample chest. She wiped it off, leaving a white streak, snorted, and told Mam it was about time this family had a healthy dose of telling it like it is. With genuine honesty.

Anna Mae looked directly into Sarah's eyes and told her if she was dumb enough to run after Matthew, all the way to Haiti, where it was hot and miserable and full of missionaries, then she guessed she'd just have to. But don't come running back for pity, she said.

Levi told her a snake would bite her. He had heard that in Haiti they grew long enough to reach from the house to the barn.

They were seated around the old kitchen table having sisters day. The married girls came home for coffee and brunch with a large spread of food. It was one of the events that Levi especially looked forward to, mostly for the food.

Priscilla looked bored with the whole thing. She had already said her piece with no effect. So after she finished her plate of breakfast casserole, she went outside to clean the forebay.

Sarah was crazy, completely nuts, in her opinion, so what was the use even trying to make her see another point of view? She was just stumbling blindly after that inflated ego known as Matthew. He'd just switched from full of himself to full of himself spiritually. Same thing.

In the house, Sarah listened to her sisters. She actually burst into great heaves of laughter when Anna Mae said if she boarded that jet and flew to Haiti, she'd be compelled to hijack it like some whacko.

"You're not going to do it," Ruthie said emphatically.

"But I can't say no to Matthew!" Sarah wailed.

"I'd have no problem in that category. Bye!

See ya! Adios!" Anna Mae said, holding little Justin by the forehead as she swiped a Kleenex across his eyes, looking for his nose.

"Watch what you're doing!" Sarah said.

"What? Oh, Justin. Sorry! Here."

He twisted his head, pushed out his round stomach, and howled for all he was worth, so she set him on the floor, his nose still dripping, her attention still riveted on Sarah's plans.

"*Butz sie naus* (Clean his nose)!" Levi yelled. "*Ach* my."

Anna Mae scuttled after her son and caught him. She leaned over and swiped viciously, getting the job done. Then she turned and went straight back to the table where she again started listing every one of Matthew's major downfalls.

And still Sarah remained unconvinced.

Chapter 11

The days that followed sisters day were the kind of days Mam imagined the writer of the "Footprints" poem had experienced firsthand.

Anna Mae and Ruthie were powerful allies, her strength bolstered by their honesty and support. But it was on her knees in her bedroom that she found complete solace, carried through the days by the strength of her faith.

Dat fasted every day, continuing in prayer and supplication, calling at the throne of God without shame. It wasn't only Sarah's leaving of the Amish that bothered him. It was the added concern that Matthew did not truly love Sarah and her willingness to blindly follow him regardless.

Another week passed until the day before Sarah's departure. It was a time of heartache for the whole family, an event so unthinkable producing an ominous foreboding for Dat and Mam.

The evening was mellow, cooler than some August nights, when Priscilla announced quietly that there was a message on the voicemail for Sarah. Surprised but pleased and thinking of Matthew, Sarah walked slowly, her head bowed, watching the way her bare feet broke the brittle, parched grasses after weeks of hot, dry wind and little rain.

Cautiously, she punched the buttons and listened to the message—a great disappointment. It was the Widow Lydia, asking her to spend the night if she could as she had something to discuss with her. Matthew hadn't called at all for at least six or seven days.

Sarah would send Priscilla to Lydia's.

Slowly she walked back to the house, torn between her loyalty and friendship to Lydia and the realization that Lydia knew nothing of her plans to leave the next day to join Matthew.

What would she say?

Guilt washed over her, sensing the betrayal Lydia would surely feel.

Greater love has no man than this: that he lay down his life for his friend. The words entered her mind, a blaze of knowledge, and as quickly, she reversed them. She was laying down her life for her Matthew, denying father, mother, sister, brother.

Mam looked up from her sewing.

"Who was it?"

"Lydia."

"Oh?"

"She wants me to come stay for the night."

"Oh?"

"Priscilla can go."

"I think you should. She asked you."

Reluctantly, Sarah threw her pajamas, toothbrush, and a few toiletries in an old bag. Without saying good-bye, she walked out the driveway, her thoughts in turmoil yet again.

The twilight was fast descending, casting shadows across Elam Stoltzfus's property, darkening the pine trees to black and the white house to a dull blue gray. Hannah had a few rugs on the line, Sarah noticed, and her mop was still propped against the back stoop.

A small car appeared out of nowhere, the headlights' glare blinding. Sarah threw up an arm to cover her eyes. Sensing danger, she stepped sideways. Something was out of the ordinary with a car moving at that rate of speed on this country road.

As she stepped into the thick uncut grass at the side of the road, the car came to a rocking halt, spraying gravel from its skidding tires. A dark-haired youth poked his head through the opening of the lowered window.

"Tell your people to watch their barns tonight."

Before Sarah had the chance to reply or ask any questions, the car took off with another screeching of tires.

Cold chills chased themselves up and down her spine. Should she turn back? Go to her parents or press on to Lydia's? Shaking, her knees weak with fright, she decided to keep going and maybe send Omar to alert Elams and her parents.

There was a light in the new horse barn, but she decided to speak to Lydia first. She found her nestled on a lawn chair in the dusk, her feet tucked under herself, an opened book laid face down on the small table beside her.

"Sarah! Oh, I'm so glad you came! Please tell me all about it."

Confused, Sarah blinked. "You mean the car?"

"No, I don't know anything about a car. I mean Matthew."

"Oh, Matthew. I didn't know you knew."

"Hannah was here all afternoon. You must be devastated. Here, sit down. Aaron, make room for Sarah."

Aaron was only two, but he greeted Sarah with a hearty "Hi!" and a wide smile before tucking himself into his mother's lap.

"What are you talking about? Why would I be devastated? I'm planning on going to Haiti with Matthew. Do you mean deciding to leave my family, or what?"

Lydia's arms fell away from little Aaron, and she turned her head and stared at the floor of the porch. A quiet groan escaped her lips.

"You don't know then?"

"What? What don't I know? I guess not, if you don't tell me."

Sarah was panicking, her voice high and shrill.

"Sit down," Lydia whispered.

Sarah sat, leaned forward, clenched her hands

till the knuckles paled in contrast with the healthy tan on her hands.

"Matthew already left for Haiti. He . . . Oh Sarah, I don't want to be the one to tell you this."

"What? What is it?"

Sarah's throat was dry, her voice ragged. Her breaths were coming in quick succession as the color drained from her face.

"He met someone and married her within a week. She's a . . . a woman of color. A nurse. She lives in Haiti."

"Noooo."

The word was a sob, a moan, a long, drawn out wail of denial. Lydia rose and gathered her in her thin, helpful arms. The calloused hands that worked side by side with her oldest son now seemed soft, soothing, angelic in their power to still Sarah.

Sarah had never known that a person could feel so much pain and still be able to bear it. How could she be holding up beneath a weight that was crushing her and squeezing the air out of her?

She had no breath left to cry. Her eyes remained dry, her mouth open as a high wail emerged.

Lydia held her, soothed her, but she was afraid for Sarah in those first minutes as the cruelty assaulted her.

"Why? How could he? Why didn't he call me?"

"Hannah said he's so soft-hearted, he just

couldn't tell you. He knew you would take it hard. He's just so kind, Hannah said."

Sarah began to shake then. Her whole body convulsed as she rocked back and forth, her arms wrapped around her waist. She hung her head as she mourned with deep grief for a lifetime of loving Matthew, now so completely lost.

"Hannah said he wrote to you."

A hot, blinding anger sliced through the life-taking sadness. Sarah sat up, lifted her head, her face white as the painted railing behind her. She spoke slowly and quietly but with terrible conviction.

"Oh, did he really? Hannah says he did? I doubt if he went to the trouble of finding a pen or spending forty-five lousy cents on a stamp."

Lydia turned her face to hide her relief. Yes! Sarah would survive. Already her resilience was showing through, her anger a sign of normalcy.

Suddenly, Sarah clapped her hands to her knees, got up in one swift motion, and stalked across the porch to look out across the lush, green cornfields of Lancaster County. She unrolled the age-old scroll of a young girl's first rejection as she attempted to decipher her own blindness for the first time. As she did so, the process began to melt away the guilt, the indecision, the awful prospect of leaving her family.

She believed God had made her decision for her.

With each wave and rustle of the deep green leaves on the cornstalks, her heart cried out her pain, but her appreciation of family and friends followed on its heels. With Matthew gone, could peace be a possibility? Her whole life had revolved around him. Now everything was black and white.

Turning, she asked loudly, "What else did Hannah say?"

"A lot," Lydia said, laughing hesitantly.

"Tell me."

As they talked, Omar came up on the porch, his lantern bobbing, followed by his faithful shadow, Anna Mae.

Sarah clapped a hand to her mouth.

"I forgot."

She told Omar about the small car. She watched his eyes widen and Lydia's face turn grim.

"Let's just all sleep in the barn," Lydia suggested.

"Should we?"

"Sure. We'll nestle down in the hay. We can watch the bats fly around and listen to the skunks snuffling in the grass. Let's do it. We'll start a little camp fire and toast some hot dogs and marshmallows. Please stay, Sarah."

Sarah agreed. She left voice mail messages for Elams and her parents, hoping they would check them before turning in for the night. Soon she found herself leaning forward from an old camping chair, gripping a long handled fork holding two hot dogs, one for Omar and one for herself.

Opposite her, Lydia brandished another fork. The two marshmallows she was roasting had caught on fire, and she waved them wildly to quench the flames. The heat left the sweet treat blackened but hot and gooey all the way to the middle.

"Mm. Oh my, I love these things," Lydia gloated. She removed a marshmallow to set carefully on a graham cracker that was coated heavily with peanut butter and topped with a neat square of Hershey's milk chocolate. Adding another graham cracker, she pressed lightly to blend the flavors before taking a large bite, melted marshmallow squeezing out the sides.

Sarah watched the warm, comforting coals as she turned the cold, unappetizing hot dog into a steaming hot, crispy, greasy goodness.

"Roll, please!" she said.

Omar immediately brought a roll, brushed the ashes off his hot dog, and handed the ketchup, pickles, and onions to Sarah. Lydia watched her friend's face, keenly aware of the depth of her pain and the courage needed to put on this front of normality.

They ate, joked, and drank homemade root

beer poured from a glass gallon jug into plastic tumblers. All the while, they kept their eyes and ears open for any unusual activity.

Cars passed on the country road, horses and buggies clopped by, and all remained peaceful. The stars appeared one by one as night followed the setting sun.

They noted the absence of bats, who usually made an early evening appearance, leaving their perches in the barn rafters to glide expertly through the night, gobbling up insects at an amazing rate. Omar said they'd be back. They just needed a little more time to adapt and take up residence in the new barn. Somewhere in the distance, a fox barked and an owl hooted as the nocturnal creatures began their nightly hunts.

Anna Mae said she was afraid. Lydia rocked little Aaron and told Anna Mae not to worry. They'd be fine with Omar here, and Sarah. Hadn't Sarah showed how fearless she could be in the face of an emergency, releasing cows and saving the Belgian on the night of their fire?

Immediately Omar spoke up, correcting his mother. "Priscilla saved Dominic."

"Oh, that's right. I forgot," Lydia assured her seventeen year old, winking broadly at Sarah.

What a comeback for Lydia, Sarah thought. The poor, tortured soul had taken only timid, little steps of recovery at first, but once she found her stride, there was no turning back. Even her face had smoothed out and her eyes relaxed. Her appearance was completely different now. She was still painfully thin, but she looked almost youthful after her recovery and healing had infused her whole being with a new sense of freedom and purpose.

They laid an air mattress, a new Coleman, on the barn floor and spread a clean sheet across it. They gathered pillows, sleeping bags, flashlights, an alarm clock, bug spray—everything they would need to stay comfortable.

Sarah lay beside Lydia with little Aaron nestled between them. Far into the night, they talked, sharing deepest feelings and emotions that had long been suppressed. They wept together, laughed together, became quite hysterical at times, and still they did not sleep.

Lydia told Sarah perhaps this hard and monumental task of forgetting Matthew would lead to her greatest happiness in years to come. Sarah quickly assured her that seemed impossible now.

"Perhaps," Lydia whispered. "But what if he turned out to be like Aaron?"

"He wouldn't. Matthew was . . . is kind," Sarah said, immediately sticking up for Matthew as she had always done.

"Aaron was kind while we dated."

There was nothing to say to this, so Sarah remained quiet.

"Did he actually beat you?"

"He hit me, yes. He hated me. I'll never marry again." The words were bitter, dripping with dark, acidic memories.

"I'm not supposed to talk about this, I know. But Sarah, I feel the hand of God has revived my empty existence with your friendship. With Matthew gone, we can be a tremendous help to each other. You'll have much of the same bitterness to overcome as I do."

"I'm not angry with Matthew. Just surprised."

There was a long, companionable silence, little Aaron's breathing lulling them softly to sleep, slowing their own soft breaths with the pungent smell of new hay as a heady perfume.

Omar stirred in his sleeping bag, muttered to himself. Somewhere off in the distance, a dog began an erratic barking. Rolling onto her back, Sarah took up her little travel alarm and checked the time.

12:38.

She rolled back on her side, whispered goodnight to Lydia, and then cried herself to sleep, thinking of Matthew on his trip to Haiti without her. She refused to believe he had married another woman. He probably wasn't married, just dating, she told herself. He wouldn't have wanted her to come to Haiti if he was already married. And certainly not to a woman of color. That just wasn't Matthew. But then neither was the flat, oily voice with the nasal twang she'd heard on the other end of the phone line.

Sarah had told Lydia she was surprised, her pride rising to the surface. Surprise was such a lukewarm term for the horror of the reality that still had not sunk in. Disbelief was much more possible. She didn't have to believe it, not yet.

With that comforting thought, she fell asleep.

A cow's bawling woke her. She was cold, so she sat up, her hands raking across the slippery fabric of the sleeping bag. As if in the distance, yet somehow close by, she heard the idling of a car engine.

The cow bawled again and rattled her chain. Sarah tilted her head, trying to catch the slightest noise. Above her, the new rafters creaked. The metal roof popped as it cooled in the night air. A truck changed gears out on the Lincoln Highway.

Slowly, the great barn door slid back as if on its own. Sarah stifled a scream. A dark form wedged its way inside, followed by another. Immediately, a piercing wand of light waved from side to side, finding the occupants of the barn floor.

Sarah leaped to her feet just as the figures turned to leave, clawing at the door.

Sarah ran. Omar yelled and caught the one figure by the shirt. Together, they rolled down the incline outside the barn door.

It was complete bedlam. Lydia screamed, and the children cried out as Omar rolled around in the grass, trying to keep hold of the writhing trespasser. Sarah sprinted to keep up with the fleeing figure ahead of her.

Pent up anger lent wings to her feet, and her long legs pumped, her arms swung. A section of the gravel cut into her bare feet, and still she ran. Past the idling car, past Elam Stoltzfus's dark house, beneath the huge maple tree across the road.

She wasn't sure what she'd do if she did catch the person in front of her. She simply wanted him away from Lydia. Away from the new barn. Away from even the possibility of bringing any sort of further destruction to that family who had already suffered more than enough.

She cried out in surprise when the figure ahead of her suddenly crumpled into the tall weeds beside the road, sobbing hysterically as if strained for breath.

"Don't hurt me."

The whimpered cry was barely coherent.

Behind them, the idling car revved to life and spun out of the widow's driveway. The head-lights dimmed, but the vehicle moved steadily towards them.

In the glare of the headlights, Sarah cried out as the small, thin figure ahead of her lunged to her feet, still sobbing, and ran crazily, panicked, after the fast moving vehicle, her thin hair flying in every direction.

"Ashley! Wait!"

Sarah ran, trying to catch up, wanting to talk to her, but the vehicle slowed and screeched to a grinding stop as Ashley flung herself into the passenger seat. The car took off, spraying dust and gravel and chunks of macadam into the dark night.

Sarah stood in the middle of the road and stamped her foot, her fists clenched in rage and frustration. It had to have been Ashley. Why couldn't she have caught her?

All those questions, that nervous wondering, the pale, skinny girl frightened of her own shadow—it all suddenly made sense. Ashley was somehow involved in these barn fires. She knew more than she was willing to admit.

Well, more was accomplished with honey than vinegar, her Dat always said, so Sarah's path was clear.

Turning, she strode purposefully back to a disheveled Omar, a wilting Lydia, and the traumatized children, all standing in an unsteady little circle of light provided by a single flashlight.

Everyone talked at once, but no one made any sense at all. It was four o'clock, the hour when weary farmers, tired of their night's vigil, relaxed and slept deeply for another hour before it was time to get up and begin the morning milking.

After everyone had calmed down a bit, Sarah

helped Omar with the milking. Anna Mae and Lydia fed the horses, the calves, and heifers.

The birds twittered as the sky lightened, heralding a new day, the navy blue streaks of night banished by the approaching orange, yellow, and pink of the sun.

They called the police, after deliberating whether or not to mention Ashley Walters' name.

If it had been her, and if the police questioned her and she denied everything, all would be lost.

If they kept the knowledge to themselves for now, perhaps more would be gained.

They decided not to reveal the name.

The police were courteous, listened to descriptions, and thanked them for the information, but as usual they didn't supply any concrete promises. They were doing all they could, which Sarah knew consisted mostly of guess work so far.

The vehicle had been small and of an indefinite light color. Omar could supply only the fact that his antagonist had dark hair and a slight build.

Disheartened, they lingered over coffee, their appetites diminished by the event in the night.

Already, the heat was intensifying, and little puffs of warm air were coming through the window screens.

Sarah picked at the edge of her French toast, swirled it in syrup, then put down her fork.

"I dread going home," she said to no one in particular.

"Stay here and help me do corn," Lydia said quickly.

"No, I should help my mother. She always has so much to do in August. I just don't want to walk past Elam's. What if Hannah stops me?"

"She won't."

With that assurance in her ears, Sarah strode purposefully home only to be confronted by Hannah, her *dichly* (head scarf) sliding off her head, her forehead already shining with perspiration, her apron as wrinkled as if she'd slept in it.

"Sarah!"

She clasped both of Sarah's hands in her large, capable ones, her mouth pursed in a show of emotion.

Wearily, resigned to her fate, Sarah lifted her eyes to Hannah's, waiting, saying nothing.

"It isn't Matthew's fault. He was confused. He's born again now, and he said God guided him straight to this lovely woman who is just the most wonderful thing that ever happened to him. He says she has a heart of gold and is so well versed in the Scripture, same as him. He told me he found his soul mate. Think of it, Sarah. His soul mate. Oh, I believe it."

She stopped, searched Sarah's eyes, then dropped her hands, stepping back.

The slow rustle of the maple leaves above them played across Sarah's flawless, tanned skin, the light in her eyes changing from yellow, green, and gold to a deep and restless gray, the hurt and sorrow of years of love and trust betrayed in the cruel manner which Matthew had chosen.

Clearly, Sarah spoke, her words precise, well placed, ringing.

"Hannah, in your opinion, nothing has ever been Matthew's fault. His whole life has been spent atop the pedestal you provided for him."

"Sarah! Don't be so . . . Why, Sarah, I hardly know you like this!"

"Well, you can get to know me if you want. If not, that's fine with me. I have been dragged through the muck by Matthew for the last time, Hannah. And you, too."

"But . . ."

Sarah lifted a hand. "Perhaps I can find who I really am, post-Matthew."

"What?"

Hannah was left standing by the side of the road, beneath the maple tree in the hot, morning breeze, puzzling about Sarah's words. She didn't know what exactly Sarah had meant by "post-Matthew."

Chapter 12

Word spread swiftly via the grapevine—known as the Amish phone shanty—and Sarah, unknown to her, became a bit of a celebrity.

She has more nerve than common sense, they said. Well, Davey Beiler's girls are all alike. Outspoken. Not afraid to speak their minds. You wouldn't think so, knowing their mother. She's so *tzimmalich* (humble).

Disbelieving individuals clapped work-roughened hands to their mouths, and with each phone call, Sarah's caper got a bit more out of hand, until the folks in Perry County actually believed Davey Beiler's *ihr* Sarah (his own Sarah) had caught the arsonist all by herself.

Well good, they said. Now the poor folks in Lancaster County can relax.

That part, at least, was the truth. Everyone figured after a scare like that, no one with brains in their head would attempt another barn fire for a good, long time. Men returned to their comfortable beds and enjoyed solid nights of sleep. Dogs returned to the safety of the back porch as the hot summer nights gave way to the winds of autumn, the time of harvest, council meeting, and communion services among the Amish.

Sarah muddled through September, half-heartedly performing what was expected of her, nothing more. At market, she made a point of strolling by the leather goods stand, appearing as disinterested as possible, but not once did she catch sight of the elusive Ashley.

The longer the girl's absence continued, the more convinced Sarah became. Something definitely wasn't right with that girl. She was almost certain she had chased her bashful friend that night at Lydia's, but she harbored doubts as well.

Even if Ashley was connected to the arsonist, she would never light a fire herself, Sarah was sure. More than likely, she was committed to a man who was the arsonist, or an accomplice.

As time crawled by on sluggish treads, Sarah became steadily oblivious to any purpose or objective in her life. She was sick of all the flour and the yeast and the shortening, the plastic wrap and endless Styrofoam trays at market. She was tired of the milking and cleaning and other countless chores at home. There was no point in anything, with Matthew gone.

Hannah no longer came to visit Mam, and Elam stayed at home, no longer bothering to walk over for a friendly chat with his neighbor. He carried the true humility of having a son gone astray, but Hannah bore her pride for her son like a misplaced banner, speaking loudly about his missionary work in Haiti without an ounce of modesty in her bearing.

Nevertheless, Mam's loyalty to her friend didn't waver. She assured Sarah over and over that this was just Hannah's way. Deep down, she was really hurting about her son's disobedience to his parents' wishes.

The air was tinged with autumn's smells, that dusty, earthy odor from the corn fodder being baled, the last of the hay put in bags.

In the kitchen, Mam's knife peeled deftly beneath the heavy skin of pale orange neck pumpkins. The garden had produced a gigantic pile of them, and Mam said they couldn't be wasted. They'd cook them down, cold pack them in wide-mouthed jars, and have all the pumpkin they needed for a few years.

Mam's pumpkin pies won prizes throughout all of Lancaster County, due in part to her own home-canned pumpkin. Better than the orange stuff out of a can, she'd say.

Without thinking, Mam remarked drily, "If there's a chance of making a wedding for you within the next few years, we'll have all the pumpkin we need."

"Thanks a lot, Mam," Sarah answered, her voice heavy with sarcasm.

"Oh, I'm sorry. I didn't mean to offend you."

"I know."

They worked in companionable silence, the

orange flesh of the pumpkin bubbling on both gas stoves, one in the kitchen and one in the *kesslehaus*, filling the house with its autumn fragrance.

Sarah was washing jars in hot, sudsy water, stacking them upside down on clean towels, when she heard a steady knock on the front door.

She scrambled to rinse and dry her hands, then peered through the screen door at a man of ordinary height. He had no distinctive features, just dark eyes, his hair cut closely to his head, a graying mustache clipped cleanly along his upper lip.

"Hello. My name is Thomas Albright."

"Hello."

"I'm wondering if I could come in and ask a few questions about the barn fires in your area."

Mam appeared behind her briefly, a quiet presence.

"We don't like to talk about them."

"But you will?"

"We'd rather not."

"Why?"

"Too much room to make mistakes."

"Well."

There was a pause. The man shifted his weight from one foot to the other as if to relieve the mounting tension in his mind.

"Is your father home?"

"Why do you ask?"

"Is he or isn't he?"

Sarah eyed the man levelly, still feeling no apprehension. He didn't appear very harmful. Sort of short and soft, baby-faced.

"He's baling corn fodder."

"Where?"

"South of the barn."

In the kitchen, Mam set a kettle of boiling pumpkin on a cast iron trivet, letting it cool long enough to put comfortably through the strainer.

"Could I ask him a few questions?"

"I doubt it."

"Smart cookie, aren't you?"

Sarah said nothing, lifted her chin coolly.

"Tell me, if you're so smart, how well do you know Ashley Walters?"

"She's an acquaintance."

"That's all?"

"Yes. We talk."

The man put his hands behind his back and tipped forward on the toe of his shoes, then back on his heels, surveying the ceiling of the porch, examining each screw holding the white vinyl in place.

"Tell me, did you give chase to her the other night?"

"What are you talking about? Of course not."

"Amish girls don't lie."

So, it was her wits against his. What did this man want from her?

"No, they don't," Sarah countered.

"But you do."

"How do you know Ashley?"

"Let's just say she's an acquaintance."

Sarah nodded.

"Mind if I smoke?"

"Yes."

"You do?"

He mocked her with his eyebrows. "So what will you do if I smoke?"

"Probably nothing."

"Good girl."

Deliberately and taking his time, he made quite a show of extracting a package of cigarettes, finding a lighter by patting his pockets. After he lit a cigarette, be began insolently blowing smoke through the screen on the door.

Sarah didn't flinch.

"Why don't you come out on the porch if you're not going to invite me in?"

"I'm helping my mother."

"She in there?"

"Yes."

He moved up against the screen door, pressing the length of his body against it, waggled his fingers, and said, "Hi, Mrs. Beiler."

"Hello," Mam said politely, then went on washing her sieve, as if he was of as much consequence as an annoying fly.

"Not very friendly, is she?"

"She's friendly."

"Just not to me."

Sarah remained silent, wishing he'd leave.

"So, when you chased Ashley the other night, what were you going to do with her if you caught her?"

Sarah didn't answer.

"I thought you Amish were nonresistant."

"We are."

"You call that nonresistant?"

When Sarah didn't answer, he flattened himself against the screen door a second time, gave a small derisive snort, and told her to stay away from Ashley Walters. Then he added that if anyone in Lancaster County thought they could relax about their barns, they were badly mistaken.

"The worst is yet to come," he growled theatrically.

With that, he flicked the burning cigarette into the shrubbery, turned on his heel, and left.

A brown SUV. There was nothing in particular to set it apart from hundreds of others. Sarah still wasn't frightened as she coolly informed Mam that he reminded her of a little Chihuahua trying to scare someone.

"He may be dangerous. You'd better tell Dat," Mam said, wisely wagging her head in that knowing way of hers.

Six fresh pumpkin pies were lined up on the countertop when Dat came in from baling corn fodder, dusty, his eyes red-rimmed with weariness, his hair clinging to his scalp.

He caught sight of the pies, and an appreciative grin spread along his lips, changing the light in his eyes. "I can't believe my good fortune. What a wife!"

Mam blushed and beamed, smoothed her apron with both hands, and said, "Why, thank you, kind sir!"

There was a happy chortle from the rolling desk chair, and Levi burst out, *"Da Davey und de Malinda sinn kindish* (Davey and Malinda are childish)!"

Dat was wily, and he knew light-hearted banter would mean a generous slice of pie, so he played right along with Levi.

Sarah burst out laughing, and Suzie threw her report card, hitting Levi's shoulder. He bent to retrieve it, leaned to one side, and slid it beneath his backside, sitting solidly on the offending item.

"Gepps (Give it back)." Suzie stood in front of Levi, hand outstretched. *"Gepp* (Give it)."

Resolutely, Levi shook his head.

"Young girls have to learn not to throw report cards."

"Levi!" Suzie howled.

"Levi!" he mimicked, lifting his face and howling.

Suzie dove into him, pushing forcefully on his

stomach, and, with Levi's feet both resting on the chair legs above the casters, he was sent skimming backward across the smooth linoleum, coming to rest with a clunk against Dat's rolltop desk. His head snapped forward, and a great guffaw was expelled from his open mouth.

"*Na grickst net* (Now you won't get it)!'"

Suzie shrieked and ran after him, shoving him against the sofa, where he spun helplessly in a half-circle, giggling wildly.

Priscilla looked up from the sewing machine, leaped to her feet, put her hands on the back of the rolling chair, and sent him flying away from Suzie, as he shrieked with glee.

Sarah stood against the counter, her arms crossed, caught Dat's eye, and gave him a wink. They both knew Levi was one of a kind.

"*Davey, die maid sinn net chide* (these girls are crazy)," he chortled to his father.

"You enjoy it, and you know it, Levi. But how long do you think we'll have to bug Mam before she'll let us eat pie?"

Levi shrugged his massive shoulders, his bright, brown eyes eagerly scanning Mam's face.

"You'll ruin your supper."

"Come on, Malinda!" Levi begged, so completely in earnest they all burst out laughing.

As it was, they ate more than one pie, sitting around the pumpkin-strewn kitchen, enjoying the perfect creaminess with just the right combination of spices. The tall shivery, custardy sweetness melted in their mouths, completely ruining the appetite that should have been reserved for healthier fare.

Priscilla said pumpkin was a vegetable so they were having a healthy supper. Levi said pie crust was a vegetable, too. Mam laughed so hard that she had to gasp for breath and wipe her eyes.

Dat said after chores Mam could just make bean soup with applesauce. Bean soup consisted of a can of great northern beans dumped into a sauce-pan of browned butter with some salt, milk, and bits of torn, stale bread. It was best eaten with dried apple pie, but if there was none, applesauce worked just fine.

Spicy red beets made a great side dish.

"*Rote reeva* (Red beets)!" yelled Levi.

There was a new calf in the barn, its white and black colors so much crisper than it mother's. It was so fresh and brand new and wobbly on its thin legs.

Sarah crossed her arms along the top of the pen, watching it struggle to stay on its feet, the mother cow pleasantly licking and nurturing it, establishing a bond between them.

Dat came up beside her to watch. "Cute little one, isn't she?"

Sarah nodded.

"Who was the man at the door earlier?" he asked.

Sarah told her father, giving all the details, and he frowned, his brow furrowed with lines of concern.

"It just doesn't sound good. I don't think we have any reason to relax or feel that the barn fires are a thing of the past. Something is definitely not right among us."

He paused. "How sure are you that it was Ashley that you were chasing?"

Sarah shook her head, her mouth in a straight line of concentration.

"Just about a hundred percent. That poor girl—I don't know, Dat. Something is not right with her."

Dat shook his head again, worry drawing vertical grooves between his graying eyebrows.

That next Sunday as David Beiler stood to preach, he cautioned the congregation about feeling smug, satisfied, full, quoting the verse in the Bible about the man who said to himself, his barns were full to overflowing, he'd build more, and have plenty for years to come.

In a spiritual sense, he cautioned against the satisfaction of feeling full as well as thinking that worldly goods were a blessing, that nothing could touch the harvest, so plentiful, so packed down and running over as it was.

Sarah sat on the girls' bench, her head bowed, perplexed. Dat made it sound so complicated. Sometimes, she still felt confused, thinking of

Matthew, but the minute she remembered his sudden marriage, the confusion left.

She wished Dat would just chill. If someone was going to burn more barns, they would. She had her own idea of exactly how Ashley Walters played into this string of fires. And she was sure it was only a matter of time until the next one was lit.

Her thoughts flitted to the night before. Saturday evenings were always hard, the emptiness, the barren land without Matthew stretching before her, year after year.

She'd just be a single, leftover blessing, as old maids were called in polite circles. She'd start her own bakery. She'd told Melvin about it. He said she was too optimistic. The last thing Lancaster County needed was another bakery. There was already one at every fence post.

She and Melvin had walked up to visit with the Widow Lydia, who was already ready to go to bed for the night, her eyes large and self-conscious, her hands constantly going to the belt of her soft blue bathrobe.

Sarah could not understand her discomfiture, until she saw Melvin watching her, standing stiffly inside the front door, tugging at his gray sleeves as if to lengthen them.

Lydia had made coffee, but the evening was stilted, stiff, and uncomfortable, the way her brothers used to describe a new pair of denims.

Finally, when conversation lagged, they'd walked home together. Melvin was strangely quiet, contemplative, a reserved manner creating an aura of distance, keeping Sarah from seeing his true feelings.

He went home early, leaving her alone on the porch in the chilly evening, the crickets still gamely chirping their songs, in spite of falling leaves and lower night temperatures.

She guessed she was like those tired crickets, knowing the end had already arrived, yet chirping anyway.

She laughed to herself, a self-mocking, unattractive snort, sitting alone, wrapped in her old sweater, her feet uncomfortably cold inside her sneakers.

She wondered if the weather changed in Haiti. Was it always tropical? Warm? She rocked forward in misery, thinking of Matthew, so tanned and fit, working hard to build homes for the natives, his wife ministering to the sick, the perfect couple working for the Lord.

Well, I'm just too Amish. Home canned pumpkin, bean soup, white cape and apron pinned to her dress, the uniform of the unmarried woman.

She had still not fully recovered from the wonder of the possibility of leaving, the excitement of actually being able go and do something out of the ordinary.

Ha, she thought again. You know better than even think about it. No, she would not want to leave, truly. It was a lust that had never been fully conceived. A thought, a desire, gone as swiftly as Matthew.

On her knees that Saturday night, she had prayed for direction, for peace, for acceptance of her lot in life, and went to bed with a strong spirit, bolstered by her time spent in prayer.

Just keep on showing me the way, O God. Didn't King David repeat that same prayer many times in Psalms?

How then, could she ever suppose God had heard her pathetic prayer? The hymn singing on Sunday evening was abuzz with the news. Rose Zook was glowing in a dress the color of bittersweet made in the latest fashion, her skin radiant from the joy within. Lee Glick had asked Rose for a date, the beginning of what promised to be a steady relationship.

Sarah sat carved in stone, unable to understand the dead weight somewhere in the region of her heart. Why?

Who could figure out why a person felt the way they did? She'd never been attracted to Lee, had she? Could she help it if he had assumed he loved her?

The songs were announced, the beautiful hymns rose and fell around her, and she sat, hearing nothing, staring at nothing, wishing with all her being she could get off the bench and go home. Home to her bed, where the pillow was soft and yielding, cradling her tired head that churned with all sorts of questions and exclamations, but always ending in commas, without a beginning and without an end.

At the close of the evening, before the snack was served, they all sang the customary congratulations to the new dating couple. Rose dipped her head, blushing and giggling. Sarah was completely taken off guard by the assault of the green monster that had many names but whose only truthful one was jealousy, pure and simple. She felt as if she hated Rose. Almost.

Sarah's cheeks flamed with embarrassment, tears sprang to her eyes, and she kept them lowered, cautiously folding her hands tightly, keeping her eyes trained on the whitening of the knuckles. Best to stay that way. If she kept her eyes on her hands, no one would know the roiling unrest inside of her.

It was only the passing of the trays of cookies, huge bowls of potato chips, and platters of cheese and pretzels that made her lift her head, smile, acknowledge comments from friends.

Oh good, no one had noticed.

Daring a look across the room, her eyes made solid contact with the devastating blueness of Lee Glick's. Instantly, her eyes left his, slid away to safety, before returning, her heart rate increasing rapidly as their gazes held, melded, touched, and understood.

I didn't know, Sarah.

I didn't know you didn't know, Lee.

In a daze, a dizzying, dangerous edge of uncertainty, with a thread of hope woven through the insurmountable, she walked to Melvin's buggy, helped him hitch up his restless horse, and then collapsed against the seat back. She restrained the urge to cry and sniff and blubber her way into Melvin's pity, sharing the whole array of misery that was her life.

"Now that's a cute couple," he observed, as they drove past Lee and Rose attaching his horse to the shafts.

"Yeah."

"She must have known what she was doing, breaking up with Matthew."

"Yeah."

"Smarter than you, maybe?"

His elbow jabbed her side good-naturedly, and she stifled the urge to slap him. She nodded her agreement and watched the stop sign flapping back and forth in the stiff breeze.

"Say something."

"Be quiet, Melvin. Just shut your mouth for one second."

"Oops. Now you're mad."

"No. Just tired and . . ."

"You wish Lee Glick would not be dating Rose."

"I don't care about Lee Glick. I don't care about Rose. Let them date and get married and live happily ever after. Who cares?" she spat out.

"You love him," Melvin said quietly, and flicked the reins.

Chapter 13

"Mam, I have to get away."

Sarah flung the statement across the table as they relaxed together with their second cups of coffee before starting the serious scrubbing and polishing, dusting and moving furniture.

Shocked, Mam choked on her hot drink, wiped her mouth, and opened her eyes wide to look at Sarah.

"You mean, away? Leave the church? Or . . . or what?"

"I just want to get out of Lancaster County."

"Sarah, stop talking like that. You can't. You have your job, and your place is right here with your family."

"How do you know?"

"Why would you question it?"

Miserably, she confided in Mam, always her refuge when things got really serious.

Her mother listened carefully, lent a patient ear, sipped her coffee, cut a cinnamon roll in half, and resolutely set one half on Sarah's plate. She shook her head when Sarah wailed about getting old and fat on cinnamon rolls on top of every-thing else, then watched as her daughter took a great bite, shook her head, and promptly took another.

"If all else fails, try pastries," Mam remarked drily. She observed the change in Sarah, the tension in her shoulders, the down turn of her usually wide and smiling mouth, the clouded eyes darkened by her own unhappiness.

"Sarah, you need to find joy in doing for others. You're so anxious about the future, and there is absolutely no hurry. Enjoy your time being single. Why panic?

"Matthew so obviously was not for you, and I'm so glad God has been gracious, sparing you the heartache of living with a man who marries for reasons other than true love."

"He loved me."

"No, Sarah, he didn't. I remain firm in that belief."

"Then evidently Lee doesn't, *didn't* either. He asked Rose."

"Your stubborn . . ."

"My stubborn what?"

"Nothing."

Mam got up, whisked the dishes off the table, barking instructions to Priscilla. She told Sarah to get up off that chair and find the ceiling mop. The attachment was in the top drawer, and she could use Palmolive dish soap since stronger cleaning solutions made streaks on the kitchen ceiling.

Priscilla sang catchy tunes, washed walls, whistled, teased Levi, organized drawers, found old postcards and letters in Mam's cedar chest, chortled to herself about her sister Ruthie's sloppy handwriting. Sarah was left to her thoughts as she plied the mop steadily across the gleaming ceiling, the tiny bits of fly dirt steadily disappearing beneath it.

Mam worked alongside Sarah, wringing a cloth from a plastic bucket of sudsy water, washing down walls, rigorously attacking any stain on the doors or woodwork.

The cleaning of the old house was a twice-yearly occurrence, usually in April and again in October, or the last of September, depending on the weather, which was the inspiration for Mam's rush to get the house cleaned now.

Dat told her he believed all Amish women were born with the instinct to clean house, like monarch butterflies or homing pigeons, drawn to the attic with a sense of purpose, an uncanny direction that sent them straight to the scrub bucket and up the stairs.

Mam chortled and beamed, said nah, no one cleaned the way her grandmother used to. She never lugged bucket after bucket of hot, soapy water up two flights of stairs to the attic and scrubbed that splintery "garret" floor, the way grandmother had. Mam swept, cleaned under the eaves with a brush and dustpan, straightened up, organized, washed windows, but she never once washed her attic floor, no sir.

That was where Mam headed next though, armed with a broom, garbage bags, window cleaner, and bug spray. She had that certain bright-eyed anticipation about her, her nostrils flared just enough to convey the bubbling of energy, and away she went, barking orders, her broom keeping time.

Later Sarah found Mam sitting on her backside beside a plastic tote, her legs stretched in front of her as she pressed a tiny blue sleeper to her breast, her head bent over it, her grief unbearable for only a moment before she got ahold of herself, as she'd say.

They lifted blankets, small white onesies, stained only a bit around the neckline, but even the stains were precious, knowing little baby Mervin had drooled there when his baby teeth were pushing through his soft, pink gums.

"Mam, seriously, do you remember this? The first time you took him to church?"

Mam nodded, her lips wobbling, a moment of vulnerability she couldn't control.

"Remember how hard it was on my pride, the fact that he wore a dress and white pinafore?" Sarah asked.

"Oh Sarah! I would have forgotten."

"You said you had to lead by example and wear a dress on poor Mervin, but I was so embarrassed!"

"Sarah, your grandmother wore a dress on Dat

until he was potty-trained. That was the old way. Now young mothers are horrified to think of putting a dress on their little boys to take them to church just that one first time."

"Some mothers still do."

"Yes, a few. But you know how times change. What was considered Plain years ago, conservative, you know, is hardly practiced anymore, it seems."

They read Mervin's baby book together, remembered the first time he sat alone, crawled, his first tooth, a lock of his hair Scotch-taped into place, but there was not one photograph.

They were oblivious to the lack of photographs. They were not a necessary or customary items for the Amish, so their absence went unnoticed.

The attic was cleaned, Mam's emotions were dusted and swept along with the floors and walls, and all was well once again.

Mam decided Priscilla's room needed a coat of paint, but Priscilla refused, saying she'd be sixteen years old soon, and then she'd decide what color she wanted. So Mam shrugged her shoulders and said alright, and that was that. They worked their way through the upstairs, wiping down the walls, and down the stairway, washing curtains and bedding and rugs. Anything washable in Mam's path was laundered in the wringer washer and hung on the wheel line to dry.

By evening, there were usually two red spots, one on either cheek of Mam's cheeks, her eyes drooping with weariness, but she was still ironing curtains, her fatigue only apparent when she snapped at Levi or answered Dat curtly.

The kitchen was the sticker, she always said. Sarah knew it, too, thinking of moving the gas stove out from its station between the cupboards, egg yolk and grease and dirt staining the sides of it, rolls of dust and dirt beneath it, the oven blackened and speckled with six months of hard and constant use.

Every half year, Mam sprayed the oven cleaner liberally, then stood up, gasping and saying, "That stuff is wicked. It can't be good for you."

But a clean oven won out, always. A few fumes wouldn't hurt, as long as that oven was sparkling, at least till the next apple pie bubbled over, or the next tray of bacon sizzled and splattered grease over the racks.

Doing the bacon in the oven was the lesser of two evils, according to Mam's way of thinking. Bacon splattered everything, but at least it didn't have to be turned in the oven. It came out nice and crispy without anyone having to touch it.

They put Levi to work that day, assigning him to polish the leaves on the fig tree growing in its big ceramic pot in the corner. He stayed at his job for hours, content to be part of the housecleaning, his face pink with the praise Mam showered on him.

Dat ate a bowl of cornflakes and chocolate cake for lunch, saying he'd been hungry for that for a while now. He didn't eat the cereal separately, but plunked a sizable square of chocolate cake right in the middle of a large bowl of cornflakes that had been liberally sugared. The bowl had also been filled with plenty of creamy milk, and it soaked into the heavy chocolate cake.

Levi said that was slop and wanted no part of it, muttering to himself as he buttered two slices of bread and plunked them on the griddle. He eyed Mam hopefully before bending to find the cheese in the refrigerator himself.

He made his grilled cheese sandwich and poured a glass of milk, then got up to make another one, resigning himself to his fate. No use begging Mam when she was cleaning house, that much he'd learned when he was young.

That was why Sarah was glad to go to market the following day. She was thoroughly tired of the intensity of housecleaning with Mam.

She felt energized and took a new interest in her work, doing her best to produce a quality product, whistling softly as she plied the dough with a spoon or the mixer or turned out flaky pie crusts.

She could hardly believe her eyes when Ashley Walters walked directly up to her, the only thing between them the clear Plexiglass that separated the customers from the employees.

"Sarah?"

The word was a question, a frightened, whispered question that hung between them, a butterfly swishing its dainty wings against the glass.

"Ashley!"

"Can we talk?"

"At ten o'clock."

"It has to be now."

"Now? Right now?"

"Yes."

Looking around, Sarah asked Emma if it was alright if she went on her break early as someone needed to talk to her.

"Sure. No problem."

"Thanks."

Quickly, Sarah grabbed her purse, asking Ashley where she wanted to go.

They sat on a bench near the front entrance, the throng of people coming and going providing a wall of privacy, a detraction, which was just what they needed to blend in as part of the life of the market, seen but not really noticed.

If anything, Ashley had only become thinner, her pale cheeks almost translucent, the blue veins in her forehead more noticeable than ever. Sarah looked closer, then drew back in surprise when she realized Ashley's lower lip was split open and partially healed. Her eyes were puffy, her skin blotchy.

As usual, she wore an oversized sweatshirt, torn jeans, and sneakers—curled, creased, and filthy.

When she spoke, her words were slurred. Sarah caught a strong smell of alcohol on her breath.

"Sarah, I have no one else. I'm in trouble. I don't have the nerve to get away from Mike, and I can't tell my dad. He'd kill me.

"There's a lot going on. There's a lot of weird stuff going on. Mike is my, well, sort of boyfriend. Sometimes boyfriend. But he, well, he's getting worse. He has a problem. I'm afraid for my life now, sort of. Not really, but just, like, sort of. I have to hide so Mike can't find me. If I go to someone Amish, I bet he'd never imagine I was there."

"What about your parents?"

"My dad hates me. My mom is in California now. They aren't together anymore."

"Your dad doesn't hate you."

"He will if he finds out about Mike."

"Well, I don't know what to say, Ashley. I'd have to talk it over with my parents. I don't know how wise it would be to hide you. Are you in trouble with the law, or is Mike? Should we call the authorities? The police?"

"I have nowhere to go!" Ashley's voice rose into a shriek of hysteria before she clapped both hands over her mouth and rocked forward, her thin hair falling stiffly forward as if to hide her somehow.

Passersby eyed her curiously. If they sat here and Ashley continued her theatrics, they would draw too much attention. Sarah got up and turned to tell Ashley to come with her, but she was knocked off balance by Ashley lunging against her, her thin hands grabbing at Sarah's bib apron, her mouth open, mewling like a lost, starving kitten, grotesque, yet so completely pitiful.

"You can't leave me here!"

"I won't, Ashley. I'll leave a message for my mother to call me. We'll decide something, okay? Just find a place here in the market and stay there, until I can tell you what my parents say."

"I'll stay in a booth at the restaurant."

"Alright. Just stay there, till I find you."

Ashley's whole body was shaking now, her lip swollen and purple, her fingers restlessly stretching the wristband on her sweatshirt as she searched Sarah's face.

"Can I borrow a couple dollars to get something to eat?"

"I'll go with you."

Could Sarah trust Ashley to be truthful? She had no idea what was going on in her life, and perhaps they'd all be getting into something far worse than they'd anticipated.

Mam answered the message on her voice mail

dutifully, the way she always did, walking to the phone shanty a few times a day to see if anyone had called.

Sarah explained the situation as best she could, interrupted only by Mam's sympathetic clucks or words of warning, placed aptly, an attempt at caution.

In the end, Mam relented, saying she'd speak to Dat, but certainly, there was no way Sarah could leave the poor, frightened Ashley at the unoccupied market later that evening.

Ashley greeted Sarah's acceptance with a nod of her head, eyes averted, bringing a storm of doubt with it. Was she doing the right thing?

A small duffel bag was the only thing Ashley carried with her as she climbed into the market van with her head lowered, her eyes downcast, a whipped animal, afraid of more punishment.

She slunk into the far corner on the back seat, slouched down as far as she could, as if to obliterate herself completely. Then she turned her face to the window and closed her eyes, shutting out Sarah and the world around her.

The usual, noisy banter wasn't completely stilled, but a respectful air permeated the interior of the van, as if the girls knew their loud joking, their fun and laughter, might hurt this sad, thin girl with the stringy, unkempt hair.

When they arrived at the farm, Ashley sat up, her eyes wide with fright, her head turning from left to right, the reality of her situation clearly upsetting.

"Sarah?" Her white hand groped for Sarah's sleeve, found it, plucked at it.

"You sure this is okay?"

"Of course. Come on."

Ashley followed her, apologizing in hurried whispers as she squeezed past the market girls' knees. There was a loud cracking of plastic breaking and a shriek from Sarah, followed by a wail of denial as she stepped down from the van and surveyed a broken plastic container with a thoroughly ruined lemon meringue pie squeezing between the cracks.

"Oh my word! Whose pie?"

"Mine! Did you step on my pie, Sarah?"

Annie, the biggest girl in the bunch, eyed Sarah with a very real sense of loss. Sarah tried unsuccessfully to hold back her laughter, but the occupants of the van heard the spluttering from her and joined in, until everyone was laughing with her.

Still chuckling as the van sped away, the two girls walked to the house, the welcoming yellow light in the windows as homey as ever.

"I'm home!" Sarah called.

Mam was at the sink washing supper dishes, but she turned, wiping the suds from her hands with a corner of her apron, a smile of welcome on her kind face.

Mam's eyes changed from the glad welcome she produced so naturally to one of shock, but she regained her composure just as quickly. She held out a hand warm from the dishwater and said, "Hello, Ashley."

Ashley allowed Mam a wild glance before ducking her head, her hair covering most of her face, the way it often did.

"I hope you can make yourself at home here. I have the guest room ready for you, and there's a bathroom you can share with the girls. Your supper is in the oven."

Turning, Mam bent to retrieve an oblong casserole and set it on the table, sliding a heavy potholder underneath.

She filled two glasses with mint tea, adding plenty of ice from the freezer, and set out a Tupperware container of applesauce and one of bread and butter pickles.

Sarah took a long drink of her tea, sighed, and lifted the lid of the casserole.

Levi appeared at the doorway, clearing his throat and gesturing at Ashley, who sat, terrified, unable to lift her glass or attempt conversation.

Wow. This is going to be rough, Sarah thought.

"Hey, Levi! How's it going?"

In answer, Levi drew his eyebrows down and told Sarah in perfect Pennsylvania Dutch that she could stop being so *gros-feelich* (proud) right now, that just because she had an English friend didn't mean she had to talk like Melvin.

Mam put at hand on his shoulder, sat him in a kitchen chair, and introduced him to Ashley, who barely acknowledged his presence. She merely nodded her head, her eyes trained steadily on the silverware beside her empty plate.

Levi, however, was delighted by the fact that they had English company, so he leaned forward, smiled, his beady brown eyes as observant as always, and bellowed, "Hi, Ashley. I'm Levi!"

Ashley cast him a wild-eyed look and nodded miserably before turning her face away.

"*Sees shemmt sich, Mam* (She's ashamed)!"

Mam held up one finger against her mouth and motioned Levi to hush, which was completely lost on him. He leaned forward, his ample stomach shoving against the table, turned his head, and told Ashley in broken English that his name was Levi Beiler and he was her friend, and he hoped she knew how to play Memory.

Ashley glanced wildly at Sarah, who nodded, smiled, put a hand on her arm, and said Levi would be a good friend, and yes, he was a champion Memory player.

That brought a small smile of recognition from Ashley, but she still refused to eat, her fingers twisting restlessly in her lap.

"Can I give you some baked spaghetti?" Mam asked politely.

Ashley shook her head.

"No?"

"I . . . don't feel very good. May I . . . Do you mind if I go to my room?" she said, her voice low and rough, as if it hadn't been put to use for a long time.

"Certainly. I just thought you might want to meet David, my husband, Sarah's father, and her two sisters, Priscilla and Suzie," Mam said hopefully.

"Okay. If I don't have to eat."

"You don't. Maybe you don't like our supper. Can I get you something else?"

Ashley shook her head, a pinched look about her nose, before looking around desperately and asking forcefully, "Is there a restroom?"

Sarah jumped up, guiding her to the downstairs bathroom, then stopped on her return to the kitchen table as she listened to the sound of Ashley being violently sick in the safety of the bathroom.

Sarah shook her head at Mam's questioning eyes, then slid heavily into her chair, her shoulders bent with weariness.

"*Sees grunk* (She's sick)!" Levi announced.

"Shh!"

"*Sees an cutza* (She's throwing up)."

"Levi!"

Getting laboriously to his feet, he shuffled to the medicine cabinet in his room, returned with a large bottle of colorful Tums, and waited patiently by the bathroom door until it opened hesitantly. A still terrified Ashley slid out between the door and the frame, as if she was too frightened to open it more than a few inches.

"Ashley! Here!"

Levi handed her the peace offering, his face shining eagerly in the light of the gas lamp, his small brown eyes as innocent as a child's and as eager to please.

Ashley stopped, turned her head, and looked at Levi with only a fraction of her guard down, but a small crack appeared in her wall of reserve. She reached out, and Levi placed the Tums in her hand triumphantly.

"Take two," he said, with an air of superiority.

"I will," Ashley said, very low and quiet.

She picked up her duffel bag and questioned Sarah with her wide, startled eyes.

"I'll show you," Sarah said quickly and led the way up the stairs as Levi sat down at the kitchen table and began the long process of presenting his case for a plateful of baked spaghetti, which would be his third for the evening.

When Dat, Priscilla, and Suzie came in from doing the evening chores, there was quite a flurry as everyone tried to tell them about Ashley at once. The din of the conversation prevented anyone from noticing someone at the front door, knocking, then knocking again, before opening the door and saying, "Hey."

Only Dat heard the greeting, turned, and said, "*Vell* (Well)!"

Surprised, the family's conversation ended, and they turned in respectful silence as three members of their community stepped inside, their faces grave and solemn. For one heart-stopping moment, Sarah thought they had come bearing tragic news, a death, another barn fire, until she remembered that kind of news was usually spread through the phone lines.

She never once gave it a thought that they were all members of the school board. She picked at the cold spaghetti on her plate, twirled her fork around and around, and ate a few pickles as she thought about Ashley being sick on her first evening with the family. She wondered what actually possessed the poor girl and chuckled to herself about how Levi had immediately taken her under his wing, like a sick kitten or a lame bird.

That Levi was a character, he surely was.

Chapter 14

When Jonas King said loudly that their school needed help, Sarah's fork stopped, the spaghetti slid off, and a wave of shock zipped from her head to her stomach. The school board! It was October, and the school board was here?

She leaned back against the kitchen chair, her breath creating a small puffing sound as it left her body.

"So, we didn't know if Sarah would consider taking on the school or not."

She heard the words through the rapid pulse in her ears, but it was followed by a high-pitched ringing that blocked out Dat's answer.

Then they all turned to look at her, their eyes kind and curious, their straw hats held politely in their hands. Their hair stuck to their foreheads, the way Amish men's hair always does after their hats are removed.

Vaguely, she saw Mam's wide eyes, Priscilla's downcast ones, Dat's questioning.

"Sarah?" he asked.

She focused on the kind eyes of her father, a shyness overtaking her, the reality of these men's visit too much to fathom.

Jonas broke into the silence.

"We have a real mess. I simply don't know how else to put it. Disrespect, disobedience, pupils simply refusing to cooperate. Mothers, parents, are taking the children's sides. I won't blame you if you refuse to help us out, but we all agree, perhaps you can. We did hear about driving off the . . . the . . . those who came into Lydia Esh's barn, and we thought maybe if you could do that, you could handle a roomful of problem pupils."

Sarah smiled shyly and picked at the tablecloth where the hem was wearing thin, leaving strands for her to pull. She didn't want to remember that night, especially not now with Ashley upstairs, so frightened of being here, her future in jeopardy.

"I . . . have a job," she said, facing the men now, able to warm up to them, inspired by the praise, which was not given easily, she knew.

"You go to market?"

"Yes."

"Well, there are market girls all over Lancaster County, but not everyone can teach a school, especially not this one," Abner Esh broke in, his rotund little form shifting from one foot to the other.

Mam asked the men to be seated. The table was cleared discreetly, Priscilla dutifully washed dishes, and Levi listened respectfully as talk swirled across the table, the problems, the solutions, the task at hand a monumental one by all accounts.

Mam served coffee and a platter of pecan bars. Sarah asked them if it was alright if she took a week to think it over. She would have to let her boss have at least a week or two to find a replacement.

"So you are considering?" Abner Esh asked.

"Yes."

It was a long time before Sarah fell asleep that night. The events of the day crowded out any relaxation as her mind picked up and examined first one obstacle and then another, discarding one solution and then the next until she became quite weary of it.

Ashley was the first problem. She couldn't just hide out here with Mam, spending her days in idleness, worrying Mam. She would have to find a job somewhere, but not in the immediate area. She had no money and no vehicle, and she was clearly more troubled than even Sarah knew.

They would let the teacher go. Fire her. Sarah knew her well. Martha Riehl. She was in the same youth group as Sarah, although not in her intimate group of friends.

She was pretty, dark-haired, very outgoing. What would she say?

They'd remove her from her teaching spot—no doubt she loved her job—and she'd be replaced by Sarah. She'd be angry, feel betrayed. And just how severe were the discipline problems?

Sarah sighed as the short hand on her alarm clock slowly crept past the twelve, and she was expected to go to market again in the morning. Would it be her last week there? She got out of bed to pull the shades down over the windows, the brilliant moonlight annoying now as she tossed restlessly in her bed.

She reached for the bottom of the shade and was just about to pull it down, when, out of the corner of her eye, she caught a slight movement, a weak light, in the barnyard beside the silo.

She stopped, straining her eyes as her heartbeat accelerated. It wasn't dark at all. In fact, everything was awash in a silvery light, illuminating the dark shapes of the cows lying in the barnyard and the pasture beyond.

There! The light was not nearly bright enough to be a flashlight. It was more like a penlight.

Watching closely, Sarah grasped the window frame, her breath coming in short, ragged puffs.

There was no wind, only the silence of the night and the beauty of the silver moon shining steadily from a cloudless night sky speckled liberally with twinkling stars.

Her eyes picked up the weak, yellowish light. It couldn't be a penlight. They had more of a bluish white light produced by LED bulbs, those new ones that used only a fraction of the energy that regular bulbs consumed. What was going on?

Suddenly a thought entered her mind. The cows weren't afraid at all. They lay contentedly, and not one got up or milled around. There was no bawling or any other sign of fright. Whatever or whoever it was, the cows were accepting it.

A dark form bent over a cow and slapped it. Dat!

The cow lunged slowly to her feet, followed by the unsteady little form of a newborn calf, wobbling along in the moonlight, aided by her father's caring hand along its back.

Dat would put the cow in a warm stall with clean straw, protecting the newborn calf from the frost of the night, which was sure to cover the fields and woods before morning.

Satisfied that the weak light was Dat's ailing old flashlight, Sarah left her vigil by the window and fell gratefully to bed, the pulled shades sufficiently darkening her room, enabling her to close her weary eyes and finally fall asleep.

It seemed like only an hour had passed when her alarm began its delirious music, much too loud and way too annoying. She was going to get rid of that obnoxious thing as soon as she could purchase another.

She sighed, weariness washing over her as she remembered the visit from the school board members. How could a person come to a sensible decision without adequate sleep?

Sarah washed her face, brushed her teeth, put

up her hair as fast as possible, and threw on her clothes without knowing exactly which dress she was wearing. She pinned on her covering and ran down the stairs, just as the headlights of the market van swept across the yard.

Mam had told Sarah not to worry about Ashley. Priscilla was good at being with people like her, so they'd be fine. Levi would win her over as well.

Sarah slumped against the side of the van, asleep before they hit the interstate on the way to New Jersey, oblivious to the girls' chatter and the roaring of the great trucks moving past in each direction.

The day was long, and her mind weary at the end of it. She packed up a few bakery leftovers without talking to anyone about the school board's visit, collected her pay, and went to the van, suddenly knowing with startling clarity what her decision would be.

She needed to get away, she'd told Mam. Out of Lancaster County, which held Matthew's memory and all the painful details in every road, every field, every farm and house and restaurant and store they'd ever been to.

She no longer wanted to see his house with the spreading maple tree across the rural road, the picket fence beneath it, his bedroom window shaded by it.

If she did go away, could she truly escape? The

pictures would remain in her memory. Perhaps filling her mind and heart with a roomful of boisterous boys and girls would be the perfect answer.

Hadn't the men said those boys were almost uncontrollable? It would take every ounce of her strength and likely more of her patience than she could produce, but she knew she wanted to try.

She imagined Matthew being chased out of Lancaster County by a group of rowdy children from the problem school and shook silently with inward giggles. Well, so be it, Matthew Stoltzfus. So be it.

Saturday evening was always a joyous time with the return home from market, the usual happiness and lighthearted talk, the anticipated end of her work week, and the long awaited opportunity to see Matthew. Now when the market van drove up to the door, the anticipation was replaced by a certain acceptance, a feeling that seemed to signal a better place, although not a perfect one.

Matthew was gone. Over and over, she had to remind herself of this fact, but no time was quite as difficult as the return from market on a Saturday evening.

She was shocked to see Mam's pale face, her lips compressed with restraint, Priscilla sitting on the couch staring into space, her eyes wide.

"What?" Sarah asked immediately, afraid for them all.

"She left," Mam said, her tone anxious.

Levi broke in.

"A white car. A little one. She went to the phone shanty. She did. She called. Someone came."

He was speaking in loud tones, clearly distraught. He had wanted Ashley to stay. She was his friend. She said she'd play Memory.

The real story came from Mam, who said Ashley had come down the stairs late, about ten o'clock or around there, refused breakfast, and asked for the telephone. She waited on the porch shivering, her coat pulled tightly around her thin frame, talking to herself, until a car pulled into the driveway. She'd gone without a good-bye or thank you. She simply walked down the steps and into the waiting car.

The driver of the car was wearing dark glasses, a cap pulled low over his forehead, and a dark coat, so there was no way anyone could tell who he was or what he looked like.

Sarah was frustrated, afraid for Ashley.

"If I knew where she went, I'd hire a driver and go look for her. But I have absolutely no idea where to start. She never told me anything about her background, her whereabouts.

"One thing is sure, she's afraid of the person she's with. He seems to have some control over her, and she knows much more about these barn fires than we think."

Mam nodded, saying wisely that Ashley held a secret about something, and it was so bad it was making her literally sick.

For now, they could only pray for her safety and hope for the best. God loved Ashley same as everyone else. He had a plan for her life, and she was important to Him.

"Just because we're Amish and have a stable home doesn't mean we're above her in God's eyes. He cares deeply about Ashley and so should we. That poor girl is so pathetic," Mam said, tears rising unbidden.

Sarah ate a slice of sweet baloney and a dill pickle, drank some tea, then poured a glass of creamy milk, and took two oatmeal cookies from the Tupperware container in the pantry.

"You know what I think, Mam? I honestly think Ashley knows who started every one of these fires. I think deep down she's a good girl, one who lives with a conscience that can barely tolerate the guilt, and I think this Mike, her boyfriend, is every bit as dangerous as she says. But I'm not convinced he's the actual arsonist."

Levi looked up from the puzzle he was assembling, his eyes shrewd, narrowing.

"I think you're right, Sarah. You know, the other day I was thinking hard. I remember the small, white car that was here the night of our barn fire, and I think the person driving the car then was much bigger than the thin guy that picked up Ashley today."

"Oh no, Levi," Mam cautioned.

"Malinda!" Levi held up a warning finger, and Mam smiled widely, the way she always did when Levi called her Malinda.

The peace that entered Sarah's life came slowly, in bits and pieces, in times she least expected it.

On her way to church the following morning, when the sunlight glistened on the frost in the hollows, wisps of fog hanging like ghosts above it and the sun so brilliant it hurt her eyes through the glass of the buggy window, she felt peace.

A calm, unhurried feeling of having cares that were not so enormous that God would not be able to handle them. Peace.

It came in many forms—the sound of the steel buggy wheels on the cold, hard gravel coupled with the dull, familiar sound of iron-clad hooves pounding on pavement, the tinkle of snaps slapping against the reigns, the homey clop of another team following them and checking the rearview mirror to see who it was.

It was familiar, home, her life, her culture. This was the only way she understood the accompanying peace.

This peace, however, was shattered by the appearance of Hannah, greeting her effusively the minute she stepped out of the buggy, chilled, eager to get into the house with her friends.

"Sarah! Oh, it's good to see you! I just have to share this with you. You'll be so happy for Matthew. They're expecting! Imagine! The Lord is surely with them, wouldn't you say? I can hardly wait to tell your mother."

Sarah nodded her head and began to walk away, but was stopped by Hannah's voice again.

"Sarah, Matthew called to tell me the good news. He asked about you. He wanted you to be the first to know. He cared very much what you thought. Oh Sarah, I can't tell you how happy he is. I can just hear the joy in his voice when he talks about his work in Haiti. He's serving in an orphanage now. Think of it, Sarah."

Sarah met Hannah's eyes, behind the glasses, eyes that sought her approval, searched for agreement, strengthening the faith she had in her beloved son.

Hannah saw the colors in Sarah's eyes change from green flecked with gold to a turbulent surf of brown and gray and restless green. She stepped back, away from the ongoing reality she saw there.

Only a whispery sigh and a hint of an accompanying smile gave away any emotion. Rachel Zook handily stepping between them, shaking Hannah's hand with a hearty good morning, as Sarah fled to the safety of the house.

She found peace was elusive, especially in the face of adversity. She listened closely as the young minister paced the floor, expounding Christ's life and his lessons, but her mind wandered constantly, thinking of Matthew, his life, his calling, his wife and the child they were expecting.

He wanted me to be the first to know, Hannah? Really?

Sarcasm and rebellion crowded out the morning's peace, and she felt torn, embattled, losing ground, her feet slipping down the dangerous slope of doubt and self-pity wrapped up with remorse and what-ifs until she couldn't concentrate on the long closing prayer in German and the final song.

She blinked back the tears that the rousing melody forced to the surface, checked every youth seated on the boy's bench, and had never felt Matthew's absence so keenly. Would it never go away?

Would his memory dog her happiness all the days of her life, a barrel of darkness she'd drag along with baler twine slung over her shoulder, crippling her, holding her back from her normal, free walk?

Well, if it did, there wasn't too much she could do about that now. She would have to do the best she could.

She dressed carefully that afternoon in a crisp

navy blue dress, pinned her cape neatly, was careful about her apron, precisely lining up the two ends of the belt, pinning it securely.

Her hair looked better than she had ever seen it now that Priscilla had introduced her to a new product from Pantene, which helped hold the curls in place even better than hairspray.

She put a new white covering on her head, satisfied with her appearance, for once.

"Think of it, Pris. When I teach school, I'll have to pin on a cap and apron every single morning. And tie my covering, then yet."

"Then yet?" Priscilla mimicked from her perch on the bed.

"Whatever."

"What's with this Pris thing? I don't want that nickname. You better not start it. I'd rather have Cilla."

Sarah laughed.

"Who's taking you?"

"Guess."

"Melvin?"

"You got it."

"How can you stand riding around with that old Melvin? He's way past the time that he should even be running around. He's not popular at all. You'll never get a husband, hanging out with him."

"Priscilla, I like Melvin."

"I know you do. That's nice. But, seriously, how old is he?"

"I think twenty-eight or twenty-nine."

"Shoo!"

"Yeah, really."

"And every time he comes to pick you up, same thing. He comes in, sits down, eats and eats and eats, talks to Dat endlessly—probably because he's closer to his age than yours—then goes through the ritual of combing his hair, and he doesn't even have any in the front. And there you sit, when I know you'd much rather be on your way to the youth supper."

"Oh well, I'm not sixteen anymore. And Matthew isn't here, so going away on Sunday holds very little excitement. The thrill is simply gone. Which shoes should I wear?"

"The flats."

"Not the heels?"

"No, you're tall enough."

"Giraffe tall?"

"No, just tall."

"Priscilla, I can't wait till you're sixteen. It'll be so fun getting ready to go away together!"

"Yeah, but you have to remember, Omar is going to take me. Melvin won't be in the picture, okay?"

Sarah raised her eyebrows, bumped Priscilla's arm with her fist, and said, "My, my."

"For someone who says there's no excitement in going to the supper, you certainly are being very careful about your appearance, which is just a nice way of saying you sure are sprucing up for someone. Who is it?"

Sarah slapped her sister playfully. Priscilla yelped and ran down the stairs ahead of her. Suzie looked up from the card game she was playing with Levi, sniffed, and went back to her game.

Dat was seated on the recliner, a large ceramic bowl of popcorn beside him, a steaming mug of coffee on the lamp stand, his white shirt and black Sunday trousers making him look younger, relaxed.

He smiled at Sarah, asked who was picking her up, then smiled again, although his eyes clouded only slightly as he watched her walk to the kitchen for a bowl to fill with popcorn.

"Mam, you may as well make another popper of popcorn, if Melvin's picking her up."

As it was, Melvin was late, and they all got into a discussion about Ashley Walters' strange existence, which seemed to escalate Melvin's opinions about the barn fires to zealous heights. Sarah watched the clock and figured the day would soon be past and she'd still be sitting there at her parents' kitchen table.

She agreed it was troubling, but if Ashley made the choice to go back to her boyfriend, there wasn't too much they could do except be patient and hope no tragedy would come of it.

Dat's eyes filled with tears of compassion, and

Levi looked somber, contemplating the loss of a promising Memory player.

When they finally got to the supper at Aaron King's, Sarah found an exuberant Rose beaming happily, waiting eagerly to extol every last one of Lee Glick's virtues to her best friend, who listened, expressed amazement, happiness, disbelief, whatever was required of her.

Aaron King *sei* Anna had done an outstanding job of planning a menu for over a hundred youth. The scalloped potatoes and ham, creamy with onions and cheese, and the green bean casserole were perfect. Sarah balanced her paper plate on her knees, ate appreciatively, talked to her friends, and rose above her heartache once again.

She whipped Rose at an intense game of ping-pong and was surprised when Lee stepped up and asked to play.

Rose acknowledged her new boyfriend coyly but handed over the ping-pong paddle, saying Sarah would never, ever beat Lee, there was simply no way. She followed that statement with a high shriek that drew exactly the amount of attention she'd hoped it would when heads turned, smiled, and watched for a while, before returning to their games.

Caught off guard, Sarah blushed and became flustered, nervous, with Lee towering only a ping-pong table's length away, his blue eyes challenging, alight with interest.

They were a match, one almost as skilled as the other, but Lee was a wicked server and won by three points. Sarah laughed, her eyes the color of spring water with sunshine dancing on its surface, her hair gleaming in the lamplight. Lee handed over the red paddle as she smiled up at him, guileless, unafraid. Unafraid or released?

He reached for the paddle, his fingers closed over hers, so firm and warm, so compelling, and stayed for seconds longer than was necessary.

On gossamer wings, the breath of attraction dipped and hovered between them, sacred, beautiful, but scarred now by the years of disappointment for Lee, by the doubt that real love could ever be possible again for Sarah.

Without a word, they wondered at it.

Chapter 15

Sometimes, Sarah thought, life goes by so fast, and quite unexpectedly a situation arises that would have been unfathomable before.

She put both hands on her desk, clasped them firmly, the fingers intertwined, took a deep breath, and said loudly, "Good morning, boys and girls," to the echoing, empty classroom, then bent forward, laid her head on the desk, and whispered, "You're going to have to help me here, Lord. It's really scary."

Teaching in an Amish one-room school was not a job that required any further studies than the eight grades she had already had. She had finished her schooling at age fourteen and then attended vocational class once a week until she was fifteen, as Pennsylvania state law required.

She remembered the order of school, the work, the way eight grades were managed. This school, Ivy Run, had twenty-three pupils distributed among eight grades, so it posed no threat as far as the number of children she would be required to teach.

The frightening part was the bad attitude, the disrespect that had run rampant the past few years, the children, or some of them, grieving their teacher terribly with blatant disobedience, among other things.

Ivy Run School was only about four miles from Sarah's home, but she rode to school with a driver rather than by scooter or horse and buggy. The school board offered to make arrangements to save her time.

The board members had been extremely kind, offering assistance, volunteering services, but so far, she had not heard a single word from any of the parents. She hardly knew who they were, anyway, so that was no big deal. She just hoped they'd be able to work with each other when things got out of hand, which Sarah felt sure was bound to happen.

It was Thursday afternoon, which left two days at market, one Sunday, and one early Monday morning, before she would stand at this desk and wish every pupil a good morning.

She wondered if her knees would support her, or if she'd faint dead away.

The school was an older brick school on Hatfield Road, set in a grove of chestnut and maple trees. The roof had been replaced a few years before, and the windows were fairly new, but the old brick structure remained the same, the porch built along the gable end, the cloak-room enclosed on one side.

The floor was a smooth, varnished hardwood, gleaming with years of hundreds of little feet walking across it. The cast iron desks were painted a shining black with refinished oak tops and seats that folded up or down.

A blackboard ran the length of the front with a white border along its top, the alphabet in cursive, print, and German on it. Rolled up maps hung just below the letters, and a row of shelves stood beneath the blackboard.

A gray metal file cabinet stood off to the right, a propane gas heater to the left. Above the heater hung a round PVC ring with wooden clothes pins attached to it with nylon string, a homemade wonder for drying caps and mittens in the winter.

The rows of windows on each side of the classroom were topped with beige, roll down blinds, serviceable when the sun blinded a row of pupils hard at work.

The artwork on the walls had been done by the previous teacher, such as it was, and Sarah could tell that had not been her interest at all as the name charts along the top of the blackboard were colored poorly and coming loose at several corners.

Perhaps, if they had time, she'd make her own name charts, colored brightly, with black lettering.

Sarah sat back, sighed, and then became quite giddy with anticipation.

The classroom was infused with a golden, late afternoon radiance, turning an ordinary room into a warm haven of light.

She stood up from the chair, stretched, and turned to get her sweater, when she heard a grating noise, a clicking.

The door.

Okay. Someone was trying to . . .

She stepped back, both hands going to her mouth to stifle a scream, when the handle turned. The door was yanked open unceremoniously, a head was pushed through wearing a beanie. The intruder's face was dirty, his coat torn in places, soiled, but the eyes as blue as always.

Lee Glick was completely taken aback, his hand going to his filthy beanie, before shaking his head, laughing ruefully, and saying, "What are YOU doing here?"

"Oh, you scared me!"

That was all they said for quite some time, Sarah standing in the middle of the aisle in the gold light, Lee standing just inside the door, his face streaked with dirt, his clothes obviously having seen better days.

He repeated the question, and she answered with one of her own.

"I came to get Marlin's arithmetic book. He's crying up a storm, because he had a stomach ache in school and couldn't get his work done, he told Anna."

"Your sister Anna?"

"Yeah."

"They come to this school?"

"Evidently. This is where I was told to go."

"I'll be teaching here, starting Monday morning."

"Are you serious?"

Sarah nodded. "They're having a lot of problems."

"Tell me about it. That's all Ben's children talk about at the supper table. You know you're in for it, right?"

"What's that supposed to mean?"

"What I said. Sarah, it's awful the way these kids act. I'm afraid for you. I really am."

"I can't do more than fail, can I?"

"No, you're right."

"I think the biggest problem, from what the guys on the school board said, is two or three families. Probably the first day I can pretty much tell who they are. Then I guess I'll go from there."

Lee grinned, his teeth very white in his darkened face. "So that's your game plan?"

"Yup."

"Good luck. You know you'll need it."

Sarah laughed. "By the way, I didn't know you mined coal for a living."

Lee looked perplexed, then a hand went to his face, and he laughed sheepishly.

"No, not coal mining. Just removing a very old slate roof and replacing it. I've looked like this all week."

"Anna's probably having a fit."

"She is."

Sarah laughed again, thinking of the over-weight little Anna, huffing around her house, cleaning, washing, clucking. She missed her and told Lee to tell her hello.

"I will."

There was an awkward silence, which surprised Sarah, their conversation having flowed so freely in the time he was there.

"Guess I should go," he said very quietly.

"Yes. My driver should be coming any minute."

He looked out the south windows, his gaze unfocused, and she looked through the north ones. It was much easier and safer that way.

Sarah took a step backward and saw her driver pull into the school yard.

"My driver's here," she said loudly, nervous now.

His reluctance to leave was apparent when he said, "Sarah, tell me. Tell me something." His voice faded away as his eyes were lifted to hers, held steady.

"Just . . . How are you doing? Are you okay? How did you feel when you found out about Matthew? I can't explain to you, the agony I experienced at . . . over the time you . . . he . . ."

The questions seemed to release a torrent of emotions as his breath accelerated, his voice rasped and cracked before he stopped, bent his head, and kicked the toe of his work boot self-consciously against a desk.

"I have to go," he said and turned.

"I didn't answer your questions," Sarah said coolly. "I am doing okay. Not fine, just okay. I will be fine." She laughed, a soft sound bordering on hysteria.

"I don't know how I felt when he left without me. Something inside of me died. I was angry, hurt beyond words, but, of course, part of me protected him, and I didn't believe any of it, but only for a short time. Hannah, his mother, is a big help. When I think of being actually married to Matthew, I can't imagine." Her voice faded away, and she shook her head from side to side.

"So, I'll teach school. I'll become a tall, skinny old maid who puts her life into the classroom, and people will call me a leftover blessing for the community. My hair will turn gray, and I'll make coffee at weddings and wait for some old bachelor or widower to ask me."

Lee laughed, tilting back his head. Then he looked closely at Sarah, the smile fading from his mouth as he held her eyes with his.

An uncertainty spread across his face, then determination as he made up his mind and closed the gap between them with two long strides, his hands came up to encircle her forearms. He tugged gently, "Sarah."

The tenderness in his voice was so real, so alive, it brought a lump to Sarah's throat. She could not have uttered a word if she had tried.

"Do you think you'll ever be able to love again? I mean, before you become an old maid?"

Sarah shrugged her shoulders and his hands fell away. He clasped them behind his back, but his face was so close to hers, she could feel his breathing.

She raised her face, found his eyes, and was lost in the blueness of them. He watched the color in hers change with emotion turning them dark with remembered pain, gray and anxious with mistrust, then vibrantly green with longing, flecked with lights of new hope.

"Sarah, I have Rose. I must honor that."

Numbly, her eyelids heavy, covering the display of feelings, she nodded.

"Yes, Lee. You do. And I wish you the best. You two are so perfectly matched. Everyone says."

"She's a nice girl. I am in awe of her in so many ways."

Leaning sideways, Sarah retrieved her new book bag, grabbed her sweater, and said, "Good. That's good. I have to go now. My driver is here. She's been waiting."

They moved as one through the door, suddenly so far apart that any words would have to be shouted in order to be understood.

They didn't look back, neither did they wave, as each one moved in opposite directions in separate vehicles.

Sarah's driver, a neighbor who was close

friends with Mam, took one long look at Sarah and asked what happened back there. Sarah laughed and told her not to worry about it.

Lee's work driver reminded him of the arithmetic book and had to pull into someone's driveway to turn around and take him back to the schoolhouse to get it.

Good thing Ben was one of the caretakers and had given him a key.

One last weekend at market, Sarah thought, as the van sped along the interstate, rain hissing beneath the tires, the windshield wipers clicking rhythmically, the fast-moving monstrous trucks spraying the van as they roared past.

The girls in the van were sitting or lying in various positions, half-awake or asleep, oblivious to the rain or the traffic, trying to grab a few minutes of rest before the churning pace of a busy market day.

Rain meant an increase in customers. It was always that way. Sarah didn't know why. Perhaps people didn't want to work in their yards or do any outdoor activities on a rainy day. They thought of a place that was cheerful and bright, filled with comfort food, especially good, hot soups and stews, warm doughnuts and cinnamon rolls and whoopie pies and cupcakes. So they'd be frantically busy today.

She'd try her best to imprint in her mind the many precious memories of the short time she'd been at market, the sights and sounds and smells of this wonderful place, filled with friends and acquaintances, people she had grown to love and respect.

The driver turned up the volume on the radio, and the van was filled with predictions of snow or ice by evening, warning motorists to use caution, especially on interstates leading to higher elevations.

That's us, Sarah thought, but she dismissed the threatening weather as they pulled up to the vast brick wall of the farmer's market.

Sarah measured flour, yeast, sugar, eggs, and salt. The great paddles of the mixer turned, thoroughly mixing the cinnamon roll dough, bread dough, and all the different yeast breads that were placed on the shelves in tempting rows.

Sarah's hands flew. She focused on her work as she rolled pound after pound of soft, delicious smelling dough into long rectangles. She quickly sprinkled brown sugar and cinnamon along the length and rolled the dough to form long pinwheels, before grasping the smooth cutter and severing one cinnamon roll after another from the long lengths of dough. She placed the rolls in foil pans and dotted them with walnuts and chunks of butter.

As she had predicted, the crowds appeared at about ten o'clock in the morning and never let up.

Sarah didn't get her first break until after lunch,

her harried boss apologizing profusely. Sarah understood and said she'd be fine, but she was so hungry she bought a soft pretzel and dipped it in cheese sauce to eat on her way to the restaurant to order her lunch.

She ordered the special there, roast beef and gravy, with French fries and coleslaw. She sat down across from Rose Zook, who was slowly spooning the perfect combination of vanilla ice cream and hot fudge sauce into her mouth.

"You know you eat an awful lot," Rose observed after Sarah had scraped her plate clean.

"You ate a bunch of my French fries—probably half," Sarah answered her friend. "But you know I had a soft pretzel on the way here," Sarah added, laughing.

"You didn't!"

"I did."

"Well, that's okay. You can eat. You work hard."

Suddenly, Rose's eyes darkened, and she toyed with her paper napkin, her head bent slightly. She sat back as both hands went to her stomach, then she spoke quietly. "I am eating everything in sight right now. It's stress."

Rose put an elbow on the table, cupped her chin in her hand, her gorgeous, heavily-lashed eyes blue but clouded with worry.

"I hardly know how to tell you, but Sarah, something isn't right with Lee. I just can't describe it. Really it's just . . . well, weird. He's nice to me, very attentive, actually, but it's like all of him isn't there or something. He seems kind of distracted."

Sarah's own hot fudge sundae now became the focus of her attention. Guilt, coupled with self-loathing and shame so all-encompassing it felt like burning fire, washed over her.

"I mean, I know Lee loves me. There was never a doubt in my mind. He just doesn't seem as if he's quite like he was when we began dating. You don't think . . . I mean, Sarah, do you think he's thinking of someone else?"

Blinking rapidly, her face flaming, she shook her head, avoiding Rose's gaze.

"What's wrong with you?" Rose demanded, suddenly.

"Nothing, Rose. Why?"

"There is, too."

"I'm just too full. My stomach hurts terribly."

"Are you serious?"

Sarah nodded miserably.

Rose laughed, a high-pitched giggle of understanding and friendship and relief all rolled into one burst of joyous sound.

"So, what do you think about Lee?"

"Oh, guys are hard to figure out, Rose. Don't ask me. I have no faith in my ability to understand guys. Look what happened to me. Fine one minute and oh so miserable the next. Who knows what they're thinking? I'm going to be an old maid schoolteacher, living in my own small house, thin and pinched and mean."

Rose whooped with laughter, then smacked the table top with the palm of her hand, turning heads as she did so.

"Sarah, that is exactly why you are my closest friend. I just love the way you express yourself. Well, good. Then I have nothing to worry about you, right? I mean, Lee sometimes, well, he mentions you. How different you are from most other girls. And . . . Well, you know, Sarah."

Rose broke off, biting her lower lip.

Sarah couldn't get away fast enough, scuttling down the aisles wanting the floor to open and swallow her.

Shamed, her face flaming now, she knew she was every bit as bad as a traitor, an adulterer.

Oh, she'd wanted Lee to take her in his arms, kiss her, and tell her he loved her, the way men did in all the novels she read, in all the hopes and dreams of her heart. Every girl yearned to be loved, it was simply the way it was.

Solomon devoted an entire book in the Bible to the love between a man and a woman, and God was pleased, Sarah felt sure.

But why? Why was she always the odd person caught in a love triangle with Rose as the prominent character?

She thought of the heart-stopping depth of Lee's blue eyes, the powerful, magnetic attraction she had experienced. His blond hair, the soiled stocking cap, the black dust on his face, the work-roughened hands clenching her arms.

Oh, Lee. It's too late, now. I ruined you with my undying love for Matthew, my stubborn refusal to see what he was. A man in love with Rose, my oldest friend. And here I go again.

And yet. He'd talked of her, to Rose.

It was hard to suppress the pinwheels of joy that cavorted freely and colorfully through her entire being, her heart soaring and swelling with a newfound awe. And yet she wondered if it would ever be possible, and now, so soon, she knew.

Too soon. It was much too soon. Her broken heart had left her vulnerable, and she'd be hurt. Again.

"Hey!"

Sarah stopped and turned, searching for the person who had called her, perplexed.

Harold from the leather goods stand stood at his entrance, his arm waving, motioning her over. He was tall, with wisps of sandy hair combed thinly across the top of his scalp, which showed through easily. His mouth was surrounded by a splattering of sand-colored stubble, a short goatee that was never quite there and never quite gone. His eyes were gray, so much like Ashley's.

Sarah stood before him, lifting her eyes to his.

"Where's Ashley?" he demanded brusquely.

"I have no idea," Sarah answered.

"Well, maybe you're telling the truth."

Sarah decided to offer no information. Perhaps he never knew Ashley had asked to go home with her. She stood quietly.

"You know she disappeared."

"You mean, completely?"

"Yeah."

Sarah bit her lip, said nothing.

"How much do you know about her?"

"Not much. We talked a few times. She's nice."

"Well, I'm going to warn you now. Stay away from her. She's bad news. She's addicted to alcohol. Does drugs. You wouldn't think it, but she's a mess. Can't handle life."

Sarah lifted her chin. "You could help her. She said you hate her."

Harold became a changed man. His face whitened, he stammered, and became extremely uncomfortable. Then he did his best to hide his discomfort by laughing, a rocky snort lacking any kind of true mirth.

"Ah, you know how teenagers are. They all think their dads hate them. She's just a kid."

Sarah faced him squarely. "She's troubled about a lot of things. Her boyfriend, Mike, for one. And for some strange reason, these barn fires that have been cropping up really bother her. She's obsessed with them."

Instantly, Harold began rambling, his words falling over one another in his haste to assure

Sarah that his daughter was mentally off with all the substance abuse, and she knew nothing of these barn fires, not one single thing. He finished with another warning.

"You stay away from her. Don't mess with her. She's . . ."

"Well, if she disappeared, I won't be able to," Sarah said stiffly.

Having spoken himself into a corner, Harold rambled on again, saying she'd come back, she always did, that's what he'd meant in the first place.

Sarah nodded, then moved on without saying good-bye, her head held high, her gaze trained straight ahead.

She'd just brush that Walters family off, forget she even knew they existed. Like a spot on a wall, they would be easy enough to wipe out of her memory, and she would be glad to be rid of them, someone else's concern, none of her own.

What Harold and Ashley Walters did or said was absolutely none of her business, and she'd take his advice and keep it that way.

From the produce stand, a husky, black-haired youth stopped hammering the board he was putting into place as he turned and watched the tall, lithe girl in the startling blue dress swing by, her movements swift and easy, reminding him of a deer, so soft, so graceful, and as lovely.

He turned, slowly, and went back to work.

Chapter 16

Who could ever have predicted that the arsonist would choose an evening when the roads were slick with freezing rain and snow to bend over his lighter and newspaper and bits of wood and start the diabolical little fire that consumed yet another poor farmer's livelihood?

Enos Miller was young, his mortgage payments on the old Hess place high. But with his wife's frugal spending habits, good management, and careful planning, they'd made it through the first five years.

Annie had born him three children. Blessings from above, he called them. His quiver was well-stocked with the three little souls God had *be-shaed* (given) them. His days were filled with hard work, and he enjoyed the fruits of his labor, anticipating the time the children would work side by side with him, building a secure foundation of tradition and trust.

They'd put the baby, Ben, to bed and covered him with an extra blanket, the sound of pinging hail on the north bedroom window calling for warmer covers. Then they knelt side by side by the foot of the high, queen-sized bed and bowed their heads as Enos prayed the German evening prayer and Annie kept her mind on his words, repeating them silently.

Annie had extinguished the kerosene lamp with a quick puff, and together they cuddled beneath the comforter brought from the cedar chest she'd received from her parents, lined with the sweet smelling wood, the flannel patchwork retaining the scent of cleanliness and home.

He kissed her goodnight, told her he loved her, then fell into a deep, restful sleep, the grateful slumber of a weary man after a hard day's work. He'd commented to Annie before he fell asleep what a good feeling it was to be finished cleaning out the box stables just as this rain turned to ice.

It was the baby's coughing that woke Annie, sleeping with her senses alert, the way young mothers do.

By that time, the fire had reached the horse stable, where the driving horses had been tied to keep them warm and dry, out of the harsh elements that night.

Annie was bewildered by the banging at first, then terrified by the high screaming of the panicked horses. She flung the bedroom door open, rushed to the hall window, and beheld a sight she would never forget.

She called to her husband in panic, her voice coming from deep in her throat, hoarse and primal, a cry of complete disbelief.

Enos felt the horror before he saw it, fumbling

with his clothes, crying out, croaking words of defeat in Pennsylvania Dutch as he pulled his shoes blindly onto his bare feet. He stumbled, slid on the ice, fell, crying out again and again as he made his way to the barn, yanked open the door, and was met by a wall of raging fire, consuming the air he had given it.

The hellish situation encompassed his senses and imprinted into his memory, the smell of burning cowhide and the black smoke, the screams of his animals in indescribable pain and suffering, the icy rain pelting his back, the red-orange inferno driving him back, away from any attempt at saving even one cow, one calf, one horse.

Still sobbing, he slid across the gravel driveway, his mind clearing enough to propel him toward the phone shanty set halfway out the driveway between the poplar tree and the wagon shed.

Just as he reached the shanty, his feet gave way on the dangerous slickness, and he fell hard on his hip, saved from a mean break by the youthful resilience of good strong bone and muscle. He crawled, then pulled himself up by the handle on the door, wet, shaking, his teeth chattering. He directed the fire trucks, giving the address, 177 Heyberger Road.

Everything moved slower that night.

The cinder trucks went ahead of the fire trucks as the township worked together with the local fire companies to allow them access to the Enos Miller farm, set back on rural roads, around turns, up hills and down, every inch of the road-way slick with ice and snow.

Mercifully, the two oldest children slept through the worst of it, their angelic little faces turned toward each other in the safety of the room at the top of the stairs, covered with a heavy flannel comforter. It was one of the ones Annie's mother, Sadie, had knotted with her sisters that day, after they found out there would be a new baby, at the age of forty-six.

The baby had settled down with his pacifier, and Annie was grateful for that as she stood inside the front door, alone, crying helplessly. She watched their hopes and dreams consumed by roaring flames, disappearing into the wet, icy atmosphere in great black billows of smoke.

Annie was quick-witted and intelligent. She remembered the last time she'd paid the fire tax. It had come in the mail, stating the amount they would owe, the Amish method of paying for their own catastrophes at times such as this.

Yes, God would provide.

As the flames leaped and danced and licked the night sky, she felt the safety of their heritage, a net designed by caring individuals, their hands intertwined to form a safe haven of care. At the root of it was God's love, the kind human beings could only obtain from a heavenly father and rely on to make life better for one another.

So she remained calm when the fire company could not respond immediately. She opened the door to call Enos and was grateful when he came up on the front porch, away from the pelting ice and rain.

She comforted her husband, fulfilling the duty of all wives, being a helpmeet, a bolster to her beloved in this time of need. He slowly regained his composure before he heard the wail of the fire sirens down on 896.

"*Ess mocht sich* (It will be alright)," Annie said, and he knew he had never heard sweeter words.

Yes, they would make it. Everything would be alright.

That statement, however, did nothing to prepare them for the days ahead, the unbelievable loss buried in the wet, blackened, stinking pile of debris. When the rain finally stopped and the cold, merciless sun shone through the clouds, it illuminated the remains of things that tore at Enos with claws of pain.

The hay wagon had been his grandfather's. His dat had given it to him, smiling, pointing out the heavy oak boards worn smooth by generations of men toiling in the hot summer sun. Now it was reduced to twisted steel wheels.

The feed cart and the wheelbarrow had both been repaired, used long past their primes, but they had served as beacons of Enos and Annie's careful planning, their balancing of a meager budget.

As always, the help arrived with horses pulling gray and black buggies, the iron clad hooves ringing in the icy wetness, the mud splashers hanging between the buggy shafts and catching all the bits of grey ice and mud before they slid off and fell back onto the road.

They disembarked, these men dressed in black doubleknit coats and black felt hats, their black trousers tucked into tall, rubber muck boots, their hands encased in brown work gloves, their ruddy faces alight with kindness yet again.

Women came, too. They turned, reached under seats, pulled out long aluminum cake pans or Tupperware containers of pies or cookies. They brought Walmart bags of crackers and pretzels, cheese and bologna, whatever they could find in their refrigerators or cellars, raiding their own pantries with hands driven by generosity.

They clucked about all the mud tracked into Annie's clean house, asked earnest questions, their eyes birdlike, inquisitive, wondering how the fire had started on a night like that. And Enoses living on a hill the way they did. *Ach* my.

The carpenter crews arrived in pickup trucks, big four-wheel drives with heavy caps on the back, carrying electric tools and portable genera-tors. Youth came wearing stocking caps and dressed almost English, but they had kind, sympathetic faces and respectful attitudes, Enos told Annie later. He had to give them that.

The children had caught the flu. They were feverish, whining their discomfort, as the house remained perpetually cold and muddy with the doors opening constantly. There was no rest for Annie.

She carried on, dutifully performing every task that needed to be done, received boxes of food, cooked along with the women, washed clothes, nursed the baby, rocked her cranky little ones, and tried to look for the good in everything.

Dat heard of the fire in the morning from the milk truck driver.

He was grave, his face lined with the bad news, his eyes concerned, knowing this fire would stir the dreaded pot of loud opinions, determination, the rumblings of retaliation that were always voiced by those who thought along the ways of the worldly.

Over and over, Dat stressed the importance of staying pure from the world, which meant not only dressing modestly and living a simple life but having attitudes and goals that were not worldly. He truly believed there were plenty of worldly men dressed in Amish clothes, secure in their displays of righteousness, but who harbored attitudes of gain and selfishness, even *schadenfreude* (pleasure at the misfortune of others), and were as worldly as if they drove around in Mercedes Benzes and dressed in brilliant hues.

But humans were just that, human, and he offered up patience and forbearance as well, striving to live by example, aware of the immense job at hand, especially at a time such as this.

He ate his fried eggs and sausage, finished his dish of rolled oats and shoofly pie, drank his steaming mug of coffee, and said he'd be glad if Sarah could accompany him, if Mam was busy at home.

Sarah nodded, willing to go, although a bit pensive, sad that her last market day had been cancelled because of the ice and snow. Well, she'd visit occasionally, or substitute if she was asked. She'd now have to accept the market days as a time remembered.

She dressed warmly and put on her new wool, pea coat and wrapped a warm green and beige plaid scarf around her neck. Then she carried out the boxes of food Mam had prepared yet again.

She loosened the latches on each side of the buggy and lifted the back on its hydraulic hinges. She loosed the seat back and swung it to the side, lifted the seat bottom and placed the cardboard boxes underneath. Running back to the kitchen, she picked up her coffee cup, the lime green to-go cup that had been a market favorite. She said good-bye, then dashed out to help Dat hitch up

Fred, who was already pawing the ground, eager to get started on the long trek to Georgetown, nearly ten miles away.

How could such a beautiful, glistening world be marred by another tragedy?

Dat remained quiet, his eyes sad, his black felt hat lowered to hide that very question.

Sarah sipped her coffee, remained quiet alongside her father, and was startled when he spoke, his voice gruff and loud.

"It wouldn't be as hard if these hotheads would calm down. And I really am afraid your cousin Melvin is behind a lot of it. He seems to be building momentum, becoming even more verbal and aggressive as time goes on. We may never find out who this arsonist is. Never."

Sarah nodded. "But isn't it dangerous, going on this way?"

"No lives have been lost. When that happens, we'll take action."

"But you don't want to wait that long."

Dat nodded, then turned to smile at Sarah. "Do you have a plan?"

Sarah laughed and stuck her elbow in Dat's side. "Of course not."

In companionable silence then, they rode the rest of the way, enjoying the display of ice and powdery snow melting in the early winter sun. Bare branches were transformed into works of art, red berries on low-growing bushes popping with color among the dark brown branches covered with glowing ice.

Giant yellow trucks clanked past, the chains on the huge wheels rattling, shoving slush and spreading salt or cinders, allowing folks all over Lancaster County safe passage to their jobs or errands.

Fred didn't seem to mind the trucks, and he stayed steadily on course when they passed, although he always picked up his head, his ears flicked backward, then forward.

"Remember George?" Dat asked once.

"Yes. That horse was crazy!"

Dat nodded.

George had been a perfect horse, trotting swiftly, steadily, until he met a truck or tractor, anything large or noisy. Then he shied so badly they often ended up in a field or up a bank, narrowly missing telephone poles or fence posts. Eventually he had to be sold, Dat proclaiming him an accident waiting to happen.

Sarah was sickened by the sight of the smoking remains of the barn, her face losing its healthy color as she struggled to gain some sense of understanding.

It was always the same. How could Dat remain so passive about this? Rage coupled with determination brought two bright spots to her pale cheeks, but she said nothing.

So what if Melvin was worldly? Nobody else

was trying to do anything to stop this senseless display of blatant hate.

Sarah didn't know Enos and Annie Miller, but they were young, Amish, and in need. And since their own barn had burned to the ground, just like this one, that was reason enough to want to help.

She was met at the door by a buxom older woman who smiled at her and asked if she needed help. The woman grabbed the cardboard box and lumbered into the house with it, calling over her shoulder that if there was more, she'd help.

Sarah winced as the woman stepped off the porch, wearing no coat, stepping solidly on the slippery steps without fear, her dark eyes alight with interest as she moved along with surprising speed for her bulk.

"Here. Give it. Just put the other one on top."

"It's too heavy," Sarah protested.

"I think not. I got it."

She hurried back, bearing the heavy boxes, and Sarah shrugged, raising her eyebrows at Dat.

"I think she's Shteff's Davey's Sam *sei* Edna."

Sarah nodded, allowing Dat the impression she knew exactly who that was, when she actually had no clue. Dat knew a lot of people.

Sarah met Annie Miller for the first time that day. She was the sweetest, most loving person she'd ever seen. She was in awe of this cherubic human who moved among the women, quietly instructing, accepting, helpful, ministering to her three whining babies, the way Sarah imagined very few young women could do, especially given the circumstances.

The young girls who had arrived first were put in charge of cleaning out the implement shed, a workshop of sorts. It was cold and very dirty, a place Sarah could not imagine being hospitable to serving food.

A handful of girls she did not know accompanied her, but they soon introduced themselves, put a straw broom in her hand, and set to work.

A group of young men had moved the plows and baler and a wagon. Shop items were moved against one wall—a table saw, a press, a drill—and covered with clean plastic.

Sarah leaned her broom against the wall, wrapped her arms tightly around her waist and shivered, surveying the dusty mess.

Outside, the revving of diesel engines could be heard in the distance. Men shouted, horses stamped their feet.

A tall, black-haired youth peered through the door. He was handed a shovel by another youth Sarah didn't know. "Come on, Alan. Make yourself useful."

The black-haired one grinned. His voice was deep and low and rough, making him sound much older than Sarah judged him to be. His teeth were very white, his smile wide and attractive. My, Sarah thought, then unwrapped her arms and set to work.

The banter flowed, girls sneezed and coughed, guys set to work cleaning the old cement block chimney. Someone brought in a woodstove, attached a stove pipe, and in no time at all there was a roaring fire to ease the biting cold.

Sarah swept, helped unroll plastic, plied a slap stapler, and became very aware of the black-haired youth's whereabouts. She knew when he left and when he returned, but her face remained guarded and uninterested as she worked in earnest.

They soon had a reasonable space to serve food, so they set up folding tables and covered them with lengths of plastic tablecloth. The women decided to serve sandwiches and soup, since the crowd would be much bigger in the coming days.

Large kettles filled with hamburger mixed with onion, ketchup, mustard, brown sugar, salt, and pepper were set on the roaring wood stove, along with kettles of chicken corn soup and one of ham and beans. Cakes, pies, and puddings appeared, as did hungry men, blackened, already showing signs of strain, the usual good will marred by an impending wall of disagreement.

Before the afternoon had waned, Dat appeared and told Sarah he was preparing to leave. Without further words, he nodded to the women and left.

Sarah was puzzled but shrugged her shoulders, went to the house, and grabbed her purse.

She looked around for the youth who had gotten her attention, but he had evidently left as well.

Oh well.

Dat was curt, his eyebrows drawn to a tense line, goading Fred as if he needed to get as far away as possible from Enos Miller's, and fast.

This was so unlike Dat. Sarah felt a wave of dread close its talons around her sense of optimism.

Everything would be alright, eventually. Everything.

"Dat?"

She spoke hesitantly.

He grunted, never taking his eyes off the road.

"Didn't you always feel that everything works together for good to those that love God?"

It was like a knife through her heart when trails of tears slid down Dat's cheeks. He placed the leather driving reins between his knees, leaned to the left, and dug around in his pocket for a handkerchief, before blowing his nose, wiping his cheeks, and replacing it with a solemn shake of his head.

"I have, Sarah, I have. But I'm not sure we can claim that promise anymore. How can we love God if we can't love our own brethren?"

Sarah nodded.

"I'm just afraid the time is fast approaching when the lessons we could learn from these fires are turning into bitter lessons, hard to tolerate. We're headed into a black abyss of hate and fighting."

"That's a strong word, Dat."

"What else is it? Unbelief? Unlove? That's only a nice way of saying the word hate. God cannot bless us this way. I'm deeply concerned, and I blame Melvin. He needs to be stopped."

Sarah cringed, thinking of Melvin. Dear, noisy, outspoken Melvin. Opinionated, yes, that too. Still she felt sorry for him.

Melvin meant well, that was the thing, and he was just sure the arsonist could be caught red-handed, by his cunning, his ability to outsmart anyone else.

Wherever Melvin went, groups of men surrounded him, slowly began nodding, seeing things his way, which, in Dat's opinion, was the world's way—to go after the arsonist, offer no second chance, no forgiveness, just slap him in jail, and let him suffer till he's sorry.

At the supper table, Dat scolded Levi harshly for upsetting his glass of water, Levi cried, and Mam's mouth turned down, taut, her disapproval unspoken but stamped on every feature.

As Sarah had experienced, things that seem so awful often turn into hidden blessings, twinkling little lights set everywhere to lighten the burden of plodding pilgrims, moving forward on the road of life.

Dat had a meeting with Melvin, one on one, which must have created a newly discovered humility in her normally brash, outspoken cousin.

Sarah sat at Lydia's kitchen table early the following evening, feeling lonely, frustrated, and in need of advice, turning once again to the pleasure of having a true friend. She unwrapped her second whoopie pie, a pumpkin one. She had already devoured a chocolate one. She chomped down on it, groaned, and peeled back more of the Saran Wrap.

"Mm! Seriously, Lydia."

Lydia laughed. It was a new sound, like rolling, babbling water, as if the happiness had to tumble over rocks to be released. Likely, it did. Her heart was probably like a rock, but it was finally breaking, softening.

"You need to start a bakery."

"I know. But I couldn't, with the cows. And now the horses. Omar is so busy, and Anna Mae is so attached to him, everywhere he goes, she's there, too. In fact, Sarah, I'm afraid she is experiencing her first dose of attraction to that Lee Glick who spends so much time with Omar. Sarah, he is so awfully nice and good-looking and sweet and good."

"I know."

"Is he single?"

"No. He's dating Rose."

"Matthew's Rose?"

Sarah nodded, finished the pumpkin whoopie pie, balled the Saran Wrap tightly, and threw it in the air.

"Yep! She always gets them!"

Lydia giggled.

There was a knock on the door, and Melvin appeared, dressed in one of the bright-colored shirts he favored, his eyes luminous, soft, his face quiet, relaxed.

"Hey!" Sarah said, glad to see him, hoping Dat had gone easy on him.

"Sarah! Why aren't you at home? You aren't even ready. Hi, Lydia," he added, turning to give her his full attention.

"Hello!"

Lydia looked up at Melvin, her smile wide and genuine, and Sarah told them both she did not want to go anywhere—not even to the Sunday youth supper. The air was cold and damp, and she was tired out from working at Enos Miller's. Besides, the following day was her first day of school, and she did not want to lose any sleep if she could help it.

Melvin nodded, then reached for little Aaron, who seemed completely at ease, being lifted from Lydia's lap and placed on Melvin's.

Melvin pulled on his hair, teasing him, and Aaron howled with delight.

Chapter 17

The evening disappeared magically, the three of them talking, sharing thoughts, feelings, discussing the barn fires, Melvin showing a type of humility Sarah had never seen.

"All I can say is that if as much good comes to Enos Millers as I have experienced, I think they can honestly say the Lord has delivered them with a mighty hand," Lydia said shyly, her eyes averted.

"Yeah," Melvin said slowly. "I guess I have to keep my mouth shut. Davey really raked me across the coals. He's the only guy I know who can do that and make it appear as if he's not hurting you. That guy just has a way about him, he does. He sure did show me the error of my ways, got me back on the straight and narrow."

Lydia's eyes were a revelation to Sarah, the look she gave Melvin bordering on worship. "Oh, what I would have given, years ago, to hear Aaron say those exact words. He just . . . he couldn't see it."

"You've been through so much, Lydia," Melvin said, the emotion in his words thick, as if tears were pressing against the back of his throat.

"I have. But God has been more than good. I have so much. And I'm learning to say I am blessed and stop thinking I don't deserve any of it, as the counselors say."

Melvin watched Lydia, and when she met his eyes, there was so much tenderness in them, Sarah had to look away. She suddenly felt like an intruder and pondered the power of attraction for some people, but just not for her.

She and Melvin had helped Lydia clean up the kitchen after the children were in bed. Sarah watched as she hovered about him, two bright spots of pink on each cheek, her eyes dancing, laughing easily, even touching Melvin's arm when she needed his attention.

Oh, how Sarah longed for something that remained elusively out of her grasp. She knew it but was helpless to change the path she had made for herself. Her own stubborn refusal to let go of Matthew, when everyone she knew had tried to warn her, had broken her heart. Now he was gone, and when Sarah ignored Lee, he had started dating Rose.

Miserably, she shared this new insight with Melvin and Lydia, who both nodded wisely, agreed. They said they supposed the right one would step out of the woodwork one of these days.

But Sarah was sure now that the right one would never come, or come again. Lee had told her that he was in awe of Rose. Everyone was in awe of Rose, she'd wailed to herself later in the privacy of her room. She was just too awesome, apparently.

Now she spoke of it, of that insecurity, to her two dear friends, and was encouraged, lifted up. She ate another whoopie pie and drank way too much coffee and could not go to sleep when she wanted to, the caffeine, the conversation with her friends, and her anxiety about teaching keeping her awake long after she had intended.

She longed for a life companion but felt she needed to accept that it wasn't for her. And that was alright for now. She was on her way to making a giant leap right into spinsterhood anyway, embarking on her teaching career in less than eight hours.

Sarah had never experienced the word inadequate before, but that was the only true description she could think of as she stood behind the teacher's desk the next morning, stoked on more caffeine and false bravado.

The classroom was damp and cold, the colorless artwork peeling away from the walls, the gas heater stubbornly refusing to ignite.

She'd punched the igniter button so often, it was only a matter of time until the whole stove exploded in her face.

She didn't know who the caretaker was, vaguely remembering Lee mentioning Ben Zook. Well, she wasn't traipsing through the cold to fetch Mr. Zook, as she was pretty sure Lee would be in the barn and find her very un-awesome, unable, and stupid, not being able to light the gas heater on her first morning.

She jumped when the door latch rattled and was yanked open by a very small, very fat little girl, her round face red from exertion and protruding from her tightly-tied head scarf like a beet.

"Good morning!" Sarah trilled, too high, too loud, and a little too quickly.

When no answer was given, Sarah cleared her throat and tried again, thinking perhaps she hadn't heard.

"Good morning!"

The little girl yanked on her head scarf, jutted out her chin, and said loudly, "It's cold in here!"

"I'm sorry. I can't get the heater started."

"Martha could."

"Well, I don't know how."

Instead of giving Sarah the satisfaction of an answer, the little girl placed both hands on her desk and glared at her, a belligerent little beet topped with unruly red hair.

The doorknob turned again, revealing a horde of head scarves, navy blue bonnets, straw hats, and multi-colored beanies, every last child wearing a black, homemade coat.

"Good morning!"

No one bothered answering, so she repeated her greeting, and was ignored again. Sarah immediately thought of the man in the Bible who sowed his seed and some fell by the wayside and withered in the hot sun.

"It's cold in here."

"That is because I can't get the heater going."

"Martha could."

Irked, Sarah said forcefully, "Yes, well, I'm not Martha. This is my first day, so how can you expect me to know how?"

A boy of about twelve gave her a look of surprise, turned to his classmates, and snickered, which started a wave of snorts and mocking sounds, which Sarah chose to ignore.

Two more boys entered, the one taller than Sarah, his face pocked with angry, red pimples, his glasses riding low on his prominent nose.

"What's wrong with the heater?" he growled, before Sarah had a chance to say good morning.

"I can't get it started."

Saying nothing, the boy padded to the stubborn heating unit, turned a dial, punched the igniter button repeatedly, and was rewarded by a low whoosh of flame.

"Oh, that's great! Awesome! Thank you!" Sarah said, meaning every word she said.

The boy blushed furiously, ducked his head, and shuffled back to the cloakroom, his hands stuffed nonchalantly in his pockets. His companions taunted him as he passed them.

The fourth time the door opened, the upper

grade girls entered, and trouble walked solidly into Sarah's life.

Tall, pretty, wearing flashy colors, their arrogance showed immediately. Their postures spoke loudly of their possession of the entire school. All four of them.

Sarah felt the color recede from her face, and she swallowed as her mouth turned into sandpaper.

"Good morning!"

The girls looked at one another, raised their eyebrows, hissed behind the barricade of their palms, and snickered in a manner so annoying it set Sarah's teeth on edge.

"Good morning!" she said again.

"We don't say that at Ivy Run," the heavy-set blonde girl said, her voice commanding everyone's attention.

Sarah considered this statement for a few seconds, then asked how they did greet each other.

"We don't greet."

That brought hysterical giggles from her three companions and a braying from the older boys.

Wildly, Sarah looked at the clock, her courage slipping away by the minute. Time for the bell.

Would they go to their seats as expected, or would they say they don't sit down at Ivy Run?

Help me, please, she begged her Lord.

She stalked very firmly to the rope in the back of the room and gave it a hard yank, adjusted her cape and stalked back, placing her feet firmly on the tile floor.

Reaching her desk, she tapped the small bell repeatedly. Nothing happened, the laughing and talking and milling about continued as if they hadn't heard any bell at all. What would she do if no one sat down? Scream and cry and grab her new lunch box and book bag and go running down the road, toward home, blatantly admitting defeat?

Slowly, one after another, the children folded themselves reluctantly into their desks, eyeing her with different levels of curiosity or rebellion, depending where she looked.

"Good morning, boys and girls!"

Only the lower graders mumbled in response. The upper graders refused to greet her, sitting obstinately in their desks, all eyes watching this new teacher.

Taking a deep breath, Sarah opened the worn Bible to the ninth chapter of Luke, stood, and began to read, her voice low, carrying well, resonant, the shaking subdued by sheer force of will.

As she read, her voice gained more strength, and she looked around the classroom, her eyes catching the upper grade boys raising their eyebrows, followed by exaggerated eye-rolling.

Tap. Tap-tap. Paper crinkling. Rustling. Feet scraping. A book hit the floor with a loud bang.

Sarah stopped reading, said nothing.

Slowly, children sat up, their eyes questioning, watching, waiting.

"As soon as everyone quiets down, I'll resume reading from the Bible."

Nervous giggles were accompanied by more feet scraping, more crumpling of paper. A small boy flipped a book closed with a loud bang, his eyes challenging Sarah to do something about it.

She stood, relaxed, and said nothing.

Someone coughed. Another pupil dropped a pencil, then looked around for smiles of approval he was sure to gain by his lack of obedience.

The heavyset girl raised her hand, clearly intending to fix this new teacher with words of rebuke.

"Yes?" Sarah said.

"You can't expect the room to be quiet. Duh!"

It was the duh that provoked Sarah to the point that she spoke firmly, her nostril flared, her gaze withering.

"I certainly can expect the room to be quiet. When the Bible is being read, it is only respectful to ask for quiet."

There was no answer, only a shocked silence.

"Now, I have to ask you to place both hands on your desks, and keep them there until I'm finished reading this chapter in Luke."

The children looked around, checking with their peers to see if it was acceptable to obey this new teacher who spoke so clearly and force-fully.

A few lower grade students put their hands on their desks, hesitantly, their expressions bordering on fright.

The upper grade boys shifted from left to right, sat on their hands, smiling widely, their eyes challenging her.

The upper grade girls giggled dutifully.

The middle grade students copied the maneuvers of the older ones.

Slowly, Sarah closed the Bible, took a deep, steadying breath, and announced her intention in a clear, careful tone.

"Alright, then. We'll close for the day. You may put your things in your desks and prepare to go home to your parents."

A small, dark-haired boy raised his hand.

"I can't," he quavered, and then a heart-rending sob filled the air. "My . . . my . . . ." His sobs cut off the words he wanted to say.

Waiting, Sarah watched the school's reaction. The sneers and raised eyebrows melted into uncertainty, leaving mixed expressions of half-hearted attempts at mockery. They were unsure how to handle this.

Going to the small boy, whose huge brown eyes filled with anxiety and the weight of being sent home to an empty house, Sarah put an arm about his shoulders, saying it was alright.

Sniffing, he put his hands on his desk. The lower graders followed suit, followed by a few of the older pupils.

"Thank you to those of you who are obeying. The remaining ones are dismissed."

A few more hands were placed on tops of the desks.

The older pupils remained in their seats, sitting on their hands, but they made no move to leave.

Sarah returned to her desk and stood behind it, still waiting. Again, the heavyset blonde raised her hand.

"We can't go home."

"Why not?"

"Well, just because. It's a school day."

"Will you place your hands on your desk then?"

"No."

One of the upper grade boys raised his hand.

"Yes?"

"Martha never made us do this."

"Martha isn't here. I am your teacher now."

"Really?"

The word was spoken with one intent—to make fun of her, and Sarah knew it. The blatant disobedience was far worse than she could have anticipated, and her heart pounded with fear. Was she taking this too far? Was it only a power struggle, her determination to prove her own superiority? She couldn't go back on her word now.

"It's up to you. If you will please obey, just this one small thing, I'll resume reading, okay? Then we'll go from there."

Her heart sank to a miserable depth as six upper grade pupils got up and went to the rear of the classroom. They noisily got down their outer wear, banged their lunch boxes in anger, slammed the door till the schoolhouse seemed to vibrate, and huddled in a dark group of rebellion in the schoolyard.

Steadying herself, Sarah finished reading the chapter, then stood with the now reduced number of children, steadily repeating the Lord's Prayer with very little help from any of them.

Sarah was no longer accustomed to saying this prayer out loud, so she stumbled over "Give us this day our daily bread," but she moved on, grateful to be able to remember just in time.

She passed out the homemade songbooks, brilliant plastic covers on sturdy binders, the pages encased in plastic, the songs typed neatly on the pages.

Someone had worked hard to supply the school with these good, strong songbooks. Perhaps it had been Martha, enthused, anticipating a successful year, only to fail so pitifully. Sympathy welled up in Sarah, and she realized she was as vulnerable, as unable to carry on successfully as Martha had been.

Sarah smiled now, as the pupils seemed hesitant, the singing class punctuated by empty spaces, leaving the class incomplete, little rows of strong white teeth with too many missing.

"Please stand together, share a songbook with the one nearest you, and let's sing page 47. I remember that song from my own school years."

The singing was pathetic, Sarah finally admitted to herself, after starting a clear rendition of "I'll Fly Away." She sang alone with only a few quavering, half-hearted attempts made by the lower grade girls.

Mostly, the pupils stood like angry little bees, their eyes bold, alert, watching her as warily as hornets protecting their nests and as ready to sting. The songbooks flopped in colorful disarray, some of them unopened, held belligerently to chests, clearly showing the students' unwillingness to participate in any form of song.

Well, she couldn't fix everything the first morning. She'd stood her ground about the Bible reading, so she'd pretend the singing class was not out of the ordinary.

After the children were seated back at their desks, Sarah introduced herself, then asked the children to wear the colorful name tags she had made with the number of each student's grade written in bold black beside their names, to make it easier to remember this first day.

No one seemed to mind, so Sarah pressed them to small shirtfronts and black pinafores, colorful dress fronts for the little girls who wore belt aprons pinned around their waists with sturdy silver safety pins.

"There!" she announced, smiling.

Ben Zook had two children in school, a little boy in third grade named Marlin, and Marianne in second grade. Sarah smiled to herself. Marianne resembled a much smaller version of Anna, her energetic little body as round as a barrel, propelled on two very small feet that were perfectly capable of carrying her swiftly wherever she needed to go.

Standing behind her desk, she told the children her name was Sarah Beiler, and she would be their teacher the remainder of the year, hopefully, if everyone would be willing to work together with her. There would be new rules, new ways, and she proceeded to read the twelve rules she'd set for the school.

A hand was raised, then another.

"Yes?"

"That's a stupid rule, about putting our hands on our desk when you read the Bible."

"You think so? Why?"

"It just is."

"Why?"

"We didn't used to have to do it."

The speaker was a fifth-grade boy named Chester, his hair as brilliantly inclined to a fiery, golden red as that of his sister Elizabeth—Liz for short—the fat, belligerent first arrival.

"I know. But it's very distracting to read from the Bible when all that noise is going on. It's unnecessary, annoying, and so I won't allow it."

"We gotta do it every morning?"

"Every morning."

Another hand was raised.

Roy, a sixth-grader, his straight brown hair hanging all the way into his eyes, shook his head as if to rid himself of the offending curtain of hair before telling Sarah that was when he learned his memory verse, when Martha read the Bible.

"Sorry, Roy. You'll have to learn the verse at home."

"I don't have time. I have to do chores, eat supper, and go to bed."

"Really? You must have an awful lot of chores, eat a long supper, and go to bed very early."

A few smiles accompanied this statement, a spark of interest shining from a number of eyes.

Arithmetic classes began with the first grade, the dark-haired little boy named Mark, a willing and eager student. Lena Mae, a small, thin girl with a perpetual frown and a pinched, weary look about her face appeared much older than her six years. Sarah wondered at the strain showing on the pale face.

Reuben and Kathryn made up the rest of the first grade, both brown-haired, quiet, and afraid to speak, which Sarah knew came from the lurking attitude of sarcasm that hovered over the classroom like a rotten stench.

Sarah had reached fifth-grade arithmetic when she heard a rapping on the front door and caught sight of two of the eighth-grade girls standing behind two older women, their faces boding no good.

Well, so be it.

Sarah went to the door, her knees almost losing the ability to carry her until her hand reached the doorknob, a much-needed source of support.

"Hello."

"Hi. Can you come out on the porch for a moment?"

The voice held no friendliness, but wasn't quite full of anger either.

Sarah stepped out, leaving the door open, the pupils turning in their seats to see what was occurring on the porch.

Ruth Stoltzfus was Rosanna's mother. She was short, squat, and clutched her sweater tightly around her waist, her brilliant red dress matching the high color in her cheeks.

"What is going on?"

Before Sarah answered, the taller, angular mother behind Ruth nodded her head, her eyes snapping, her mouth turned down in a stern frown. Sarah imagined a snapping turtle wearing a black bonnet but dismissed the thought immediately.

"I asked the pupils to stop making noise while I read the Bible for devotions. When that didn't work, I asked them to place their hands on their desks."

"Whatever for? I never in all my life heard such a thing. That's way too strict. You can't send children home from school because of such a little thing. I mean, who would listen to such a ridiculous rule?"

These words were forced from the angular mother's mouth, the frown bobbing up and down as she spoke, the nodding head of Ruth Stoltzfus accompanying the words of her friend.

The two eighth-grade girls watched Sarah, triumph an ill-concealed victory they claimed more fully with every word their mothers spoke.

"What should I have done?"

There was no answer immediately as the mothers looked at one another, then to the victorious daughters, before sputtering, shaking their heads.

Finally, the tall one with the black bonnet spoke. "Well, you wouldn't have had to go to such drastic measures. It's simply unnecessary. They wouldn't have HAD to put their hands on their desks. Being sent home is serious business."

"Yes, I agree. But if I'm supposed to teach Ivy

Run School, we need to be able to understand each other. If you would like to know what needs to happen in this school, then we'll have a parent teacher's meeting on Friday evening.

"If you won't attend, then you may as well take your girls out of school now. Putting their hands on their desks is only the tip of the iceberg, believe me."

After the last pupil had disappeared down the road, walking or propelling their scooters homeward, Sarah sank into the swivel chair, leaned back, and folded her hands on her stomach. She propped her elbows on the cracked vinyl arm rests with tufts of white fibers protruding from them, and she knew this day had been the beginning of the end.

She'd already failed, and it was only her first day. The mothers were right. She'd been too strict.

Love never fails, and she had reacted to disobedience with a hard, angry stance, a refusal to back down, and now all was lost. She'd be so ashamed. The only girl in Lancaster County who'd taught school only one week before having to give up.

Well, she also held the dubious title of being the only girl whose fiancé had run off to Haiti and married an English woman as well as the title of being the one caught in a web of intrigue as far as Ashley Walters was concerned. She'd failed her, too.

Chapter 18

Dat said the barn raising at Enos Miller's went well. In fact, it was enough to rekindle any love that had ever been lost among the community.

It was the overwhelming number of men, the orderly manner in which things occurred when each one was willing to take instructions from the seasoned older men who had directed the raising of many barns before this one, that reduced him to a lip-quivering, tear-filled man of gratitude.

The weather had been unusually fine. The mud and debris had all been shoveled onto a blackened, odorous heap that would continue smoking for days.

The sun warmed them as they erected the skeleton of the building. The fresh, yellow lumber smelled of hope and faith yet again for Dat.

Opinions had been shelved for the day of the barn raising, as the charity among them built a shrine to love in action, a kind of holiness about the building that didn't allow gossip or hating or backbiting.

Dat was inspired, rejuvenated, his faith in his fellowmen firmly entrenched.

In his mind, he chose to look for the good in

each one, tolerate the opinions that he didn't agree with, and live each day trying to look at the world through the eyes of a benevolent Savior.

"If God has so much mercy on us—each day it's fresh and new—then we need to acknowledge this same mercy for our *mit and neva mensch* (fellowman)."

As he spoke, the family was still seated at the supper table, Levi at his right, Mam at his left. The old doubleknit tablecloth covered the oak extension table and was laden with Mam's Corelle dishes. The serving dishes were now half empty, containing mashed potatoes and beef gravy and corn and buttered noodles. Smaller glass dishes held applesauce and coleslaw, and one had only a bit of red beet juice covering the bottom, the last red beet egg having been speared by Levi, salted well, and enjoyed with great relish.

The evening sun was casting deep shadows in the corners of the large farmhouse kitchen, so Mam got up and flicked a lighter beneath the propane lamp in the oak cabinet, illuminating Sarah's face and highlighting the misery that had been her day.

Levi, as always, trumpeted the news headlines, having heard every detail from Sarah herself, as she wailed out her disastrous day, alternating between complete refusal to think her teaching career was salvageable to fighting for her own way, refusing to accept failure. It was alright for

Dat to give this whole *schtick* (piece) about love and looking for the good in each person, but she simply couldn't run a classroom on love. That was all there was to it.

"*Die Sarah wahu un heila* (Sarah was crying)!" he announced with importance, snapping his suspenders for emphasis.

Dat looked at Sarah sharply.

"You were crying? *Ach* my. And I completely forgot to ask you about your first day at school. Was it really that bad?"

"Every bit," Sarah said, nodding. She proceeded to relate her entire day in her own words, Dat listening carefully.

"So now you have this parent teacher's meeting Friday evening, right?" he asked finally.

"I guess. I don't know. Mrs. Turtle—oops!"

Sarah clapped a hand over mouth, her eyes already begging Dat's forgiveness.

"What?" he asked, grinning as he dabbed at a few spots of grape jelly on the tablecloth.

"Oh, one of the mothers looks like a snapping turtle."

Levi looked sharply at Sarah, then burst out laughing. Suzie snickered, then joined in, and Priscilla grinned widely, enjoying Sarah's description.

Dat remained sober, and Sarah was chastised by this alone. "You say the whole school is infested with mockery and sarcasm. I think perhaps some must have found its way home."

He told Sarah, then, that to expect perfection had been drastic. In disbelief, shame so acute she visibly squirmed in her chair, she listened as he told her in soft tones that he had experienced this type of uprising many times as a minister. He was expected to lead but often found that serving was the better approach.

"What you did, we would all like to do, but it was a huge bite for your first day. I wish you the best, having this parent teacher's meeting, but don't be surprised if not too much is accomplished. Your goal is to get those children to want to obey your rules."

"It's impossible!" Sarah burst out, on the verge of tears.

"Go halfway. Go to school in the morning, and see how many hands are placed on their desks, see how long it goes until they feel awkward, sitting on their hands. They can't do much, with their hands under their . . . um . . . backsides."

Mam shook up and down, her eyes twinkling.

"But Dat, they're so disobedient. So openly *fa-schput* (mocking)."

"That didn't start overnight, and it's not going to go away overnight. Try and win them. Stand firm."

"I just want to quit."

"I've wanted to quit many times. These past

few years have probably been the hardest ever, with the differences in opinion where the barn fires have been concerned. Now a group of ministers thinks anyone who talks to reporters should be *schtrofed* (chastised), and I think that's a drastic measure."

"Like the hands on the desks."

"Afraid so."

Dat looked at the clock and rose to do the evening chores, whistling under his breath as he pulled on his boots.

"Oh, I forgot to tell you all. That Lee Glick that's helping the Widow Lydia's Omar with his Belgians? He was driving a mare double with that half-trained stallion. It was a sight, I tell you. Every head was turned when they drove into Enos's with a load of hay. I've never seen a neck on a Belgian like that. He sure does have a way with horses. I think he must be a special person, the way that Omar looks up to him. Not often you see such adoration."

Side by side, Sarah and her mother washed and dried dishes, discussing the school day as the land around them settled into darkness. Yellow squares of light appeared at the cow stable windows as the diesel purred into action, providing power for the milking machines and cooling the fresh, warm milk poured into the gleaming bulk tank in the milk house.

Levi sang loudly as he resumed shuffling his

Rook cards, and Suzie came banging through the *kesslehaus* door, filling a bucket with hot water from the hose attached to the wall, faithfully doing her chores, feeding the new calves.

Mam shook her head when Sarah asked why Suzie didn't get her hot water in the milk house, so she let it go. Perhaps she was much more controlling than she knew.

She swiped viciously at a burnt pan, added a few sprinkles of dish soap, and attacked it once more, before rinsing it beneath the faucet and stacking it in the dish drainer. Then she leaned back, her hands propped on a corner of the sink, lowered her head, and shook with laughter.

"So, this is how my spinsterhood begins. I have to have you and Dat to set my priorities straight. Seriously, I'm so ashamed."

"Oh no, Sarah. Please don't be ashamed. You're so young. We learn by our own mistakes. Everyone does. Some learn faster than others, but we learn, eventually."

"What would I do without my parents?"

Sarah slid an arm around her mother's waist, leaving a trail of white suds, and her mother wrapped her in her arms, holding the red and white checked dish towel behind Sarah's back.

In the background, Levi sang, "We'll work, we'll work till Jesus comes, we'll work, we'll work till Jesus comes."

The clock struck six, steam rose from the

teakettle on the coal stove, and Sarah knew she was blessed beyond measure.

As she packed her lunch the following morning, the world seemed like a better place, loaded with endless possibilities. It was amazing what a good night's sleep could do for her spirits.

She spread mayonnaise on a slice of whole wheat bread, layered Lebanon bologna, cheese, and lettuce on top, then added another slice of bread. She shoved it into a Ziploc bag and turned to find a small container to hold some bread and butter pickles. Another bag of potato chips, a few carrots, and one small molasses cookie went into the insulated pouch, and she was done.

Today she was wearing a dress the color of her eyes, a deep sage green. She pushed up the sleeves as she prepared her lunch.

She'd wear her Nikes and accompany the children to the playground, if she could cajole them into playing an organized game.

She had never seen children huddled in individual groups without playing a single game at recess. She guessed it wasn't considered cool to play games, and some of those pupils surely could use some physical exertion.

The job was monumental, no doubt, but her energy motored along, fueled by a healthy breakfast of granola, vanilla yogurt, and a sliced banana. When her driver showed up, she ran out to the waiting vehicle, waving briskly at

Dat, who stood at the door to the milk house.

One by one, or in groups, the children sidled through the door, watching their new teacher with varied degrees of suspicion or curiosity.

No one answered her round of good mornings, but with Dat's advice intact, she could let it go. The upper graders slouched in various positions, their desks suddenly a place to display any outlandish way of sitting they could devise.

She chose to ignore that, knowing they were baiting the trap. Get the teacher mad and we have the upper hand, they seemed to say.

"Good morning, boys and girls!" Her voice quivered, straightened, steadied.

The murmurs were low, somewhat garbled, and came mostly from the first and second grade, as two upper grade boys flashed mirrors, combed their hair up over their heads, turning the mirrors to view the results of looking English.

Sarah began reading the Bible, as she had done the day before, asking no one to put their hands on their desks. Timidly, a few first graders placed them on their desktops, the little knuckles white from clenching them so hard.

Bewildered, unsure, the remaining students looked around, lifted eyebrows, mouthed questions. Their hands remained in their laps or hung loosely at their sides as they were unsure exactly how to proceed.

But it was quiet—clock-ticking-on-the-wall, beautifully quiet.

They stood and repeated the Lord's Prayer, Sarah stumbling over the same passage, a few more pupils reciting along with her than the day before.

Singing class was a study in disorganization. No one stood straight or even tried to put any heart into the song, so Sarah asked if they would like to learn new songs instead of repetitively singing the old ones.

No one bothered to answer, the girls' eyes half-closed with boredom, the boys much too cool to notice the fact that she'd spoken at all.

That set the tone for the whole day. Disinterest, rebellion, outright anger, refusal to accept rules, probably everything that could have gone wrong did.

At the end of the day, her shoulders ached from being held stiffly in place, her right ear was throbbing seriously, and the beginning of a major headache was hovering somewhere in the region of her right temple.

Not once had any child spoken respectfully to her.

The games at recess hadn't happened, the boys informing her the only game they played was baseball, and it was too cold for that.

Sarah suggested Prisoners Base or Colored Eggs, which brought such a display of mockery that Sarah dropped the whole idea.

Many students failed their lessons, scoring percentages below sixty-five, and refused to tackle the list of do-overs, so that at the end of the day, Sarah lay her arms on her desk and sobbed great tears of defeat and remorse. She wished she'd never started this impossible task. She wasn't cut out to be a schoolteacher. Unqualified—that was the word. And she still had that daunting parent teacher's meeting to live through.

When the doorknob turned, she wasn't afraid, figuring one of the students had forgotten a book or a paper. Then she seriously considered dropping on her knees and crawling under her desk, where she would stay till Lee Glick went away.

Why? How could he pop into her classroom unannounced? Her curly hair was completely out of control, her eyes were sore and swollen, her face blotchy, her nose red from wiping it repeatedly, and there he stood, dressed in clean, casual clothes. No work clothes this time.

"Sarah?" The word was a question, an inquiry with a polite, kind tone carrying it.

"*Ach* Lee. I . . ." Helplessly, her hands fluttered to her face. "I'm a mess."

He strode toward her desk, and she lowered her eyes. She felt him standing behind her chair and stifled a gasp as his hands came down on her shoulders.

"You look like you've had a rough day."

"Yep."

"May I massage your shoulders? Not in a . . . um . . . you know. I'm just a friend. Let me."

"Okay."

Whether it was right or proper was completely forgotten, the healing comfort in his hands restoring her sense of well-being.

She felt the headache dissipate, the sharp pain between her shoulders loosen, as his hands massaged away the frustration and hopelessness of the day.

"Feel better?"

He stepped back, flexing his fingers, and Sarah felt a sense of loss as sharply as any physical pain, accompanied by the absolute knowledge that he had no business being here in this schoolroom giving her a "friendly" massage. Lee was a two-faced deceiver giving her hope now, even though he was dating Rose.

She didn't answer, letting the waves of betrayal and anger take control.

He repeated the question.

Sarah faced him, her eyes golden at first, but they darkened by the first wave of unrest, then changed color again as the wave receded, leaving room for a swirling gray of emotion.

"No, I don't feel better, Lee. Just go away. Go away and leave me alone. You're Rose's boy-friend, and she's supposedly my best friend. You're in awe of her. You said so yourself. So just go. I'm sick of tagging after Rose Zook. I'm sick of . . ."

Her face crumpled, and she began crying quietly, her head lowered, her hands coming up to her face in one graceful movement.

Her future had been long and cold and barren before. She could take it again. If she just looked at it once and accepted it, gave herself up to it, in Mam's words, it would be alright.

It was just unfair to have Matthew living in Haiti with his wife, and Lee dating Rose, and Melvin finding far more than he had ever dared to hope, a situation turning into the sweetest love story Sarah ever hoped to attain.

But it was not alright that Lee was here. She grabbed a Kleenex from the box on her desk, turned her back, miserable and ashamed.

Again, she felt him behind her, his hands encircling her shoulders. She could feel his breath, like the wings of a butterfly.

"Sarah, I came to tell you, I broke off my friendship with Rose."

Sarah remembered seeing the words "broken arrow" on the blackboard, where she'd demonstrated the adjective broken describing the arrow. The feeling of rapture began in her feet, but it all came together, filling her entire being with music, subtle, soft, cymbal-crashing, drum-beating music, all at once.

She couldn't face him. Not now.

"I can't forget you, Sarah. I'm not being honest with myself or God if I continue dating Rose. Half the time, I'm thinking of you. It's been that way since the day I saw you at your barn raising. I know I don't have much chance. I think you are the kind of girl who loves only once, and you certainly . . ." His voice faded away.

So Rose had been right! She knew, too.

"Say something, Sarah. Anything."

The space of a heartbeat, the length of eternity —she didn't know how long she waited, until, slowly, she turned, her eyes downcast, standing before him, mysteriously unable to tell him everything she wanted to say.

"It's okay. I'll give you time. I probably should have waited longer. I know you're not ready. Maybe you never will be. You have this thing about spinsterhood."

In spite of herself, Sarah smiled, a small, trembling grin that slid away before she met his eyes.

His gaze was blue, so magnetically blue, and for long moments she was lost in the beauty of meeting his eyes without thoughts of Matthew wedging their way between them.

She understood the meaning of giving herself to a man. It was almost spiritual, the way they stood apart, allowing their eyes to convey what their spirits already knew.

"I'll wait," he whispered.

Sarah nodded. "Yes."

"We need to be sure. We need to . . ."

Brokenly, still saying words that made no sense, the music in her ears completely erasing any speech, he reached for her, brought her against his chest with a sigh of longing, a repressed love, and held her there, her heart beating against his, an ageless symphony of a love announced, examined, accepted.

"Sarah."

She was afraid that if she answered, the spell might break, so she said nothing. She wanted to stay in the safety of his arms, her heart beating in unison with his.

"Sarah?"

It was a question now, so she tried to step back to see the question in his blue eyes, that haven of safety, but his arms did not release her.

"Does this . . . does us being together mean anything to you?"

In answer, she lifted her face, raised herself only slightly, and touched her lips to his, to that wide, kind, perfect mouth.

Her touch was no more than a whisper, a breath, but it was her way of assuring him that, yes, he had a chance, that as long as their hearts beat strongly, she would be there for him.

When she pulled away, his grip tightened. He lowered his face, and his firm mouth sought hers again, until the room spun and she pulled away, a soft laugh breaking them apart, unthinkable to him, but so necessary she knew.

"Does that mean . . . ?" He was smiling, but his eyes were dark with longing, tortured by the years she had always been just beyond his reach because of Matthew Stoltzfus.

"I should not have done that," she murmured, low and soft. "I don't know what got into me."

"Sarah, don't. Don't feel guilty."

"I don't want you to think I'm bold, or brazen, or . . . you know."

"I have never been as close to anything that I imagine heaven to be, as when you kissed me. It was unreal. I still can't believe you just did that."

He touched his lips with his fingers, shook his head, and gave a soft laugh, barely loud enough for Sarah to hear.

Softly, her hands rested on his shirtfront, and she asked if it was alright to wait awhile. It wasn't proper for them to begin dating now.

"I can't wait. It seems as if the minute you're gone, this will be one long dream, and I'll wake up knowing I can never have you. How are we going to see each other? Just not get together, ever?" he asked suddenly.

The raucous honking of a car horn brought them rudely to reality, and Sarah searched wildly for her book bag and the red pen she wanted to take home.

"My driver. Oh my goodness. I wonder how long she's been out there."

Lee reached for her again.

"No. Lee, oh, we can't. Not now."

"When can I see you?"

"Don't come to my house. You just broke up with Rose. I . . . Melvin goes to play . . . um . . . Scrabble at the Widow Lydia's, so . . . you're there sometimes, right?"

"Yes! With Omar!"

"Don't let on."

"I won't."

"Bye."

"Bye, Sarah."

She locked the door behind them both, and he untied his cold, impatient horse. She rode away looking straight ahead, and he had an awful time of it getting into his buggy, his horse standing on his hind legs and pawing the air with his front hooves, coming down in a flying leap with Lee only half in the buggy, scraping his shin painfully on the cast iron step.

He decided he needed to spend more time with this crazy horse and less time with Omar Esh and his Belgians, until he remembered what Sarah had told him and his heart swelled with emotion. His head in the clouds, he pulled out in front of a gray Toyota with an irate driver behind the steering wheel, pumping his fist in the general direction of the buggy.

Mam had a fit. Only the second day of school and here was Sarah, her despairing daughter, suddenly bouncing into the house, her eyes alight, pink blossoms in her cheeks, her smile wide and genuine, her face glowing.

"Teaching certainly suits you today," she commented.

"Yes, Mam. It does. So much has gone better today."

Sarah began a vivid account of the Bible reading, the quiet, the newly acquired sense of accomplishment, completely pulling the wool over poor Mam's eyes.

Mam peeled potatoes, slowly gouging out any sprouts or black spots, and thought seriously that Sarah might actually remain an unmarried lady, an old maid, a spinster, choosing to live alone all her life and pour herself into her pupils.

Well, it wouldn't be too hard on Mam's pride. After all, single women were a blessing in a community—as schoolteachers, storekeepers, and they often helped out after a new baby arrived. The list went on and on.

Or she could marry a widower. She had a way with children. Imagining that, Mam cried furtive tears into the muddy water in the dishpan.

Wouldn't that be a touching day? she thought. Sarah so sweet, such a light to the community. Now that Priscilla was different. She liked her boys.

Chapter 19

The night of the parent teacher's meeting arrived, in spite of Sarah's panic. Most of the parents attended, stepping through the entrance to the classroom with serious expressions, greeting one another gravely, brows furrowed.

This was serious business, a meeting called the first week of Davey Beiler's Sarah being the new teacher. They'd heard she was a go-getter, not afraid to speak her mind. Well, she'd better watch it.

The school board had come early and heard Sarah's grievances, which were mostly due to a lack of respect from the students. Then they opened the meeting with a moment of silence, stated the reason for the meeting, and allowed Sarah her time.

"I'm sorry for making everyone leave their work just to come here tonight, but I truthfully don't believe any of you have any idea how bad the attitudes of the students really are."

She let that statement rest where it might, before plowing through the stares of hostility, disbelief, and some of outright rebellion.

She described her first day in detail, her father's advice, and her willingness to work with the parents, but if she had no help from them at home, she may as well leave now.

All in all, the meeting was a surprise hit, the men especially agreeing with Sarah and the school board, the women whispering in the cloakroom afterward but coming to tell Sarah they wanted to know if their children were not behaving.

How could a teacher describe students who weren't really misbehaving but whose characters were soaked with the poison of rebellion and a lack of discipline, enabling them to freely voice their disrespectful opinions without conscience?

But it was a start.

Ben and Anna Zook stayed long after the last parent had gone through the door. They sat in the upper grade desks and shared their thoughts and opinions, the *frade* (joy) they'd felt when they heard Sarah would teach and the hopelessness of poor Martha Riehl, which hadn't been entirely her fault.

Anna was as little and round as ever, barely fitting into a school desk, her hair and covering neat as a pin as always, Ben smiling and nodding at all his wife's antics.

They were slowly coming to grips with the fire that had destroyed their old barn and were accepting of it now, although Ben had to see a doctor and take a good antidepressant for more than a year.

"He just couldn't handle some of the things,

the financial part, mostly," Anna concluded, clucking like a protective little biddy hen.

"I couldn't have pulled through without Lee. Her brother. He's something else. He has a talent for planning ahead, then seeing that the work gets done. He was a real pillar of strength for me."

Sarah acknowledged this bit of information with a dip of her head.

"Well, such is life," Anna remarked. "It goes on, gets better with time. Barn fires aren't fun, but you get a new barn in the end. It looks nice, our barn does. I like the color of the metal siding. It's cool."

She smiled a genuine smile of pleasure, including her husband in its brilliance, then announced the fact that she was hungry. Why didn't Sarah go along home with them and she'd make stromboli?

"At ten o'clock?" Sarah was incredulous.

"Shoot. I could eat stromboli, easily," Anna announced happily.

"Come along home, Sarah," Ben urged.

"No, I can't. Mam would worry. I'd have to call my driver, and there's no telephone here. No. Maybe some other time."

After they'd gone, Sarah was vastly relieved, in spite of the temptation. How could she and Lee have hidden their feelings from Ben and Anna? Could she have pulled it off?

She had asked the driver to pick her up at ten thirty, which meant she had another half hour to wait.

The night was warmer than the previous ones, so she turned off the propane lamp, locked the door, and sat on the cement porch steps listening to the night sounds, watching the half moon in the star-filled sky, listening to the whispering of the wind in the willow tree down by the fence.

She heard singing, didn't she? Or was it the willow tree playing tricks with her senses? There it was again. High, a bit reedy, but a voice singing.

Headlights loomed in the darkness, putting the fence, the privy, the willow tree in plain sight. The singing stopped as the car slowed.

There were voices, a car door slammed. Then a high shriek, followed by a man's angry voice.

The wail of despair that followed tore at Sarah's heart, and she rose from her seat immediately and walked toward the sound before deciding it wasn't worth the risk. It would be foolhardy, putting her life in jeopardy.

A car door slammed again.

Sarah cowered by the brick wall of the school as a figure hurtled through the night, feet pounding the pavement, followed by desperate shrieks.

"No! No!"

How could she just stand against the wall and listen to that?

Sarah ran toward the open gate, calling, "Does anyone need help?"

The vehicle sped up again and then screeched to a stop. A dark figure leapt out and grabbed the fugitive, hauling him or her into the car as Sarah stood, afraid to intervene, afraid to step outside the boundaries of the schoolyard.

The small white car was not a Volkswagen. That was all Sarah knew for sure as it careened past, tires squealing, leaving her standing along the rural road watching it speed away.

It could have been Ashley. Who else would be in trouble around here, followed by a small, white car?

Another barn had burned to the ground, and the Amish still just sat, taking all the hatred and violence, bowing down, and saying, "Thy will be done."

Sarah was so upset when she walked into the kitchen at home that she strode purposefully to her parents' bedroom door and rapped smartly, her heart thudding in her chest until she heard her mother's muffled voice.

"Can we talk?" she hissed.

"Of course."

Bed springs creaked as her parents left their warm bed and appeared at the kitchen table where Sarah sat, the lamp lit, the teakettle heating on the gas burner.

Her parents slid into kitchen chairs, their eyes

wide with worry, and Sarah immediately launched into a vivid account of the runaway person, the small white car, and the fact that they never did mention Ashley Walters to the police. What if she was in grave danger?

"Dat, you know she is!" Sarah burst out.

Dat nodded, listening, stroking his beard with a large calloused hand.

"But you don't know if it was Ashley, do you?"

"No. But I have a feeling."

"So you suggest we call the police and tell them everything we know?" he asked.

"Yes. Ashley knows something that bothers her terribly. I really do think she knows who is starting the barn fires. It's just an intuition, a hunch, but as time goes on, it becomes more clear. You know that rude guy who came to the door? When we were canning pumpkin? He warned us to stay away from Ashley. Her father, the man at the leather goods stand at market, said the same thing."

Dat pondered Sarah's words.

Mam rose when the teakettle's whistle pierced the air, unhooked three mugs from the wall, dropped a tea bag into each of them, and poured the hot water.

Long into the night, they reasoned among themselves, Dat pulling in the direction of passivity, Mam steering toward finding out more of Ashley Walters' lifestyle, and Sarah leaning heavily toward Melvin's way of thinking.

"You know, Dat, someone is going to get hurt, or even killed. At first, everyone in the whole Amish community was afraid. After a while, we relaxed. Then there was another fire, we rebuilt, and the rage and fear and everything else just flooded in again. It's a vicious circle without an end. The barn fires are not going to stop until this person is caught. And I feel as if we know enough to try and do something about it."

"But is it right?" Dat asked, after a long pause.

"What do you mean, is it right?" Sarah asked.

"Our forefathers would not have fought in a war, neither would they have gone to court, or hired a lawyer to defend themselves. We are a nonresistant people. If a man smites one cheek, give him the other. If he asks you to go with him one mile, go with him twain," Dat quoted quietly.

"And if a man burns your barn, give him a bunch more to burn!" Sarah exploded.

Mam burst out laughing, and Dat smiled hesitantly.

"It's only common sense, Dat. This last fire just got my blood boiling. I mean, here is this humble couple, never hurt a flea, live their lives as best they know how, deny themselves anything wasteful or frivolous. You'd think God would smile on them always, but some lunatic creeps through the night and lights their barn. Why wouldn't we want to help them, Dat?"

"It's not our way, Sarah."

Mam raised her eyebrows, watched her husband's face, and kept her peace.

"I'm afraid if we try to put the law on Ashley, we'll be raking in a whole load of trouble we didn't bargain for. We surely don't have much evidence."

Defeated, Sarah bade her parents goodnight and went to bed, frustrated, still committed to finding out what she could about Ashley. Dat was too old-fashioned, always bringing up that old forefathers thing.

Remembering Lee, she touched her fingers to her mouth, smiled softly, let the light of his eyes soothe her, and fell into a sweet and restful slumber.

A few days later, Sarah was shocked to see Ashley Walters when her school driver stopped at a Turkey Hill market for gas, the needle on the gauge of her old Chevy hovering just above empty.

Sarah's lips were chapped, a brand new cold sore popping up, so she ran into the small store to purchase a tube of Blistex. She stopped short when she saw the unmistakable profile of the thin, tormented girl behind the cash register, her hair falling forward as always, a curtain to shield her from the harsh realities of life.

Should she reveal herself? Or turn and leave?

Ashley was as shy as a wild deer, and Sarah

desperately wanted to avoid spooking her. She didn't have much time, so she found the Blistex and walked boldly toward Ashley with what she hoped was a welcoming expression. Ashley's eyes met Sarah's before a wave of fright opened them wider, but she struggled to calm herself and remain professional.

"Hi."

"Hi, Ashley. How are you?"

"I'm okay. Back with Mike. We're good."

"I'm just so glad to see you. To know you're okay."

"Yeah. Well, that'll be a dollar and seventy-nine cents."

Sarah handed her two dollars, accepted the change, and was dismissed coolly when Ashley said, "Next," to the customer behind her.

"See you soon," Sarah said hopefully.

Ashley waved a hand while addressing the lady behind her.

Ivy Run School had turned into four brick walls of challenge, literally.

Once Sarah understood that the parents were not actually against her (except perhaps Mrs. Turtle), she caught her stride and dove headlong into each new day, making subtle changes that surprised her as the pupils allowed the changes to occur.

Bible reading remained a quiet, devotional time, and gradually more of the pupils spoke the

Lord's Prayer. She introduced new songs, which didn't do much to increase the enthusiasm for singing class, but it was a start.

The first day she mentioned a game of baseball, the loud jeers and boos infuriated her, and she firmly told the intimidating upper graders that it was either baseball or staying in their seats.

"I'd rather stay in my seat," Steven Zook growled, slouched in his desk, his huge feet splayed disrespectfully in the aisle, a fine powder of brown dust surrounding them from the dried mud.

"Yeah. Who would, like, WANT to play baseball?" Rosanna chirped triumphantly, daring Sarah to challenge the rules Steven and she had created.

"Me," Sarah said.

"Well, good for you."

That day, Sarah made a deal. Whoever would participate in a game of baseball would get five points, and five hundred points would mean a field trip.

Of course, they all mocked the field trip. Who wanted to go traipsing across some farmer's pasture dodging cow patties to hear a few sparrows warbling?

Sarah swallowed the hot anger that rose like bile, threatening to choke her. She was terrified to feel a warm wetness in her eyes as a lump of defeat settled over her.

Unexpectedly, a quavering voice announced, "I'll play."

"Elam! That is seriously wonderful! Great! So, we have Elam and me. We can play batty in and batty out, unless we get more volunteers."

Hesitantly, two more hands went up—the sixth-grade boys, Christopher and David—followed by one fifth-grade girl.

That first day, there were seven players, and they played a dreadful game of Round Town. The students missed balls and struck out, not one of them skilled at the ageless game of schoolyard baseball.

The remaining pupils lounged around the porch or the horse shed, ate their endless snacks from Ziploc bags, jeered, tripped the little ones who dared venture close, and, simply put, did their best to make recess miserable for anyone who didn't hang out with them. Sarah chose to ignore them.

All through the month of November, recess remained the same. Sarah could barely control the urge to swat the two eighth-grade boys with the baseball bat.

The weather turned cold and damp, and still they kept playing. The lower graders established themselves, playing kickball with the good soccer ball Sarah had purchased, their cheeks rosy from the cold, their eyes snapping with excitement and good health when they crashed through the front door, whipped off their coats and scarves and beanies, and slid into their desks when the bell summoned them to their seats.

On the day when Sarah announced they had accumulated five hundred points, her eyes shone with anticipation.

"That is so exciting!" she said, speaking as if the entire school had participated.

"Our field trip will be a tour of the Strasburg Railroad Museum and a ride on the train!"

A great cheer rose from the pupils, especially the lower graders.

"For lunch, we'll go to my house, and my mother will make stromboli."

Another enthusiastic roar greeted this announcement, and Sarah dared peek sideways at the disgruntled upper graders who had refused to play and would not be joining the field trip. She found varying degrees of embarrassment, remorse, and a watered down mockery, perhaps.

"I have a brother, Levi, who has Down syndrome, and he will have a surprise for everyone as well."

"What's Down syndrome?" Reuben asked.

"He was born with a handicap. Years ago they called these people retarded, but he's just a little mentally and physically challenged. His mental capacity is about the same as an eight year old's. But he's so excited when the school comes to visit."

Rosanna raised her hand, her lower lip protruding petulantly. "What are we going to do?"

"You'll have to stay home that day."

Sarah actually felt sorry for those who had refused to play baseball. The jeering and rebellion suddenly felt as if it was running low on fuel, sputtering, dying but still gliding along, an airplane with no fuel gauge, unaware, above the clouds.

"That's against the rules. You can't make us do that."

"We'll see."

After third recess, Rosanna marched to Sarah's desk, leaned across it, and said briskly, "If we play baseball from now till you go, can we go, too?"

"What do you mean by we?"

"We. Everyone else. All the upper graders."

"Let me think about it."

Rosanna's eyes were a mixture of arrogance and shyness, which was so encouraging that Sarah burst through the door, threw her book bag on the table, and yelled for Mam the minute she got home.

Sarah missed two weddings in the month of November, refusing to allow a substitute access to the fragile foundation she had built so far.

The weddings were for distant cousins, relatives on her father's side who she wasn't well acquainted with, so she didn't feel too bad when she decided against going.

She thought of Lee constantly, wondered if he'd ask to take her to the supper table, the Amish tradition where the bride and groom coupled their friends for an evening of food and hymn-singing.

She saw him only from a distance on week-ends, averted her eyes when he did come close.

Rose cornered Sarah, of course, one of the first weekends after Lee broke off their friendship, wailing unhappily about life's unfairness, and what was she supposed to do now?

They were seated side by side on the small sofa in Barbie Ann Smoker's bedroom. Her parents, Levi Smokers, had arranged to have the supper for almost 150 youth.

Sarah admired the solid oak bedroom furniture, the double windows dressed in purple drapes, the matching floral comforter, and listened sympathetically as Rose rambled on.

Rose had lost weight. Her face was pale, her cheekbones etched sharply against the rich purple of the window coverings.

She was even more beautiful, her large, blue eyes limpid with sadness and misery. Her dress was a powdery blue, matching the color of her eyes, and Sarah could truthfully say she was astounding.

"I should have kept Matthew. I miss him now."

Sarah exhaled a derisive puff of air.

"Tell me about it." The words tumbled out before Sarah could recapture them.

"You really did love him, didn't you?"

"Oh yes. Definitely. I loved him all my life."

"I know. You loved him even when I dated him."

"No."

"Yes, you did."

"I know."

They burst into giggles and then became hysterical. Sarah held Rose's thin form as she cried pitifully against her shoulder. Sitting up, Rose sighed and blew her nose, before a fresh wall of tears tumbled down the porcelain face.

"We'll just be old maids. Buy a market stand. Sell doughnuts. Or make hoagies. Have a deli. Weight three hundred pounds and enjoy our lives."

"Immensely," Sarah nodded.

"No pun intended," Rose said sourly.

Then they became hysterical again, and Sarah decided a friendship like theirs was rare. It had withstood the ravages of unstable relationships with Matthew, gossip, and attractions to Lee. But would it be able to survive if Lee actually did begin a serious friendship with Sarah after allowing the proper span of time to elapse?

What if Lee was just another Matthew? Hadn't Matthew been fiercely attracted to her that day at the Beilers' barn raising? But nothing had come of it, really.

Sarah was consumed by fear and dread, the thought of Lee being untrue or insincere rendering her motionless.

"Sarah, did you know that your eyes turn dark when you think something deep or disturbing?"

"Do they?"

"Yeah. You have such a golden look about you. I often think of you that way. Your eyes and your skin sort of match your hair."

"You mean I look like a dog or a cat?"

"Oh now, stop!"

That day their friendship was cemented once more, the camaraderie between them a solid, binding thing.

Rose could not have known about the moment Lee found Sarah's eyes, and for long seconds, one yearned for the other, the attraction equal, complete, leaving Sarah in a fine misery afterward, pulled in two directions by her loyalty to Rose, her feelings for Lee. Why was life always so complicated?

Through the cold night air, Sarah walked alone, searching for Melvin's buggy after the supper. Suddenly a tall figure appeared beside her.

"Looking for a ride home?"

She stopped, turned.

"I'm Alan Beiler. I think I saw you at Enos Miller's, right?"

"Oh yes. Yes, I was there."

"Hello."

The hand that was proffered was large, firm, cool to her touch, and she looked up into two dark, dark eyes with a warm light in them.

"I'm Sarah. Beiler. Same as you."

"Yeah. Your dat's a minister. We're not related. Well, maybe fourth or fifth cousins. I checked the Fisher book."

Sarah was flattered. He'd checked the Fisher book. That announcement was pretty serious. Often, if a young man was interested or curious or attracted to a young girl, he only had to look up her family in the Fisher book, a recording of every family in Lancaster County and the surrounding areas.

"You need a ride?" he repeated.

"No. My cousin, Melvin, is around here somewhere."

And Sarah was suddenly relieved that he was.

Chapter 20

A bleak, windy Saturday in December found Sarah walking into the Turkey Hill on Route 340, determined to talk to Ashley.

No one knew she had gone except Mam, who believed the story Sarah had given her about going to Country Cupboard for prizes, little objects to be handed to her pupils when they deserved a reward.

She tied Fred securely, blanketed him, and wrapped her coat tightly around her shivering body as she walked to the door.

It was better than she'd hoped. Ashley was on her knees, stocking shelves, and there was a glad light in her eyes.

"Sarah!"

"Hi, Ashley."

"It's good to see you."

"I came here to talk to you, Ashley. I really would like some information. Can you . . . do you have time?"

Ashley looked at the clock on the opposite wall.

"A few minutes."

They stepped off to the side, allowing a customer access to the coolers, and Sarah took stock of her friend's face, the healthy glow, the wide eyes, no longer hooded, frightened.

"You look good."

"I am. I'm in a good place in my life. Mike is really straightening up, and we're better. I'm better. Actually, Sarah, I want to thank you for everything you've done for me over these past few years. You saved my life, really. I want you to know I'm grateful. You know, like, appreciative."

"I didn't do anything," Sarah said.

"Oh yes. Yes, you did."

"Can I ask you one question, please?"

"Sure."

"How much do you know about the barn fires?"

Ashley stood still, her eyes averted, the shapeless sweatshirt hiding her thin figure, her fingers clutching the bands of the long sleeves.

The door opened and closed, the cash register whirred quietly, voices mingled, and still Ashley remained quiet.

Finally she sighed.

"A lot, Sarah. Way too much. It has to end, I know. In the past, I was afraid. I'm not anymore. It's weird, but I don't care anymore. He can just kill me. He threatened too many times. But his . . ."

"Ashley!" A large, buxom woman called from the register, her eyes snapping, her arm motioning Ashley over.

"You're needed on the other register!"

There was nothing to do but leave. Sarah

walked by the register, waved, and was astonishingly rewarded with a genuine smile from Ashley who put her hand to her mouth, then flung it outward, a kiss thrown with a quick smile of love and friendship.

"Thanks!" Sarah mouthed, then hurried out of the market and dashed across the parking lot.

Deep in thought, she loosened the nylon neck rope and swept the heavy horse blanket off Fred's back with one swoop. She grabbed the reins and made a short turn, the steel rims of the buggy wheels grating against the cast iron roller on the side of the buggy, strategically placed to allow such turns.

Straining to see, holding Fred to a standstill, she waited patiently as the line of cars crept past. Then she loosened the reins and chirped, urging him out onto the busy roadway, the main route between Lancaster and the village of Intercourse.

Christmas wreaths, roping, holly, doors decorated for the season—houses everywhere were decked in holiday finery, Sarah observed. A wonderful time of the year, she thought.

Sometimes she wondered what it would be like to decorate a tree or hang a wreath or string bright lights along the eaves of a house. Keeping the Plain tradition, these things were viewed as frivolous, unnecessary, but Sarah enjoyed them on English houses, nevertheless.

She was always glad for the gifts they gave

and received, the Christmas cards they sent, the cookies and treats they made, keeping the spirit of Christmas alive in their simple, Amish way.

Happiness was doubled for her, thinking of Ashley's recovery, the light in her blue-gray eyes.

Well, the problem wasn't Mike, her boyfriend, evidently. Who had threatened her? Surely not her father.

She watched absentmindedly as four mules pulled a manure spreader over the half frozen ground, their ears bobbing randomly, flopping up and down as their heads moved in time to their steps. The manure spewed out of the rattling spreader, inexpensive fertilizer for the fields, a boon for next year's corn crop.

Fred plodded along, slowing as they neared Bird-in-Hand, trying to veer off the roadway onto a side road leading toward home. Sarah had to open the window and slap his rump lightly with the reins.

"Come on, Fred. You're just lazy," she called, then closed the window and snapped it shut, satisfied when Fred changed his gait to a brisk pace.

She wiped the top of the wooden glove compartment with a gloved hand, opened the door only a crack, and shook out the accumulated horse hairs.

In winter, the horses' coats grew thick and heavy. The loose hairs somehow found their way into the smallest openings, clinging to lap robes and purses and gallons of milk or containers of food or plastic grocery bags.

At the Country Cupboard, Sarah greeted the cashier, then placed a few small tablets, packets of erasers, key chains, balloons, anything she imagined would please the children into her basket.

She thought wistfully of having a Christmas program but immediately changed her mind, knowing she had a long uphill road to travel before that was possible.

She picked up a package of clothespins for Mam and a few dishcloths, then stood in line at the cash register.

"Hey, Sarah."

Sarah turned to see Hannah, Matthew's mother, directly behind her, her eyes bright with interest, but a certain wariness in them as well.

"Hannah! My, it's good to see you. I miss you. You never come to the house anymore to see Mam."

"Oh, Sarah. I know. Too many things happened between us. Too many."

Sarah nodded as tears came unbidden.

"Matthew's coming home!"

Hannah leaned forward and whispered, her eyes shifting, making sure no one overheard, as if Matthew's appearance, his return from Haiti, would be heralded with the same welcome as a tornado or some other natural disaster.

"Really?"

"Yes. He's coming alone. His wife is ill."

"Why would he leave her then?"

"Oh, she has her parents, he said."

"I guess."

"Yes. She's really close to them."

"That's good."

"Come visit when Matthew's here."

"Why would I?"

"Well, Sarah, you're friends. You're good friends. He'll want to see you."

Sarah's face reddened. She said good-bye, exiting the store as quickly as possible, blindly loosening the neck rope, almost driving directly into a parked mini-van.

No, we're not friends. I am still Matthew's broken-hearted girlfriend, a recovering love addict. The sight of him would be enough to make me relapse completely.

Hannah would never understand.

It was on the front page of the *Intelligencer Journal*, the Lancaster daily newspaper. It was on the local radio station, on CNN and Fox News, but of course, the Amish people didn't know that. Only the ones who received the daily paper scanned the article, clucked, and shook their heads at the girl's young age.

Only twenty, they said. *Hesslich shaut* (Such a shame).

There were no alcohol or drugs involved.

Ashley Walters had been flown to Hershey Medical Center, air-lifted after a horrible wreck, the small, white Honda she was driving folded like an accordion beneath the stainless steel tank of an oncoming milk truck.

She died there, alone, only a few minutes after she arrived at the vast hospital.

Sarah found out when she came home from school. She listened, openmouthed, as her mother brought her the daily paper. She crumpled immediately onto a kitchen chair, her head bent over the paper, one leg folded beneath her.

"Oh, Mam!" she wailed after she finished reading the article. Mam stood behind Sarah, a hand on the back of her chair.

"You don't think she did it on purpose?"

Sarah shook her head as tears streamed down her cheeks. "No, no. Absolutely not. The last time I spoke to her she was happier than I've ever seen her. I just can't grasp this."

Levi was saddened by Ashley's death, saying it really was *unbegreiflich* (unbelievable). He asked to be taken to her viewing, if Dat and Mam would take him.

Sarah wished Ashley had not been so alone when she died. She hoped fervently she had been conscious of nothing after the wreck. Sarah couldn't eat her supper, couldn't fall asleep, thinking of Ashley hitting the underside of the unyielding tanker, so small, so innocent, so alone.

She threw back the covers and got down on her knees beside the bed, cupped her face in her hands, and stayed there, praying, even though she knew Ashley had already died. What sense did it make praying for her soul? But it was comforting, instilling a certain peace throughout her.

What had Dat said about Ashley?

God loved her, too. She was important to Him.

Sarah figured God cared very much about Ashley's soul and would take care of her, *fersark* her.

Who could tell what upbringing the poor girl had had? Her mother living thousands of miles away, her father threatening. Or had he been? Would they ever know?

Three evenings later, the Beiler family dressed in funeral black. Dat and Levi wore blue shirts, crisp, homemade, ironed carefully, their high-topped, black Sunday shoes gleaming, their felt hats placed securely on their heads. Mam wore her black shawl and bonnet, the girls their woolen pea coats.

It seemed like such a short time since Mervin's viewing had taken place, and now they reached out to whoever had loved Ashley, broken family or not. Death was a universal bond, grief a language everyone understood. No culture was unique at the time of a death, the sorrow keenly felt by those who had experienced it before.

They helped Levi into the van, using a step stool and steadying his shaking legs, Mam's hand on his back, Dat holding onto the stool in the cold, December wind, his *mutsa* (Sunday coat) blowing up as he bent over.

Levi grunted, pulled himself up, and sat heavily in the front seat, his eyes alight with bird-like curiosity, before asking, "Who is the driver?"

The name was supplied—Randy Stover, a man who was fairly new in the business of driving the Amish.

"Well, good evening, Randy. I'm glad to meet you. I'm Levi Beiler."

Randy smiled, politely exchanged pleasantries with Dat, and listened carefully as Levi informed him he was going to the city of Lancaster and not to a dentist or doctor.

"Nothing's going to hurt this round, Randy," he announced, giggling jubilantly. Then Levi turned to his father. "Can we stop at McDonald's, Dat?"

When Dat gave no immediate answer, Levi informed him that the last time he had had a Big Mac it was summertime, hot.

Dat smiled and said alright, Levi, which satisfied his inquiry.

The city of Lancaster was a frightening place on a dark December night, even if lights illuminated every sidewalk and street corner.

The funeral home was a lavish, stone building on King Street, a fancy canopy erected over the front stoop, brick pathways winding between exotic shrubbery and trees.

The parking lot was empty, or almost, and Sarah's heart felt dark and heavy for her friend. Surely someone was there for her. Someone cared.

They helped Levi down from the high van seat, explaining patiently that this was a viewing, like Mervin's, and he had to stay nice and quiet. If he obeyed, they would buy him a Big Mac at McDonald's on the way home.

Silently, they moved as one. A small group of Amish people dressed in black, going to pay their last respects to a new acquaintance.

There was no one standing in line. A handful of people were gathered at the end of a long corridor, an open book on a gleaming wooden stand nearby. Heavy carpeting muted their steps, and Dat stood respectfully aside as Mam bent to sign their names.

He took off his hat then, carrying it by his side, whispering to Levi to do the same. Levi had a steady look of concentration on his face, so Sarah knew he would obey perfectly, his reward a calorie-laden treat.

The coffin was set in a warmly lit alcove, a few bouquets of flowers set at attractive angles around it. Surprisingly, the coffin was opulent, lined with white satin, lavishly carved and decorated, a cascade of white lilies spilling across the top.

Sarah recognized Mike, who appeared extremely nervous, wild-eyed, as they approached.

A handshake from Dat changed that, a hand to his shoulder altered the look completely, as his face crumpled and he turned away, his shoulders heaving.

Instant tears welled up in Sarah's eyes as Dat stayed with Mike, speaking kind words of condolence to the distraught youth.

They moved on to greet the man and woman standing at the head of the coffin, shook hands, introduced themselves. Mam was pulled into the elegantly dressed woman's embrace, then each of the girls in turn.

Dat repeated his kind gestures to the man, who was dressed in an expensive suit, his face openly curious.

Finally, the woman introduced herself as Ashley's mother from Fresno, California.

"My husband, Andrew."

Sarah stood and looked at Ashley, lying so still and lifeless, her face patched together and barely recognizable to her.

So young, she thought as tears slipped down her cheeks. As they talked, Sarah was shocked to discover the couple was named Andrew and Caroline Walters, Ashley's true biological parents.

"You, you aren't separated?" she asked softly.

"No. Oh no. Ashley came to Pennsylvania for

college. She was estranged from Andrew and me."

Caroline was suddenly overcome with emotion, dabbing daintily at her tears. "I know this sounds lame, but she literally got in with the wrong crowd. We talked sometimes, but the sad part is there wasn't much we could do."

They talked for awhile, the Walters longing to learn all they could about their daughter's last years. Then the Beilers' stepped aside as a few people from the farmer's market made an appearance.

Where was Harold from the leather goods stand? He was the one Ashley had claimed was her father. Confused, Sarah turned to greet Tim, the owner of the farmer's market.

Tim then said hello to Levi, who watched his face with curious eyes, both hands clutching the brim of his hat. But Levi would not open his mouth to acknowledge Tim's greeting.

Bewildered, Tim asked Sarah if Levi was mute.

"No. Oh no. He was told to be quiet at the viewing and then he'll be allowed to go to McDonald's."

Levi nodded, his eyes sparkling.

"Big Mac!" he mouthed, then checked hurriedly to see if Dat or Mam had overheard his breach of contract.

Quietly, the Beiler family moved on together,

leaving the Walters to greet the handful of well-wishers and acquaintances.

Confused and sorrowful, Sarah walked back to the van.

"I'm just so glad she has parents to take care of her burial. It seems less devastating somehow," Mam mused quietly.

"But she said her parents were separated," Sarah said, her voice unsteady, troubled.

Dat was true to his word, and Levi enjoyed his sandwich, complete with the highly-regarded French fries and ketchup and a large Coke to boot, which he enjoyed to the fullest. Then he tossed and turned the remainder of the night, finally getting up and helping himself to a spoonful of Maalox and a long drink of water, keeping Mam awake until three o'clock in the morning.

Even Dat was grouchy at the breakfast table, drinking cup after cup of black coffee, his thoughts a thousand miles away. Finally, he spoke.

"It wouldn't be so bad, if we could only have obtained more information about these fires. Clearly, Mike is terribly afraid of us."

"I don't think he had anything to do with them," Sarah said.

"What makes you say that?" Dat growled, setting them all a bit on edge.

"Ashley as much as told me. I think he was

mischievous about them, enjoyed scaring people, even wanted us to think it was him, but he was too immature, too childish. I don't think he'd be brave enough to do something like that."

"But the bottom line is still that our only source for information about the fires is gone."

"You didn't want to question her."

Abruptly, Dat left the table, which was completely unlike him. Sarah knew Ashley's death troubled him more than he would admit, which proved to Sarah that he struggled the same as everyone else, desperately wanting an end to the danger of yet another fire.

A heavy cloud of oppression hung over the rest of the family. Suzie kicked the table leg, saying she didn't feel well and asking why she had to go to school if she was sick.

Levi ate oatmeal and bananas, belched loudly, and didn't ask to be excused until Priscilla reminded him sharply.

He said it was the Maalox.

Sarah went to school with a heavy heart, her face pale, her shoulders drooping.

She told her pupils about the accident, about knowing Ashley, and was gratified when even the older boys seemed interested. It was a small start at building a relationship with them, but it was at least a start.

At recess, the heavy, red-faced little girl named Leah came up to Sarah's desk, leaned across it, and watched her, the bright, beady gaze never leaving Sarah's face. Sarah put down the red ballpoint pen she was using and looked at her.

"What can I do for you, Leah?"

"Nothing."

Quickly, Leah swept away. Sarah raised her eyebrows and went back to work, checking the first grade's penmanship papers.

Five minutes later, Leah was back, watching Sarah's face.

"What?" Sarah asked.

"You know Ashley?"

"Yes."

"She got eggs from us."

"She did?"

"Yes. Her and Mike."

"Really?"

"Yes, they did. She gave me some bubble gum."

Quickly, Leah looked around to make sure no one saw her.

"Here."

She thrust a small bag containing a very squashed chocolate cupcake in Sarah's direction. Her small bird-like eyes gazed steadily into her face before she opened her mouth, then closed it again.

"Don't tell anyone, but I pity you, because Ashley died."

Then she catapulted her round form away from

the desk, shot out the door, and hid her face the remainder of the day.

Every small moment like that was a rosy victory for Sarah, making each day at the teacher's desk worthwhile. She ate every bite of the chocolate cupcake, finding it delicious, a symbol of the effort she put into each day, a small reward perhaps, but a huge accomplishment. What an angry little girl Leah had been that first day!

They made candy canes from red and white construction paper and hung them from paper chains, planning to stretch them from the center of the classroom to the four corners. Sarah decided to ask the two eighth-grade boys to do it.

"Sam, would you and Joe like to hang these paper chains?"

There was no response. Both boys slouched in their seats, reading tattered copies of old books brought from home, questionable paperbacks Sarah did not have the nerve to discuss.

No use opening that can of worms just yet, she thought wryly.

"Sam?"

Joe raised his hand.

"We usually don't help the teacher."

"This isn't usually."

No response.

Sighing, Sarah let it go but felt as if everything

she'd accomplished had just slipped out of her grasp, leaving an oily residue that she could not wash away.

Teaching school was a trail with so many highs and lows, the highs like Mt. Everest, the lows an unexplainable abyss, a place full of hopelessness.

Six weeks, and what had she accomplished? Worse yet, five barn fires, and they were back to square one with Ashley gone. Sarah folded her arms on her desk, laid her head on them, and closed her eyes.

Chapter 21

Sarah spent the following Saturday evening at the Widow Lydia's, her house cozy and warm, every corner lit with scented candles for Christmas.

There were wrapped presents on the old library table, and homemade bells hung from the window blinds.

They'd cut egg cartons apart, folded aluminum foil over the small cups, strung them on red and green yarn, and tied red ribbon around them.

They had just finished another batch of caramel popcorn, adding pecans to it this time. The house was infused with buttery, sugary smells. Lydia's face was glowing, her hair gleaming smoothly in the lamplight.

She confided in Sarah, whispering behind a hand raised to her face, that she felt guilty, but this Christmas she was simply going all out.

She had spent almost thirty dollars for a set of Legos for Ben, she confessed. Sarah stepped back, surveyed Lydia's face, and said that was fine, absolutely, not extravagant at all.

They made a double batch of Rice Krispie treats and decorated them with green and red icing, for Aaron, the toddler.

Sarah was washing dishes, thinking how easily

marshmallow succumbed to hot water, when someone spoke, directly behind her.

"Hello, Sarah."

Turning, her hands still in the dishwater, she found Lee Glick, his blue eyes conveying his gladness at seeing her there. Sarah wanted to fling herself in his arms, right then and there, but she slowly took her hands from the dishwater and dried them on a towel before she said, "Lee."

"How are you?"

"Oh, I'm okay. You heard about Ashley Walters?"

A great shout went up when Melvin suddenly appeared, his shirt the color of new grass in spring, his balding head shining like a freshly washed egg, his nose as crooked and dear as ever.

"Surprised you, right?"

Sarah laughed but acknowledged that yes, he had, while she blushed furiously. Melvin howled with glee, savoring her embarrassment.

Lydia stood shyly in the background, her eyes giving away the beating of her heart.

Melvin turned to her, and the look they exchanged needed no words, a rare and beautiful thing.

Omar had gone with his friends for the weekend, so Anna Mae and Rachel were thrilled to have company, making coffee, serving pretzels and cheese, obviously enamored with Melvin.

He held court with a kingly air, seated on a throne of his own imagination. To say he was in his element was an understatement, and Sarah watched him, marveling at the change in her cousin.

The candles flickered, the coal stove glowed, the smell of freshly-brewed coffee mixed with sweet smells from the kitchen. Sarah's happiness was complete when Lee turned and smiled at her, his face warm and filled with more than a welcome.

When they discussed the latest event pertaining to the barn fires, Melvin said there was no doubt in his mind that they had missed their chance by taking Dat's advice instead of allowing the police to interrogate that girl, and now look, she was dead.

Sarah mentioned the fact that Mike was still around. Lydia agreed. It might be worth a try.

Lee became somber, slouched in his chair only a bit, saying nothing as Melvin waved his hands for emphasis, explaining in his ringing voice why he thought the law should know about Ashley and Mike.

"You know, the police are a lot more intelligent than we are. They'll know which steps to take, which way to go. I don't know why your dat can't see that."

Sarah shrugged. "I thought he put you in your place."

"He did for awhile, but I got so upset at Enos Miller's it wasn't funny. They are the nicest couple, so simple and humble and God-fearing."

"About the opposite of you," Sarah teased.

Melvin made a face, while Lydia's eyes worshipped him.

Far into the night, they sat around Lydia's table, playing board games as the candles burned low in their glass jars. The coal fire needed stoking, and the children dropped off to sleep, one by one making their way upstairs to their soft beds to snuggle beneath thick comforters.

Melvin suggested they stay awake till four o'clock, then all do chores together. He didn't have church this Sunday. Lee did, but he said it was alright to skip services, because he had other important matters to attend to—milking Lydia's cows.

Melvin really laughed about that, winking broadly, and Sarah slapped him, just for fun. The cousins exchanged a knowing look, and Sarah was rewarded by the warmth, the approval of Lee, in Melvin's eyes.

In the month of January, all of Lancaster County turned into a vast, arctic landscape dotted with white barns, farmhouses, and clusters of multi-colored homes forming quaint, homey villages.

Farm wives stoked the fires. Cornmeal mush sizzled in cast iron frying pans, liverwurst heated beside it in sturdy saucepans, fuel for shivering, hungry men when chores were finished.

In some of the new, more modern Amish homes, the husbands grabbed their lunch pails and thermoses, said good-bye to their wives, and were whisked away in diesel-powered pickup trucks, going their ways with framing or roofing crews to build townhomes, offices, garages, homes for a steadily-growing population centered around the Garden Spot of America.

It was called progress.

Others hurried off to welding shops or cabinet shops, manufacturers, builders of fine, timeless furniture or farm equipment. They wolfed down quick breakfasts of bagels or cold cereal, while the hungry farmers ate their fried mush and liverwurst, eggs and stewed crackers, and home cured bacon.

When the sun rose, spreading light and a thin warmth across the land, hundreds of Amish households were up and moving, making a living however they could, blessed to be dwelling in a land where freedom of religion was practiced and respected.

Almost every Sunday morning, a minister some-where would mention the fact that the congregation could travel to church with their horses and buggies, freely and openly, worshiping without fear. Their forefathers in Switzerland had crept through dark fields at night, worshipped secretly in caves, were hounded, jailed, burned at the stake for this. This freedom.

And what were we doing with this wonderful, God-given thing?

That was the question that clung to David Beiler's conscience, wrapped tightly around it, never quite allowing him to let go in the face of a persistent adversary—the towering flames that had devoured too many Amish barns in Lancaster County over the past few years.

The forefathers, *die alte*, had ingrained in them the principle of nonresistance, taking the verses in the Bible quite literally.

They were Jesus's own words, weren't they? Love your enemies, do good to them that hate you, pray for those who use you and persecute you.

Liebe deine fiende (Love your enemies). There was no way around that.

He imagined that if spirits could be seen by the human eye, comprehended by the lowly under-standing of mere mortals, a civil war of sorts would be raging in the frigid air today, on one of God's wonderful mornings.

For some reason, the burning of Enos Miller's barn had set off a fresh wave of indignant wrath. After coming together in unity for the barn raising, brother again rose against brother in fresh battles of opinion as verbal swords sliced through the air, and harmful charges and feints were executed.

Sisters days and quilting days and market stands became part of the darkness of verbal combat, as mothers, friends, sisters, and cousins voiced their opinions about the barn fires, the spirit of disagreement as thick as pea soup.

Bent and aged, their thin white hair almost completely hidden by their large white coverings, old *mommies* (grandmothers) shook their heads and said among themselves, "It wasn't always so."

Women were taught to be silent, obedient, and if they had anything to say, to say it to their husbands. And here were these young women, laughing uproariously, devising ways of catching the arsonist, including steel-jawed traps, among other outlandish devices.

They couldn't help it if their shoulders shook silently with mirth, though, could they?

David heard of these accounts from Malinda, who attended sisters days and quiltings all through January, coming home with her shoulders stooped with care, but often a twinkle in her eye as well.

For one thing, their two daughters, Ruthie and Anna Mae, were the works! Malinda just didn't know where they got their outspokenness. They claimed that if the Amish pooled their resources and paid for a private detective to follow Ashley Walters' boyfriend around, the fires would come to an end, and they meant it.

When Mam had protested, they said a private detective and a lawyer were two very different things. It was ridiculous, in this day and age, they said, taking this suffering like sitting ducks. No wonder he kept right on burning barns. Nobody even tried to do anything about it. And they were their own daughters saying this.

The next morning, David Beiler absent-mindedly cut the baler twine on a bale of straw with his Barlow pen knife, then hung it carefully on the large nail pounded into the post for that purpose. He took up a block of straw and threw it into the horse trough. He was rewarded by a nicker from Fred.

The winter sunlight found its way through the dusty windows, and he reached up to turn out the propane lantern, then made his way across the cow stable, into the milk house, still wet with steam from the scalding, hot water Sarah had used to scour the milking machines.

The fact that she was still here on the farm, living in peace and harmony with her family, washed over him and infused his thoughts with gratefulness, engulfed his spirit the way the steam warmed the milk house.

God had delivered them with a great and mighty hand, as He had with the children of Israel in days of old, and it still had not ceased to amaze him.

But why was God waiting so long about the

barn fires? Did He allow them to continue because of the *tzvie-drocht* (dissension)—the backbiting, the disharmony, the hateful attitudes? Have mercy on us, David begged as he stepped out of the milk house into the blinding light of the morning sun.

Seated at the breakfast table, smelling of the strong lava soap he'd used to wash his hands and face, David bowed his head. His wife and children followed suit as they clasped hands in their laps and thanked God for the good food spread on the table, then raised their heads and promptly began passing dishes and platters.

Levi was cold. He announced in grumpy tones that no one had *fer-sarked* the fire, and his toast was burnt.

"Just a little dark, Levi," Mam said gently around a mouthful of sausage and egg.

"Don't talk with your mouth full, Malinda," he snapped.

Priscilla burst out laughing, spraying orange juice across her plate. She choked, coughed, covered her mouth with her hand, and went to the sink for a paper towel.

David Beiler smiled broadly, caught Sarah's eye, and winked. Sarah smiled widely, winked back.

Suzie said, "Don't boss Mam, Levi."

"Mam should swallow first, then talk. That's what she says to me."

Suzie looked at Levi without smiling, and he returned her look steadily, unblinking, before saying, "Did you hear what I said?"

Suzie nodded, and Levi tucked into his eggs and sausage, stopping only to tell Mam the toast was so burnt there were little black things smeared in the butter, and he didn't like that. She should be more careful, making toast.

Dat told Levi it would be a great idea for him to make toast. He could pull his chair over to the gas stove, put the homemade bread on the broiler, and keep checking it until it was just the right shade of brown, then turn the oven off and remove it.

Levi's eyes turned bright and cunning, and he saw the opportunity to show off his ability as a helper in the kitchen, latching onto the idea like a pit bull, never letting go. All day long, he begged Mam for the opportunity to make toast until she relented, and he ate perfect toast for lunch, as a snack, and for supper.

While Levi was either making toast, thinking about it, or eating it, Sarah was fighting her own private battle at school. Her courage fled completely when Hannah Stoltzfus brought her sister to visit the school, sitting in the back of the classroom, two sentries of disapproval, every bit as formidable as hungry vultures. Why had they come?

Sarah's hand shook as she called first grade to

arithmetic class, attempting to hide the fact that she'd noticed anything amiss.

At recess, Hannah fluttered up to Sarah's desk, her face flushed, her sister firmly in tow. The color in her face was high, her eyes popping, as if her high blood pressure was actually pushing on her eyes, shoving them up against her glasses, which were spattered with grease.

Her old sweater was torn at the seam on one shoulder, and white lint clung to the front like dandruff. Her stockings sagged over her large, black Sketchers, so inappropriate for a woman her age, but Hannah's choice for comfort.

"Sarah! My, oh. I'm surprised how well you teach."

"Thank you," Sarah said coolly.

Her sister nodded her head in agreement, all her chins wobbling as she did so.

As Hannah leaned close, Sarah was subjected to a decided odor of something fried emanating from her sweater that had likely hung from a hook in her *kesslehaus* for years without being washed.

Mam did the same thing with her everyday sweater, that ratty old black thing that served a multitude of purposes, but Sarah often grabbed it and threw it in the washer with the last load of denim trousers.

"Did you hear about Matthew's wife?"

Just for a moment, Sarah steadied herself by

placing her hands on her desk, before raising her eyebrows in question.

"Her name, you know, is Hephzibah, just like that Bible woman. Sarah, she's such a good person. I feel as if Matthew has been rewarded for his life-changing conversion.

"Anyway, she is sick. She's *unfashtendich grunk* (very sick). Matthew calls every day. They are in the hospital, and they can't really find the cause of her fever. It just doesn't go away."

"Malaria?" Sarah asked.

"What do you know about that disease?" Hannah asked abruptly.

"Not much. I just know it's a common disease in tropical climates, a mosquito-borne illness."

"Are you telephoning Matthew?" The question was sharp, bitter, an arrow tipped with the poison of suspicion.

"Of course not."

Hannah's sister's eyes widened, and she drew back as if to gain a better perspective to watch this interesting exchange.

"Well, don't. He's married now, and I know it's very hard for you to give up. It always was. But you'll be alright, in time. But just don't call Matthew. It wouldn't be right."

Out of the corner of her eye, Sarah saw Joe push little Ben into the corner of the horse shed, heard the little boy's terrified howls from inside the sturdy walls of the schoolhouse, and quickly asked to be excused.

She met a shaking little second grader, blood pouring from a nasty gash on his forehead, his eyes showing the pain and fear of having collided with a sharp metal corner, his nose and eyes running.

Herding him into the cloakroom, she moistened a clean paper towel and held it firmly to the wound and sat him on a folding chair as she examined the cut.

It was deep but not very long. She felt sure a firmly applied butterfly bandage and some B and W salve would begin the healing process just fine.

Hannah, however, insisted he be taken to a doctor. She knew Ben's parents. She'd take him home, and his mother would want to take him. Why, that gash would leave an awful scar.

So she bundled up poor frightened Ben and trundled him out the door, clucking and going on all the while, her sister exclaiming and waving her hands, leaving Sarah with a discipline problem, a sour stomach, and a desperate need to run after Hannah and tell her to go home and stay out of her life, out of her business. And would she please never ever mention her son Matthew's name to her again?

Courage eluded her the remainder of the day, driven away by Joe's loud sneers, his swaggering shoulders, his demeanor challenging Sarah to try and do something about everything she'd seen.

He knew. He knew she'd seen him eating pretzels in class and pushing Ben on the playground. But her mind reeled from Hannah's visit, her senseless accusation. It robbed her of the ability to confront Joe.

By the time the afternoon arrived, Joe had tried her patience to the limit, laughing, whispering, flirting with Rosanna in an unthinkably bold manner. When Sarah finished her third-grade English class, she said "Joe Beiler!" very firmly and very, very loudly.

He jumped up, snickering.

"You need to stay in for recess, so we can talk."

A deathly silence folded itself over the classroom, the clock's ticking suddenly magnified.

They had never heard their teacher speak in such a terrible voice.

When the pupils were excused for last recess, Sarah was actually surprised when Joe remained seated, as she had been prepared to watch him openly disobey and follow the others out the door.

Seated, but slouched as low as possible, he fiddled with his ruler, scraping it across his desk with a grating sound that jangled Sarah's already harried resolve.

"Joe, you know you've been doing crazy things

all day just to try my patience. What is up with eating those pretzels in class?"

He shrugged, became sullen, his eyes hooded.

"May I have an answer, please?"

"I didn't have any breakfast."

"Really?"

"Yeah."

"Why? Surely you had time for a bowl of cereal."

"Yeah."

"Why did you push Ben?"

"He made me mad."

"How? Joe, he's only seven years old."

"He's a pest."

"Not Ben. He's afraid of everything."

Suddenly, Joe sat up straight, his brown eyes flashing dark fire, and he burst out, his adolescent voice breaking into unmanly squeaks. "You sound exactly like my mam. 'Shut up, shut up,' she says. 'They're little. They're only three or four.' She hates me. You know why I ate pretzels? I had to finish hanging out the wash because she was fighting with my dat. So there."

Ashamed, he turned his face away.

Sarah was speechless. She had never known a mother who would tell her son to shut up. Or argue so forcefully she couldn't finish the laundry. And get her growing son no breakfast?

For a long moment, she watched Joe, saw the bad skin, the acne engraved in his quivering cheek. She looked into the eyes that appeared rebellious, brash, sneering, curtains of dark brown hiding pain and a ceaseless yearning for love, patience, and understanding from two parents who were blind to their son's needs.

Sarah knew there were nine children in the Beiler family. Joe was the oldest at 13.

Still, he could have eaten the pretzels on his way to school.

"Joe, I'll tell you what."

Sarah sat in the adjoining desk and made him meet her gaze.

"Don't do it again, okay? And try and be careful on the playground. Ben was hurt pretty badly. And I guess we have to learn to get along if we're going to be stuck in the same schoolhouse until May, right?"

Joe shrugged, shifted his brown eyes.

She spoke to him about flirting with Rosanna, saying they were much too young for such things and was rewarded by a dark, painful blush creeping over his face.

"No speeding ticket this time, young man, just a warning," she said, touching his shoulder.

That day was a memorable one, a turning point.

Chapter 22

Mam paged through her vast array of seed catalogs, clucked, licked her thumb, slurped the lukewarm tea by her side, cleared her throat, scratched her arm, and did just about everything else Sarah could imagine that could completely annoy her.

She was seated at the kitchen table, towers of workbooks beside her, steadfastly plodding her way through them. The lamp hissed, and the cold air swirled around her legs as the mean January blast rattled the spouting at the corner of the house.

Priscilla was curled up on the sofa, reading, and Suzie looked as if she'd fallen asleep at the opposite end, a soft, navy blue throw tucked securely over her shoulders.

Levi was in the shower and had been for the past fifteen minutes, singing a loud, off-key rendition of "Silent Night," a fragment of the old song lodging somewhere in his brain, a leftover from the holidays.

Dat was stretched out on the recliner, but the only thing Sarah could see was an open newspaper, the tips of his fingers, his legs, and stocking feet.

It was almost nine o'clock.

Sarah yawned, threw down her pen, shivered, and said loudly, "Priscilla, would you consider helping me check my books?"

Reluctantly, Priscilla lowered her book, eyed Sarah and the stack of books, and prepared to get off the couch. "I can, I guess."

Mam mused out loud. "I think I'm going to try a different kind of pea this year. Sam King *sei* Arie said Green Arrows are the best, but I disagree. And instead of zinnias, I'm going to plant hardy salvia. I'll start the seeds on the porch."

The porch was Levi's room. It was already decked out with Mam's geraniums, dropping brown leaves all over the shelves, tedious to clean around. All the porch needed was dozens of tiny, square pots full of soil and minuscule seeds, waiting to be knocked over by large bumbling Levi, muttering to himself in the dark of night.

When they heard a loud knock on the door, it surprised all of them, including Dat, who lowered his paper, raising his eyebrows.

"This time of night?" he asked, to no one in particular, then pushed back the footrest, got up, and walked to the front door, laying the folded newspaper on the table beside Sarah's stack of books.

When he opened the door, a whoosh of icy air was unleashed into the room, and Sarah drew her feet under the chair.

Sarah didn't recognize any of the three Amish men, all dressed in long, woolen overcoats and black felt hats, heavy boots on their feet, their faces somber, mouths pinched in grim lines.

The family knew without being told to exit the room, except for Mam, who would be invited to listen if she desired.

The girls shivered their way through their showers, emerged steaming, and leaped into their cold beds, wearing soft socks and long flannel pajamas, homemade pieced comforters piled high on top of their blankets.

It was seriously cold at zero degrees with a brisk wind. All she remembered before falling asleep was the low murmur of voices, never changing, never stopping, a ceaselessly moving creek, a stream of opinions. She could gauge the nature of the visit by the looks on her parents' faces in the morning.

Dat was quiet while they milked, came in late for breakfast, his face inscrutable, nodding briskly at Levi instead of giving his usual hearty "Good morning." He picked at his food until he suddenly laid down his fork, looked around, and asked if anyone had overheard the conversation the night before.

Mam kept her face lowered. The girls shook their heads.

Levi stopped chewing, watched Dat's face.

"Except you, Levi?"

"Well, Davey Beila!"

Clearly ashamed, he turned his attention to his plate.

Levi had been stuck in the bathroom without his pajama pants, the path to his bedroom a wide expanse in full view of the visitors. Levi became more undecided and upset by the minute, brushing his teeth over and over, combing his hair, stalling for time, till he finally gathered enough courage to call Dat and, in typical Levi fashion, announced very clearly that he was stuck in the bathroom without his pants.

"*Hop ken hussa kott* (I had no pants)!" he said now, justifying having had to ask Dat to leave the table, where his serious visitors were left trying to look as sour as they had before.

Dat chuckled, his eyes twinkling. "You could have gone to your room, Levi."

Levi shook his head vehemently, "*Oh nay. Hop rotey knee* (Oh no. I have red knees)."

Everyone laughed. Suzie giggled and snorted, rapping her spoon on the table. Levi looked around appreciatively, glad he could make his whole family laugh, especially on a cold morning like this.

Dat continued telling his family about the visit from the three men. Melvin had spoken to the local police, asking for night patrol between Bird-in-Hand and Enos Miller's in Georgetown. This had been picked up by the media, somehow, and became instantly blown out of proportion, followed by far-out assumptions and half-truths. A Philadelphia newspaper had run an article called "Non-resistant?" with Melvin's picture and his words in bold, black print.

Sarah's oatmeal turned tasteless, the thick creaminess sticking in her throat. Oh no.

So he had actually gone ahead and done it, this thing he'd long cultivated on his own, wagging a finger, threatening, the need to make his opinion known, overriding everyone's advice.

Dat sighed. "So I suppose all the words I spoke to him were pretty much worthless." Defeat was threaded through his voice.

Sarah felt a pity so keen it was physical. Her father had done so much for the community in the past years, treating his congregation with respect and kindness. He did not deserve this outright disobedience.

Anger welled up on the heels of her sympathy for Dat.

"That Melvin!" she said, her eyes blazing green.

Dat shook his head. "Sarah, you agree with him sometimes, don't you?"

She felt the heat rise in her cheeks.

"I do. Sometimes. But Dat, do we ever really know one hundred percent of the time how we really feel? Do you?"

"I think I do. I can't move past turning the other

cheek. Forgiveness. It's the whole, complete message of Christ. It is."

The last two words were spoken firmly, as if to reassure himself that this was really true.

Mam laid a gentle hand on Dat's arm, picked nervously at the button on his sleeve.

"It's hard, Davey. Truly hard to cling to a message of love when the fires have occurred, one after another. The verse in the Bible about forgiving your brother seventy times seven suddenly becomes almost impossible and hard to understand. How is it possible?"

"But it's necessary."

"Absolutely necessary."

Priscilla's eyes met Sarah's and flashed. "It's only going to get worse since Ashley's death."

"I don't know about that," Dat responded. "Remember the night of her viewing? I don't believe that Mike is a criminal. He was clearly devastated by her death. It was only when I spoke to him, touched him, that he began crying like that. My heart went out to him, as I would have felt toward anyone in a time of grief."

At school, the students spent recess sledding, playing snow games, building snow forts. Sarah joined her pupils during the lunch hour. The sun shone on most days, and icicles formed along the eaves, turning the brick schoolhouse into a picturesque building nestled in a grove of leaf-less, winter trees.

Wet stockings, boots, beanies, and gloves surrounded the propane gas heater that whooshed dutifully to life, true to the temperature on the thermostat, a modern-day wonder in Sarah's opinion.

She clipped the smaller children's gloves to the homemade PVC ring that hung from its hook above the heater, allowing the wet articles to dry quickly and efficiently.

Joe and Sam, and Rosanna and her cohorts still refused to go sledding or participate in any running games. They opted to slouch against the wall of the horse shed, although the snickering had all but disappeared. Occasionally, they would trip one of the smaller children or roll one in the snow, but Sarah never let it go, always following the misdemeanor with words of rebuke or having them spend time at their desks.

Her days went by fairly well, although she constantly had to balance discipline with common sense, patience, and encouragement, working to instill that elusive ingredient into the school—a willingness in most of the children to want to obey.

There were small victories, the smashed chocolate cupcake, Joe's outburst of confession that day, Rosanna asking to go to the Strasburg Railroad, the long awaited trip that had gone very well without the stubborn upper grades after Sarah had refused to give in.

Not having a Christmas program had made Sarah sad at first, but she knew she had saved herself hours of frustration by giving it up.

Now she was secretly contemplating a spring program around Easter, waiting to see how the pupils would respond to discipline by the end of February.

Always, just when she felt she was gaining ground, some of the older pupils would get out of their seats to walk around without raising their hands, just to see how far they could go without Sarah calling them back to their seats.

Or their refusal to work on their scores would start all over again, leaving her in a black mood with no hope of ever changing anything.

Catherine, a sixth-grader, raised her hand just before school let out one day when Sarah's head felt like an over-filled balloon, ready to pop.

"Yes, Catherine?"

"What are we doing for Valentine's Day?"

Sarah stopped and thought.

"I forgot about Valentine's Day."

"We want to do something, don't we?"

"Certainly. Of course. Any suggestions?"

"Stay home, like, all day," Rosanna said loudly, looking around for any signs of approval.

When none were forthcoming, Rosanna slid to the side of her seat and leaned over as if she was searching for something in her desk. When she sat up, her face was red, and she was blinking self-consciously.

Sarah was thrilled, glad to see her discomfiture. It was, by all appearances, a good thing when no one acknowledged her wise cracks.

"So, any suggestions?" she asked, pointedly ignoring Rosanna.

"Pizza?"

"Hot lunch?"

"Valentine's Day party?"

The suggestions came thick and fast, assaulting Sarah's headache, but welcome, nevertheless. It showed enthusiasm. Even if it was for something as frivolous as a party, it was still enthusiasm.

So Sarah traveled home, happily chatting with her driver, took two Tylenol as soon as she came within reach of Mam's medicine cabinet, and flopped on the recliner before she closed her eyes, breathing slowly, deeply, allowing the tension of the day to evaporate.

It was unusual to see Hannah striding up on the porch, her breath coming in short, hard puffs, her hair disheveled by the brisk wind, her coat pulled like sausage casing around her ample waist. As in former days, she didn't knock, just pushed the door open a sliver and yelled, "Hey!"

Quickly Mam turned the gas heat to low, checking the potatoes with a deft hand, and wiped her hands on her apron as she hurried to the door.

"Hannah."

"Malinda."

The words were unspoken questions.

Mam paused, then said, "*Ach* Hannah, you don't come anymore the way you used to. I miss that." The words were a healing balm, covering old wounds, cleansing them of harmful bacteria, the kind that fester and grow, turning a good, steadfast friend into a foe.

"Well, Malinda, a lot of water has gone under the bridge since Matthew dated Sarah. It's just awful, just awful now. His wife is dying. They say there is nothing more they can do for her. She has some sort of rare virus. They'll lose the baby, too. He is completely devastated. I want him to bring her home for better medical care, but he can't."

Sarah felt her mouth go dry. The room spun, tilted, and righted itself as the blood drained from her face and her hands began a ridiculous quaking completely on their own.

What if Matthew's wife passed away? That would leave him free to marry again, to return to the Amish, come back to the fold, resume life as . . . as what? As it was meant to be? Or as her heart still yearned? Who was to know?

Her thoughts out of control, Sarah gripped her hands to still their shaking. She squared her shoulders and bent her head, noticing the intricate pattern in the linoleum, the perfection of the copied pattern, so similar to real ceramic tile with grout between the squares.

Which was real? When was love genuine and when was it counterfeit, only a replica of the original product?

She heard Hannah's voice, recognized Mam's answers as Priscilla's large green eyes watched them, as keen as a cat. But it was all secondary, as if in another realm. Would Matthew return?

"If she passes, I guess Matthew could return. But I can't see him coming back to us, to be Amish again. He knows so much more about the Bible now. He knows more than our ministers, I'm sure. He can talk about the Bible for hours. He's so interesting.

"Elam is afraid he'll mislead me yet, but I told him, *ach*, what would an old biddy like me want in another church? I'm about as Amish as they come. You know, Malinda. But Matthew is just something else, so he is."

Mam answered Hannah with only a polite nod of her head, her smile becoming fixed, lopsided, as she struggled to keep a hurtful opinion to herself, victory showing as her smile righted itself.

Mam knew Matthew was firmly glued to the pedestal of his mother's pride, slowly turning from flesh and blood into various metals, hardening into an idol she would worship her whole life long. No mere words of advice would ever change that.

She listened attentively to Hannah's praise of her son, and when the potatoes boiled over, she was genuinely relieved to have Hannah glance sharply at the clock and say she must go as she had cornbread in the oven—nothing better in the dead of winter. She pulled her black men's gloves over her chapped hands and took her leave.

With a sigh of resignation, Mam sat down, shaking her head, as if a great weariness had taken up residence in her body.

"Sarah, what if Matthew returns?"

A blinding, fluorescent joy shone from Sarah's eyes, and Mam shivered in the face of it. "Do you think he will?" Sarah whispered, the hope still brilliant after the initial flash of rapture.

Mam shrugged, then got up from her chair, whipped the pot off the stove, and began beating the mealy potatoes with a vengeance, the potato masher clacking against the steel sides of the pot in harried circles. Mam's nerves supplied ample muscle power as she resisted the very thought of that cunning wolf showing up again on the front porch, opening up all the fears and sleepless nights yet again, just when they thought God had taken mercy and answered all their prayers.

Well, if she had anything to do with it, he wouldn't. Her eyes flashed, and her cheeks took on a color of their own as her arms pumped away at the potatoes. Turning, she snapped, "*Grick da dish ready* (Set the table)."

Sarah cast a frightened look at her mother.

"What in the world, Mam?" she breathed.

Mam's composure slid away as her shoulders slumped, tears leaking from beneath her sturdy glasses as she told Sarah in an unsteady voice of the fear in her heart.

"Matthew has such a strong hold on you, Sarah. I'm so afraid if he does come back, he'll want you, but not his heritage, not his Amish background, and he'll persuade you again."

That was how Dat found them—Sarah shocked, her face suppressing untold emotion, his dear, faithful wife in tears, which were not often seen, especially not without good reason.

Quickly, they tried to remedy the situation, and as quickly, Dat insisted on knowing what Hannah had wanted. When they had told him, he sat down heavily, the breath leaving his body, a furrow appearing on his brow as the only sign of his anxiety.

"Well," he mused, before his mouth widened into a grin. "This reminds me of a story in one of the old reading books—the one about the bride-to-be who went to the springhouse and found a hatchet imbedded in the ceiling. Till it was all over, the what-ifs, traveling from person to person, had resulted in numerous calamities and suspicions forming in the minds of the villagers. Don't you think that might be the case here?"

Mam nodded, shamefaced, but to save her pride, she insisted it was only she and Sarah, not a bunch of others, who had been speculating.

"I heard it!" Levi bellowed from his chair by the window, where he was identifying birds with his binoculars, the bird feeder stationed just outside for his enjoyment.

"These women act like the birds. Such a *ga-pick* (picking) and *ga-fuss* (fuss) they have!" Levi said, shaking his head.

In spite of vowing to keep everything in perspective, Sarah had a difficult time keeping her thoughts and emotions from spiraling to untold heights.

The only thing that remained to keep her anchored was Lee, the agreement they had to wait until the proper time to begin dating, and the love she felt for him. Or was that only desperation to relieve the hurt from Matthew?

Clearly, if Matthew returned, she would find herself in the most difficult situation of her life, a crossroad piled with insurmountable obstacles, all labeled with puzzling, life-altering choices yet again.

Priscilla entered her room late that evening, a

towel twisted around her hair like a turban, her warm fleece robe tied around her waist, her feet cozy in woolen slippers.

"It's so cold in here, you can see your breath," she complained as she plopped on Sarah's bed, bouncing her and causing her pen to make a dash across her diary.

Leaning over, Priscilla raised an eyebrow.

"I'll give you five whole dollars to read your diary."

"More like five hundred, and then it's not guaranteed," Sarah muttered.

"You know, hopefully, you're just crazy." This sentence was spoken flatly, dryly, without emotion.

Sarah turned sharply, her eyes wide, as she found Priscilla's, the question hovering between them.

Not waiting for a response, Priscilla plunged ahead.

"What is it going to take? What will have to happen before you are finally shaken to your senses? Sarah, I can see it in your face. Matthew, or the thought of him, is still as precious to you as he's ever been. What about Lee? What about the sweetest, best-looking guy who would do anything he could for you? Are you just going to throw him away like a piece of trash, disposed of—CLUNK!—in the waste can? And he's already given up Rose for you."

"We're not dating."

"But you agreed to start as soon as the time is proper."

"Well."

"Well, what?"

Sarah shrugged her shoulders. "She didn't die."

"But she will."

"That doesn't say he'll return. Perhaps he loves Haiti and will stay there."

"And if he does, and if he calls for you, you'd swim the Atlantic for him."

When Sarah laughed, Priscilla unwrapped the towel from her head and shook out her long, beautiful, blonde-brown hair. She took a large, black brush to it, wincing as she did so.

"You disgust me." The words were harsh, accusing, hard stones of misunderstanding.

"Don't judge me, Priscilla. You've never been in love."

"You're not in love with Matthew."

Sarah laid her diary carefully on the nightstand and turned to look at her sister, holding her gaze without guilt.

"Sometimes, I'm not sure I know what love is," she said finally, quietly.

Priscilla nodded, then whispered, "I do."

Sarah raised her eyebrows. "At sixteen?"

"When I was still fifteen."

"Omar?"

Priscilla nodded.

"Love is not hard to figure out, for me."

Sarah nodded.

Outside, snow pinged against the window as another snowstorm approached the county. The cold seeped between every crevice around the baseboards, between the window frames, sending a shiver up Sarah's back.

Was it the cold, or was it a premonition? Some strange dread of the future, an intuition that lurked around the perimeters of the farmhouse, finding its way into her soul?

Chapter 23

When Hephzibah died, the unborn child going with her, Hannah was one of the first people to know, and she lost no time in coming to tell the Beilers, her tears already streaming down her face, the gulping sobs coming without restraint as she reached the door. Mam ushered Hannah inside, putting a hand on her heaving back and a box of Kleenex at her disposal as she offered a gentle word of sympathy, her fear and foreboding tucked deep inside, where Hannah had no access to it.

Hannah's description of the situation took Mam to the primitive Haitian hospital, the heat, the rejoicing in the Lord as she passed into His arms, bringing tears to even Mam's eyes. Without a doubt, this woman had been a special person. The light of her Master's love had enabled her to serve selflessly, ministering to the poor and the needy, with a heart that was joyous in doing so, and Matthew's life had been blessed by her.

On and on, Hannah sobbed, bringing wadded tissues to her bulbous, red nose as more tears streamed from her squinted eyes. Over and over, she removed her glasses, wiped them, and replaced them, before a fresh onslaught of grief overtook her.

Mam realized, wisely, of course, that this was no ordinary grief. After all, Hannah hadn't even known the girl, this woman named Hephzibah. She put two and two together and decided Hannah was crying all the tears for another reason. Maybe these were the tears she had never cried for Matthew's leaving.

Malinda remained kind and sympathetic. She put on the coffee pot and brought out a tray of pumpkin cookies frosted with caramel icing and another plate of good, white sharp cheese. She added some Tom Sturgis mini-pretzels to the spread and a roll of Ritz crackers and some grapes they'd had on special down at Kauffman's Fruit Market.

Hannah grasped the hot mug of steaming coffee, laced it liberally with cream and sugar, and began dunking pumpkin cookies into the thick liquid as fast as she could break them in half and retrieve them with her spoon.

"*Ach* my, Malinda. *Ach* my. How can I doubt your friendship? You always know what I need, don't you?"

"You mean pumpkin cookies?" Mam asked sagely, and they threw back their heads and laughed until Mam wiped her eyes and straightened her covering.

She always did that when she felt guilty for laughing too much, as if the adjustment of her large, white covering could pay penance for her lack of holiness. Hannah knew this gesture well and had often teased her about it. So now, when Mam reached for her covering strings and gave them a good yank, Hannah shook her finger under Mam's nose and said ministers' wives were allowed a good laugh, now, weren't they?

Their friendship once again restored, Hannah poured out her longing to have Matthew return to the fold. Wouldn't it be wonderful if he and Sarah could get together again, simply resume the friendship where it had left off? she asked.

Mam remained level-headed, agreeing, but clearly stating her fears. She told Hannah that Sarah had promised to serve Christ among her people, and she would be heartbroken if she broke her vows.

Oh, Hannah understood this. Indeed, she did. Halfway through the pack of Ritz crackers, the block of cheddar cheese dwindling rapidly, her stomach full and her spirits mellow, Hannah lowered her head, leaned forward, and confided in Mam. She admitted that Matthew made her so angry—just sometimes, not always—but he could come back and live among his lifelong friends and family and behave himself. Even if he was well-versed in the Bible, he better watch out or he'd be as bad as the person in the Bible who lifted his face and thanked God that he wasn't as bad as other people, and she meant it.

With that, she nodded, clamped her mouth

shut, and said there was a very real possibility of Matthew being too big in his own eyes.

When Hannah polished off the last of the grapes and headed home, Mam's spirits were strangely uplifted, and she sang quietly to herself as she worked on her quilt, the light of the sun on the snow more than sufficient, her needle quickly rising and falling in and out of the soft fabric.

Who was she to map out God's ways? One simply never knew what He had planned, or what He was thinking, exactly the way Davey said.

At school the next day, Sarah sat down hard, the unforgiving wooden seat of the toboggan rising up to meet her backside before she was quite ready. "Ow!" she yelled, and the third-grade girls howled with laughter.

"Ready?" Martha Ann called.

"Ready."

Sarah gripped the narrow shoulders ahead of her and hung on, yelling with the rest of them as they careened down the icy trail that had been there for too long, the noontime sun turning the snow into a dangerous, slick path of pure, unadulterated terror.

The speed with which they shot down the hill was absolutely unsafe, but it was the thrill of each school day, the pupils arriving breathless, their entrance into the schoolhouse accompanied by their answers of, "Morning!" when Sarah greeted them. It was rarely "Good morning," just

"Morning," but it was sufficient as long as her eyes were met, her presence acknowledged without hostility.

Constantly, Sarah reminded herself to be content with baby steps, little steps of progress, small differences in the children's attitudes, small changes, but changes, nevertheless.

In school, the turmoil in her heart was stilled, the challenges of the day occupying her mind as she focused her attention on the children and the work, constantly striving to be the best teacher she could be.

Dealing with the students in the one-room school, with all eight grades in such close quarters, was as challenging and nerve-wracking as it had always been. But, slowly, there were differences.

Geography lessons turned into discussions, in spite of the eighth-grade boys initially refusing to co-operate and instead tapping their fingers, fiddling with their pens, and making annoying sounds, which were all duly ignored. When Alaska was chosen as a project, with its vast expanses of unspoiled acreage, pipelines, and animals of the tundra, the lure of the exploration proved to be too much, and they were slowly drawn into the discussion. Their drawings and maps were truly phenomenal.

Joe proved to be an outstanding artist, although not without constant praise, words of admiration spoken whenever an appropriate moment pre-sented itself.

The parents who occasionally took time off from their hectic schedules to visit the school were in awe of the artwork, the projects done so precisely, the pencil drawings and intricate designs done so well. And by their own children! My, oh, they said later. I didn't know Henry could draw like that.

Praise was hard to come by for the teacher, however. No one mentioned the artwork to Sarah, they just walked along looking at the drawings on the walls, their arms crossed around their waists. They sniffed, spoke in low tones to one another, and then changed the subject before approaching her.

That was alright. Sarah understood the need to withhold praise in order to keep someone humble, on the straight and narrow. She really did.

But a wee bit of affirmation would be nice, an unexpected ray of warmth on a chilly day.

When Lee's sister, Anna, showed up that week, she was so effusive with her loud words of admiration, it was as if the blazing summer sun itself had entered the classroom. Sarah's face grew flushed with heat as Anna repeatedly threw up her hands, squealing in amazement, turning to Sarah repeatedly, asking how she could get these children to draw like this.

Anna's youngest boy was entirely engrossed in cleaning out Rosanna's desk, books thumping on the seat, pens and pencils rolling across the floor, but it all went completely unnoticed by his awe-struck mother.

Sarah winced when Rosanna spied the boy and pulled him away with an impolite jerk of his arm. This was followed by an indignant howling that brought his mother scurrying, flustered and apologetic. Her apologies were received coolly by the queenly Rosanna. Sarah felt like slapping her, but, of course, she didn't.

Anna settled herself on a folding chair, her son perched on her short legs, her hands holding him closer than was necessary, her eyes alert, eager, radiating good humor.

Sarah conducted classes as usual, and the children sang three of their favorite songs for Anna. At recess, Anna was close to tears, praising Sarah's teaching ability with a deluge of admiration, holding nothing back. Leaning close, she nudged her rounded shoulder into Sarah's and whispered, "I heard! Oh, I'm excited. I can hardly believe you are actually going to date. It's an answer to prayer!"

Sarah smiled, but her smile was followed immediately by a wave of horrible guilt, knowing that Matthew's potential homecoming had largely occupied her thoughts, enveloping her days with anticipation.

Perceptive, smart, Anna watched, her eyes like a bird.

"What? Isn't everything okay?"

"Yes. Oh, of course."

"Good. Sarah, for real, you have no idea how thrilled I am, how thrilled we all are."

A smile that felt untrue, somehow, was all she could manage, but it would have to suffice. At least she hadn't spoken words that were not quite truthful. She hadn't said anything at all.

Sarah completely underestimated Anna's perceptive abilities. She was taken by surprise, to state it mildly, when Lee knocked on the door of the schoolhouse late that afternoon.

Her heartbeats multiplied, skidded, steadied, but her face still showed alarm when she opened the door.

Ever since the night that car had followed the girl with Sarah watching the fight, hearing the heated exchange of words, she did not feel completely safe at school after the children went home.

She was jumpy, lifting her head at any unusual sounds, going to the window to be positive nothing out of the ordinary was going on, telling herself it was foolish. Was it, really?

"Oh Lee."

"I didn't mean to frighten you."

"I'm . . . No, you didn't."

"May I come in?"

"Of course."

Sarah stepped back.

She forgot how tall he was. She forgot how blond his hair was, how tanned his skin, how clean-cut his profile. His eyes were so blue they were ridiculous.

Before she could say anything, he found her gaze and held it with his own.

"Sarah, I came to ask if it's true. Is Matthew returning?"

Sarah lowered her head. Her eyes noticed the dust on the high gloss paint in the intricate pattern along the side of a wooden desk. She thought she should clean it.

"Yes. He . . . Well, his wife, um, died. I don't know if it's really true that he's coming back here. To stay. Hannah, his mother, thinks he might."

A silence hung over the empty classroom like a suffocating blanket, cutting off Sarah's air supply.

Finally, Lee spoke.

"And when he does return, will things change between us, Sarah?"

Sarah answered too quickly.

"No. Oh no."

Still her head was bent, her eyes hidden from his, the top of her head the only way he could gauge her emotions, which was a lot like looking at a broken thermometer.

"Sarah, look at me."

It was impossible, and she knew it.

When he said nothing, the suffocation from the unbearable blanket of silence increased, and her desperation mounted until she knew there was no way out. The despair folded her into a child's seat. Her arms rested on the desktop, her head on them, as shameful, terrible sobs shook her body. The sounds were muffled, polite, even, but they put a dagger through Lee's heart.

When he didn't place a hand on her shoulder, when he didn't crouch by her side to murmur condolences, the sobs became shorter, then weaker, then stopped entirely, before Sarah lifted her head long enough to look, search, bewildered. Had he gone?

He remained in the classroom, standing stiffly by the window, gazing through it at the late winter light, his hands clenched behind his back.

When he stayed silent, Sarah cleared her throat and said very softly and quietly, "Lee."

He turned at the sound of his name, his expression unfathomable.

"I . . . I . . ." Completely at a loss for words, her voice faded into silence.

When he spoke, his words were restrained, his tone soft.

"I thought Matthew's leaving was a clear, bold answer for me, straight from God. Now I'm not so sure. I guess perhaps if someone loves the way you loved him, there is never a time when that goes away completely. In other words, even if you choose to date me, I will not have you fully. A part of you will always love Matthew."

Sarah's denial began with a slow back and forth movement of her head, her eyes still lowered to the desktop.

Lee sighed, walked over, and stood so close to her, she could feel his presence. She could detect the odor of lumber and steel nails and strong hand soap, even the leather from his work boots.

"So Sara, I think the right thing to do in this situation would be to set you free. How does that old saying go? If you're not sure something—someone, in this case—is yours, set it free, and if it doesn't return, it never was yours to begin with. How does the rest of it go?"

She didn't think before she spoke. She just lifted her head and looked into his blue eyes and said, "If it comes back to you, it always was yours. Or something like that."

"Yeah. Something like that."

He walked away, toward the door, and Sarah opened her mouth to protest, then closed it again when he stopped.

"You're free to go then. Just forget about the fact that we had planned to begin dating, alright? When Matthew comes back, you'll be completely unfettered. You alone must choose."

Suddenly, the significance of that tremendous

impasse loomed before her, a fire-breathing dragon of impossibility, hopelessness, coupled with the knowledge that she was clueless, holding a key to her future that was securely locked, and what if the key was all wrong? What if it didn't fit?

When Lee buttoned his work coat and placed a hand on the doorknob, her eyes took in the shape of his shoulders, the tilt of his head, as if she could store away the memory, a keepsake, something to hide in the deepest recesses of her heart. She had loved him, hadn't she?

Guilt made her cry out. "Lee?"

He froze.

"Don't. I mean . . . I . . ."

Without another word, he let himself out, closed the door softly behind him, and did not look back.

Sarah repressed the urge to run after him. What would she say if she did catch up to him? How could she begin to tell him she did love him, but she loved Matthew more? Matthew Stoltzfus's whole life was intertwined with her own. He was the missing piece of her, the way he filled up every loneliness, every moment of longing. She could not make Lee understand this.

Sighing, she stood and watched the road for a glimpse of Lee. When there was none, she simply didn't know what to do, so she sat back down, staring straight ahead, seeing nothing, until her driver arrived and pressed her palm against the steering wheel, emitting two loud honks. The sound brought Sarah quickly back to reality.

When Mam looked into Sarah's eyes and saw all the dark misery threatening to dissolve into tears, she wisely did not press the issue. She just turned away and said nothing.

Sarah mumbled something about not feeling well and went upstairs slowly. She flopped on her bed and wished there was someone she could confide in. Someone who understood.

Mam walked around with her mouth pressed in a firm line of denial, boding no good. Priscilla told Sarah unabashedly and repeatedly that she was crazy. And Dat was too involved in the meetings and goings on about the barn fires.

That was another thing. Sarah was completely fed up with all this talk of a dangerous person on the loose and people speculating about what to do. Men from the community just kept showing up in the kitchen, placing blame on Dat, on members of the community who clung to the old ways. What exactly was he supposed to do?

She felt a great pity for her father. He had aged many years in a short time. Over the winter, his cough would not go away, no matter how many different home remedies Mam spread on his chest or how many bottles of tincture or piles of herbal pills he swallowed. The cough wracked his body relentlessly.

He kept at his work, doing chores, hauling manure, oiling machinery, doing the things every farmer did during the winter, but he never quite got ahold of the rasping cough.

Even when he preached in church, he coughed, and it seemed to embarrass him. Perhaps he thought it was a sign of weakness and was ashamed.

Whatever the reason, Mam talked in hushed tones to Sarah, saying she knew why Davey coughed like that. He was under too much stress. There had never been a time like this for as long as she could remember. The way brother turned against brother, valuing his own opinion above everyone else's—it was turning into a battle of senseless speculation, and not one of them really knew anything.

Mam said that was the whole trouble with the world, the way no one could stay silent in the face of unexplainable situations. They all tried to figure it out, when in actuality, they were all helpless. Even the world, the *Englishe leid* (English people), did not know what to make of the repeated disasters.

As Sarah sat on her bed, staring into space, she heard Dat's cough in the kitchen below, then a murmur of voices, and she knew her mother would be clucking, fussing, hurrying to heat water for a bracing cup of peppermint tea.

She tried to imagine her life with Matthew as

her husband, comfortably living in a house together, talking of ordinary, mundane subjects, the way they always had in school, at family get-togethers, their whole lives. They had been so close. Dating, seeing him every weekend, and often on week nights, living her dream.

He would have changed a bit, of course, which was only to be expected, living a different life-style. He had probably adopted different mannerisms, the way his people talked openly of their faith, freely expressing their beliefs, whereas Amish people preferred their worship in silence, their views often hidden.

But Matthew would return. He would come back to the Amish way. Sarah felt sure. If she couldn't believe in that, she didn't know Matthew very well, and she did. She knew him better than he knew himself, she told herself.

Sighing now, she leaned back on her pillow and let the anticipation of the future envelop her, seal her safely inside, secure, the doubts and fears kept outside. For now.

The candle on her nightstand flickered. Headlights beamed across the room as a car approached on the road, arcing across the ceiling as it turned.

Downstairs, Dat coughed again. A cow bawled from the barnyard, where the black and white Holsteins frolicked about, getting a bit of exercise in the still, cold air, their breath a whoosh of steam expelled from their warm nostrils.

Levi sat by the window, dressed in clean flannel pajamas, his hair wet, combed properly, his teeth brushed furiously. A jar of Vicks stood on the nightstand at his bedside for the long night ahead of him, when his sinuses would close, causing him grief and long hours of sniffling and honking dryly into piles of Kleenexes.

His eyes were tired, drooping at the corners, but it was only a quarter past seven on a cold winter evening. He'd finished his jigsaw puzzle. That one had been easy, and he didn't feel like playing a game with Suzie, so he thought perhaps he'd just go to bed.

He grasped the arms of his chair and started to get up, when he thought he saw someone, something.

He reached for his glasses, polished them on the tail of his flannel pajama shirt, and plunked them on his nose, squinting.

Slowly, he reached out and pushed a pot of geraniums aside, brushed off a brown leaf that fluttered to his lap. Aha. Some chap was walking up to the fence.

Tilting his head, he peered out the window between the leafy geraniums and watched. There. This chap sure was bold. Not ashamed of anything. What in the world? Was he just going to stand there and look at the cows?

It was too dark to see exactly what was going on, but Levi saw the animals stop and watch, their ears held forward, their wet noses held high, sniffing.

Levi's eyes slide toward the kitchen, where Dat sat hunched over his tattered German Bible, a cup of tea at his elbow. Well, he didn't need to be bothered. This was Levi's sighting. All his own. And so he sat, a still form peering between the geraniums.

Chapter 24

For several long moments, Levi sat as still as the most experienced hunter stalking his prey, completely engrossed by the spectacle before him. As he tilted his head one way, then another, he figured he'd have to get rid of some of these geraniums if he wanted to know what was going on.

He turned his head, saw Dat was alone as he read, no Mam or Priscilla. Suzie sprawled in front of the black coal stove, so he reached out with calculated precision and set two coffee cans of geraniums on the sewing machine to his left, soundlessly.

There, that was much better. He had a full view of the chap by the barnyard. With snow on the ground and the waning, half-moon's light providing illumination, Levi could plainly outline the man's dark form, standing stock still, looking up as if he was checking out the barn roof.

He figured the man was doing no harm. He certainly was not driving a small white car, so it couldn't be the man that had "struck the barn on," as the Amish often said. Likely this man was out for a walk, maybe taking pictures of the cows in the moonlight.

The man turned his head and looked at the

house. Levi's breath came quick and fast. He could not tell who it was. Better tell Dat.

He had just opened his mouth to call Dat when a pair of headlights came slowly in the drive beneath the maple trees, their trunks inky black, lined up like sturdy sentries but allowing the car access to Davey Beiler's farm, the tires crunching quietly on the frozen snow.

Good, Levi thought. Now he'll be afraid and run across the field. Instead, the man turned, waiting beside the driveway, as the vehicle pulled up slowly. He looked toward the house.

Levi did his best, peering intently through the lenses of his thick spectacles, his breathing accelerated now. He looked like that other man. Not the man from California, the other one. That night they'd gone to Ashley's viewing, there where she had lain so dead in that great big fancy casket, with all those flowers.

Levi watched as the man opened the passenger door and lowered himself into the car. It moved off slowly, the crunching of the snow audible to Levi's ears.

Well, they were taking their time, he reasoned, so they weren't going to stick the barn on. And the car was not white. Levi couldn't really tell what color it was in the darkness.

When it turned around out by the implement shed, Dat lifted his head, coughed, and looked toward the window above the kitchen sink, as if he thought he heard something, but then he lowered his head and resumed reading.

Levi kept his eyes on the car as it drove slowly out the drive, turned left, and continued down the rural road.

Quietly, Levi replaced the geraniums, picked up the withered brown geranium leaf, and placed it carefully in the trash before shuffling out to the kitchen with his empty water pitcher.

David Beiler looked up as Levi approached, smiling at him absentmindedly, his thoughts on the verses he had read.

"*Bet zeit* (Bed time)?"

Levi nodded.

"*Brauch vassa* (Need water)?"

Levi nodded again.

"Did you take your garlic and echinacea?"

"No."

"You better would."

"Garlic stinks."

Dat chuckled.

"It does you a lot of good in winter, Levi."

"It still stinks."

Muttering to himself about his plans to hide the plastic bottle of garlic capsules, Levi took a tray of ice from the freezer, twisted it, and shook the cubes into the small plastic water pitcher. Then he opened the tap and filled the tray with water.

Mam emerged from the steaming bathroom, her face rosy from the heat, her navy blue bathrobe belted securely, a white *dichly* (head scarf) knotted around her head.

"Ready for bed, Levi?"

"*Ya. Vett an snack ovva* (I would like a snack)."

Mam's eyes twinkled. "We have good oranges."

Levi gave her a baleful look and shook his head from side to side.

"*Vill* (I want) shoofly."

"No, Levi, shoofly pie tomorrow morning, for breakfast. Oranges tonight."

"I don't like oranges. They're sour. Hard to peel."

"How about an apple?"

"Apple pie?"

His face was so hopeful, his expression so woebegone, Mam's heart melted like soft butter, and she went to the pantry, got down the freshly-baked apple pie, and cut a sizable wedge for her perpetually hungry son.

Wreathed in smiles, Levi thanked her profusely, grabbed a fork, and enjoyed every bite to the fullest, then sat back and wiped his face very carefully.

"*Denke*, Mam," he said.

"You're welcome, Levi."

He thought he should tell Dat, the apple pie suddenly escalating his goodwill toward his beloved parents.

"Davey."

"Hmm?"

"There was a man standing by the barnyard tonight."

"Aw, come on, Levi."

"There was. I saw him."

Dat shook his head, "No, Levi."

Levi nodded. "A car came and picked him up. He looked at the house, then he looked at the barn."

"After he was in the car?"

Dat was fully alert now. He picked up his German Bible and took it to his desk with the rest of his German books, coughing again.

"No," Levi said slowly.

"Before?"

"*Ya.*"

"Why didn't you tell me? Why didn't I see or hear anything?"

"You were reading."

"Hmm."

Mam watched Levi's face intently.

Suzie rolled over, sat up, yawned, and said Levi told *schnitzas* (fibs) if he felt like it. She hadn't heard anything.

Levi said the man did not want to stick their barn on, and he was not driving a white car. He looked like that other man.

"What other man?" Dat asked sharply.

"Not the one from California. The other one."

"See? He's just making this all up," Suzie yelped.

"Hush, Suzie."

"Which man from California? When? Where?" Mam asked, bewildered now, hurriedly placing the apple pie back into the Ziploc bag, keeping order in her kitchen even if other events in the world appeared unsolvable and disorderly.

"That dead girl. When we ate at McDonald's."

Dat looked hard at Levi, glanced hurriedly at Mam, went to the window, and looked toward the barn for a very long time without saying anything.

When he turned, his face appeared pale, and he spoke tersely, "Time for bed, Suzie, Levi. Where's Sarah and Priscilla?"

Going to the stairs, Mam called the girls, who appeared obediently soon afterward. They sat on the couch quietly as Dat reached for the German prayer book, nodding his head.

In perfect unison, they turned, kneeling as Dat read the old prayer, the evening prayer from the same *Gebet Buch* (prayer book) his father had read at the close of each day, his voice rising and falling as he pronounced the words, so dear to his heart, so comforting to Mam's.

As the rest of the family slept through the cold wintry night, David Beiler could find no rest. He paced the kitchen floor, turning repeatedly to stare out the window, the one above the sink, gripping the countertop unknowingly, his shoulders tense, his mind tumbling with unanswered questions.

Was he putting the community at risk with his refusal to talk to the media and allow better coverage? What if Levi really had seen a suspicious person on their property that night?

Over and over, his anxiety led him to the window, his mind reliving the horror of his own barn fire, the terror, and poor Priscilla, losing Dutch, now not even caring whether she had a horse or not.

Cruel. It was all so cruel. And Priscilla had been just one victim of the arsonist. Still, it didn't hurt for children to give up their own wills. That was old knowledge passed down for generations, and it never failed to amaze him. Discipline served as a boundary of love, producing caring adults for society, over and over.

As long as there was love to balance the discipline, it worked. Traditions were dependable, safe. But always? Even now?

In the face of this fiery adversary, who was he to say? Old John Zook exhorted them over and over to forgive. God had allowed the barn fires to take place, so he would provide a way, if they stuck to their beliefs.

Christ had suffered so much more, and He without sin, and here they were, ordinary sinners, beset with flesh and blood, and they couldn't forgive without rising up in anger, insisting on vengeance.

In his heart and soul, he knew it was wrong.

Upstairs, lying beneath the heavy comforters, Sarah struggled with her own private battle, without confiding her fears to Priscilla, who had flounced out of her room after asking what was up with her sour mood and telling her she was crazy yet again.

Jagged edges of fear taunted her, restricted her from looking forward with a clear gaze, unable to decipher an uncertain future.

Torn between a great love for Matthew and an unexplainable misery about Lee, sleep eluded her completely. She lay on her back, staring wide-eyed at the dark ceiling as her thoughts chased away every last shred of peace.

What if Matthew did return and refused to acknowledge her? What if he denied the fact that he had ever cared for her?

He wouldn't. Would he?

Hannah told Mam he'd likely be home in the spring. Six more weeks! Not even two months.

Would he appear different? Older? Wiser? Ready to admit his mistakes? Would he grieve for his poor, deceased wife?

Suddenly, she remembered the Widow Lydia's words, a precise pinprick inserted into the magical bubble she had built around herself. She had bowed her head, Lydia had, in that way of hers when she was contemplating a weighty matter, as Sarah's words had rained around her, happy little dashes of anticipation, exclamation marks of joy punctuating every sentence. Matthew was coming home! That seemingly was all Sarah knew or cared about.

When Lydia finally spoke, she simply said, "Hopefully, Lee is an extraordinary man and understands this."

Sarah's face had flamed. Reaching up now, she touched the tips of her ears, remembering the searing heat of her discomfort. There had been no words to justify her anticipation of Matthew's return.

Melvin, of course, had his usual lack of tact, bluntly telling Sarah that he wanted nothing to do with Matthew, and he certainly hoped she felt the same. He said that if she didn't watch it, she'd be left high and dry, turning 40 and not being able to figure out what had happened.

"I can't think of it, but there's a word for girls like you," he finished.

Sarah looked up sharply.

"Fickle?" Lydia asked shyly.

"That's it. You can't be trusted, Sarah."

But what did Melvin know? He was one to talk. Going on 30 years old, unmarried, and now, by all appearances, completely enamored by Lydia. If he was a bit off the beaten track, why couldn't she be?

Besides, he didn't know if Matthew would return to the fold or not. Opinionated trouble-maker.

Flipping onto her side, she peered at the numbers on her battery-operated alarm clock. 12:42.

Sighing, she resigned herself to a day of tired irritation at school. She began breathing slowly in and out, relaxing her shoulders, cleansing her mind of troubling thoughts about Matthew.

Just before she fell asleep, she thought she heard Lee say, "See you, Sarah."

Startled, she jerked awake, her heart hammering. Was she really losing her mind? When all else failed, she prayed fervently, asking God to direct her path and help her lean not on her own understanding.

She prayed for guidance, prayed for her pupils at school, for her ability to teach them with wisdom and understanding. Peace enveloped her, covering her softly as she fell into a deep sleep.

In the morning, a soft temperate wind moaned around the house, whistling along the eaves, gently tossing the small branches of the bare maple trees in an undulating dance of promised spring.

Water dripped off the roof's edges, and icicles broke loose and crashed to the ground, burying themselves in the dirty snow. Everything melted together in a sluice of water, creating a fine, sticky mud anywhere there was bare earth.

Brown grasses huddled in sodden little heaps as the white snow around them dissolved into frigid water, slowly moving in little rivulets to join the large stream of water gushing from the downspout on the implement shed's corner.

Sarah jutted her chin comfortably into the confines of her dark head scarf, tying it securely as she walked to the barn to join Dat for the morning milking.

Ah. She lifted her face, felt the soft wind, heard the melting snow running along the eaves, and thought how lovely, how absolutely deliciously lovely, it was that spring was on its way.

Her eyes were dry and itchy, so Dat found her standing in the milk house, rubbing them with two fingers, blinking, then yawning.

"Didn't sleep?" he asked as his morning greeting. Just then a yawn caught him, his mouth gaping open tremendously, followed by a shaking of his head, a bleary look, and a grin of humility.

"No."

"Me either. What was bothering you?"

"Not much."

Time to start milking, Sarah thought wryly. Subject closed.

They worked together in silence, the cows munching their silage, the milking machines chugging with a homey sound, just the way they always had.

Sarah fed the calves, her gloved hands getting wet as she laughed ruefully at the strength of the day-old calf's jaws as the little animal bucked and fought, ravenously hungry, willing the calf starter to come faster.

Stars twinkled overhead, and a thin streak of dawn appeared in the east, the promise of a beautiful day.

She rubbed the stubby black head of the last calf, withdrew the plastic bottle from its greedy little mouth, leaving it standing bewildered, wondering why the milk was already gone.

She washed the milkers and scrubbed the gleaming sinks, finishing just as Dat entered, hanging up an extra lantern for her.

"So, you didn't say why you weren't able to sleep," he said, leaning against the bulk tank, eyeing her quizzically from beneath his tattered chore hat.

Sarah lifted her hands from the hot water and wiped them on her bib apron before turning to face her father, shrugging her shoulders helplessly.

"Oh, just, you know, stuff."

"Same here. Stuff."

She caught the twinkle in her father's eye, and they laughed softly together.

Dat said, "Matthew?"

Sarah nodded, shamefaced.

Dat thought of all the things he would like to tell her to keep her from having to learn the hard way. Oh, how he longed for her to see!

"Just remember to pray each day, Sarah. Read your Bible, for in those inspired words lie wisdom. Remember that God comes first, and then earthly joys—guys, you call them, romance, whatever."

Did his face take on a reddish glow?

Sarah smiled genuinely at her father, encouraging him, knowing he was awkward when discussing matters of the heart.

"I'll be alright, Dat. I really will. Matthew will return in about six weeks, and then I guess I'll figure it out, don't you think?"

Dat nodded, placed a hand on her shoulder. "I think you will."

They walked together, splashed through the rivulets of icy water, the softness of the dawn caressing their faces, waiting for the first rays of the morning sun. They knew that each day is new, God's mercies as fresh as the dawn, renewed all over again as if each day was the very first day of creation.

Whatever lay before both of them—decisions, crossroads, events, mountains that seemed immovable—they knew their faith would somehow sustain them.

Sarah bent swiftly, picked up a handful of snow, and squeezed it into a snowball of sorts. She drew her arm back, took aim, and fired a hefty shot at her father's broad, denim overcoat.

The resounding splat brought a surprised yell

from her father, followed by a grand swoop, and a pile of snow landing directly in her face.

Spluttering, laughing, Sarah bent for another solid handful but was stopped by the sound of a window opening. Levi appeared, clearly delighted by Davey's antics, and he was yelling at the top of his lungs.

"*Grick an, Sare* (Get him, Sarah)!"

Dat cried, "Uncle! Uncle!" and Levi bounced up and down with genuine glee.

Laughing, they entered the *kesslehaus*, where the smell of frying mush greeted them, warm and crisp and cozy, the smell of home, tradition, and genuine happiness.

The Glossary

Ausre gmayna—A Pennsylvania Dutch dialect phrase meaning "other churches."

Bann—A Pennsylvania Dutch dialect word meaning "excommunication" or "ban." The Amish practice this when they believe someone in their community has violated the Amish understanding of faith and the practices that flow from it.

Bet zeit—A Pennsylvania Dutch dialect phrase meaning "bed time."

Dat—A Pennsylvania Dutch dialect word used to address or refer to one's father.

Dichly—A Pennsylvania Dutch dialect word meaning "head scarf."

Die alte—A Pennsylvania Dutch dialect phrase meaning "forefathers."

Doch veggley—A Pennsylvania Dutch dialect phrase meaning "carriage."

Englishe leid—A Pennsylvania Dutch dialect phrase meaning "English people."

Ess mocht sich—A Pennsylvania Dutch dialect phrase meaning "it will be alright."

Fa-fearish—A Pennsylvania Dutch dialect word meaning "misleading."

Fa-schput—A Pennsylvania Dutch dialect word meaning "mocking."

Fer-sark—A Pennsylvania Dutch dialect word meaning "to take care of."

Frade—A Pennsylvania Dutch dialect word meaning "joy."

Ga-fuss—A Pennsylvania Dutch dialect word meaning "fuss."

Ga-pick—A Pennsylvania Dutch dialect word meaning "picking," as in picking on someone.

Ga-mach—A Pennsylvania Dutch dialect word meaning "to do."

Gebet Buch—A Pennsylvania Dutch dialect phrase meaning "prayer book."

Geduldich—A Pennsylvania Dutch dialect word meaning "patient."

Gepp—A Pennsylvania Dutch dialect word meaning "give it."

Gros-feelich—A Pennsylvania Dutch dialect word meaning "vain" or "proud."

Ivver vile—A Pennsylvania Dutch dialect phrase meaning "soon."

Kalte sup—A Pennsylvania Dutch dialect phrase meaning "cold soup."

Kesslehaus—A Pennsylvania Dutch dialect word meaning "wash house."

Kindish—A Pennsylvania Dutch dialect word meaning "childish."

Mam—A Pennsylvania Dutch dialect word used to address or refer to one's mother.

Mitt leidas—A Pennsylvania Dutch dialect phrase meaning "sympathy."

Mutsa—A Pennsylvania Dutch dialect word meaning "Sunday coat."

Naits—A Pennsylvania Dutch dialect word meaning "thread."

Nay—A Pennsylvania Dutch dialect word meaning "no."

Ordnung—The Amish community's agreed-upon rules for living based on their understanding of the Bible, particularly the New Testament. The *ordnung* varies from community to community, often reflecting leaders' preferences, local customs, and traditional practices.

Rumspringa—A Pennsylvania Dutch dialect word meaning "running around." It refers to the time in a person's life between age sixteen and marriage. It involves structured social activities in groups, as well as dating, and usually takes place on the weekends.

Schadenfreude—A Pennsylvania Dutch dialect word meaning "pleasure at the misfortune of others."

Schnitzas—A Pennsylvania Dutch dialect word meaning "fibs."

Schtick—A Pennsylvania Dutch dialect word meaning "piece."

Schtrofed—A Pennsylvania Dutch dialect word meaning "chastised."

Sei—A Pennsylvania Dutch dialect word meaning "his." In communities where many people have the same first and last names, it is customary for the husband's name to be added to that of his wife so it is clear who is being referred to.

Siss net chide—A Pennsylvania Dutch dialect phrase meaning "it's not right."

Tzimmalich—A Pennsylvania Dutch dialect word meaning "humble."

Tzvie-drocht—A Pennsylvania Dutch dialect word meaning "dissension."

Unbegreiflich—A Pennsylvania Dutch dialect word meaning "unbelievable."

Unlieve—A Pennsylvania Dutch dialect word meaning "hatred."

Vassa—A Pennsylvania Dutch dialect word meaning "water."

Vissa tae—A Pennsylvania Dutch dialect word meaning "meadow tea." It is made by pouring boiling water over fresh mint or spearmint leaves and then sweetened with sugar.

Yoh—A Pennsylvania Dutch dialect word meaning "yes."

Zeit-lang—A Pennsylvania Dutch dialect word meaning "longing."

The Author

Linda Byler was raised in an Amish family and is an active member of the Amish church today. Growing up, Linda loved to read and write. In fact, she still does.

Linda is the author of the *Sadie's Montana* series, which includes these three novels: *Wild Horses*, *Keeping Secrets*, and *The Disappearances*. She has also written the *Lizzie Searches for Love* series, which includes these three novels: *Running Around (and Such)*, *When Strawberries Bloom*, and *Big Decisions*. She is also the author of *The Little Amish Matchmaker*, *The Christmas Visitor*, as well as *Lizzie's Amish Cookbook: Favorite recipes from three generations of Amish cooks!*

Additionally, Linda is well-known within the Amish community as a columnist for a weekly Amish newspaper.

Center Point Large Print
600 Brooks Road / PO Box 1
Thorndike, ME 04986-0001 USA

(207) 568-3717

US & Canada:
1 800 929-9108
www.centerpointlargeprint.com